The Chosen One, My Ass!

Michelle Summers

Charming Lil Penny

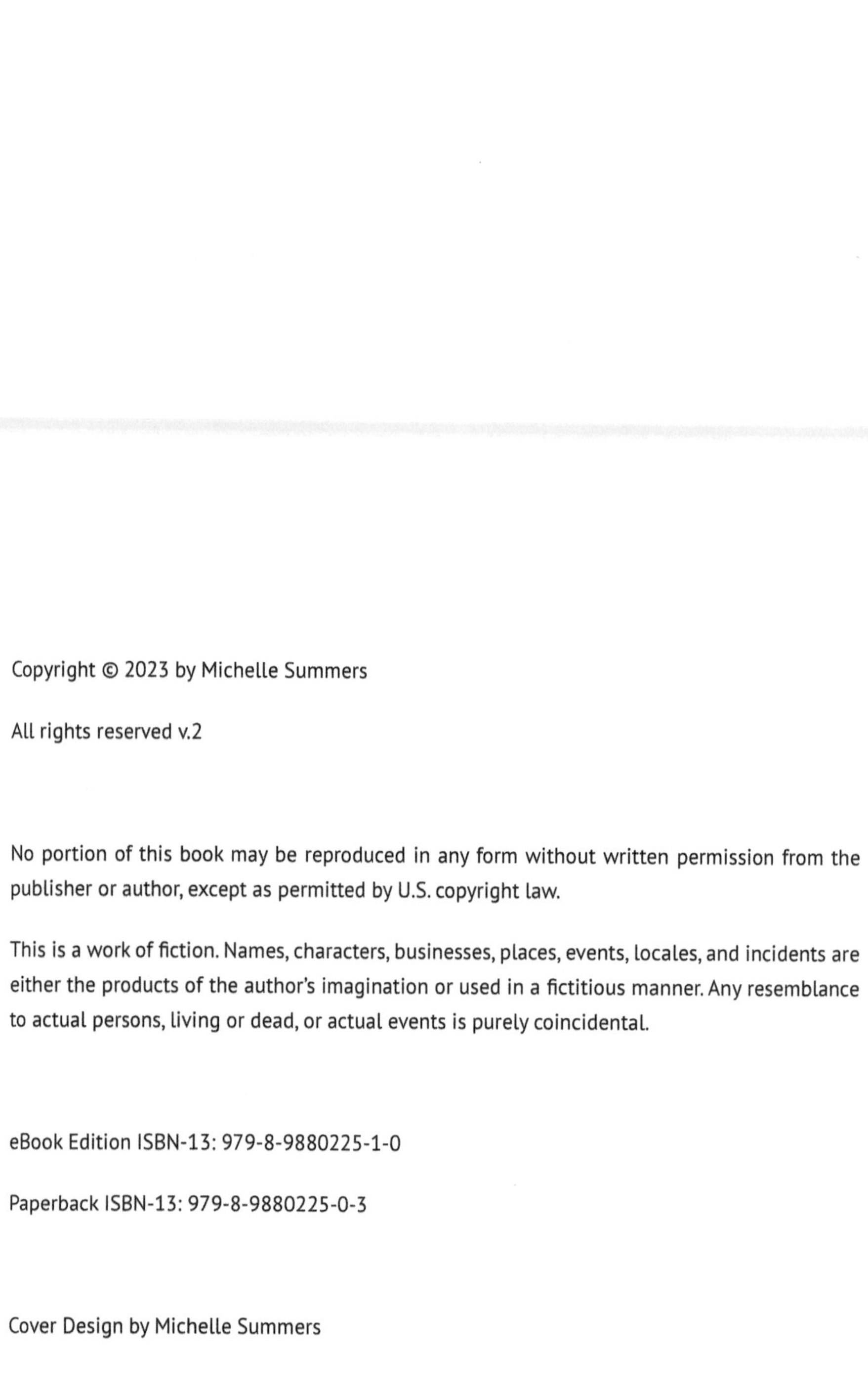

eBook Edition ISBN-13: 979-8-9880225-1-0

Paperback ISBN-13: 979-8-9880225-0-3

Cover Design by Michelle Summers

For Danika, the most badass mother I know,
and DaiSempai, my quintessential Guardian,
you're the real superheroes.

WANT MORE?

Be sure to check out Michelle's latest books, get free excerpts and updates through her newsletter, and connect with her on social media by scanning the code below:

Contents

Prologue

The inside of the warehouse is dark, but I can still see as if I am outside on a bright summer day. It's a strange feeling, and I wonder if I'll ever get used to this new ability, not to mention my new super hearing. Of course, all I can see are boxes stacked to twice my height and a twisted pathway running throughout. I can sense someone running on the far side of the room to my left. I stand still and close my eyes, tracing their path around the room with my hearing, like some freakish bat lady. Whoever, or whatever, that is, they have entered the maze.

Quite frankly, this entire situation is utter bullshit, but if I need to fight monsters *and* listen to my kids fighting on eleven now, I'll just use this machete thing to stab myself right here and be done with it.

I can make out the ragged breathing of whatever is in here with me. It is somewhere behind me and sounds like it holds a whole lotta breath. I'm not ready to turn around, but I can tell it's getting closer.

What the hell did he put in here with me?

Why did I do the one thing that I, as a woman, have learned not to do from the time I could comprehend personal safety: trust a random guy I just met? Big mistake.

Chapter 1

Miranda

I am not ready to open my eyes when the alarm on my phone starts to screech. The ear-piercing chime is the only one that can wake me up, but that's only because I hate it so much. I look at the screen to check the time. I'm not sure why since my alarm goes off at the same time. Every. Goddamn. Day. 6:15 a.m. Yuck.

I used to be able to hit the snooze a few times before I really had to get up. But my eldest, Jessie, is in eighth grade now, and she has to be in school practically before dawn for her science club. My two elementary schoolers, Natalie and Sam, get dropped off next. If they aren't in school before 8 a.m., then they have to be signed in as tardy. My sixth grader, Phoebe, is dragged around with her siblings because she doesn't need to be at school until 8:15 a.m. When I was their age, I didn't need to be at school until 9 a.m. Forcing kids (and their parents) to be up so early is crazy to me. My husband, Jake, is the one who usually handles the daily drop-off marathon.

I pad into the bathroom and feel a little sweaty from the heat blowing out of our vents. We have hit the time of year when the morning has a delicious crisp chill, and none of my children will get out of bed if they can even sense it. As I wash my hands, I look at my reflection and the twenty extra pounds I have hanging around. Okay, more like fifty. Fine, it's seventy pounds. After I turned forty, taking off weight has been getting harder and harder. Granted, I haven't really tried all that hard.

I notice that the silver is starting to shine in my dark brown curls. But at least after forty-two years, I finally learned how to take care of my hair so it is shiny and soft instead of resembling steel wool. I use my cooling applicator to apply a little eye cream and hope it makes the perpetual dark circles lighten a bit. I trace my upper lash line with a soft brown liner and brush on a touch of mascara so that people can at least tell I have eye lashes. They used to be so dark and long and lush, but they got lighter and lighter with each of my four pregnancies. I used to only use makeup on special occasions. Now I don't feel human, or at least not remotely feminine, without my liner and mascara.

I brush my teeth, grab my bathrobe, and return to my room where I flip up the light switch.

"Time to get up!" My voice has a singsong tone but is still insistent.

Jake mumbles through his arm draped over his face to block the sunlight. "Mm, okay, Miranda." Jake is still curled up with Sammy, our seven-year-old, youngest, and only son. My husband's hair is hanging in our son's face; he needs a haircut. Well, not needs—not to me anyway. It's getting a little floppier than he prefers though. I stare for a second nostalgically.

When we first got together, he was in a band, and he was a bit of a bad boy. His medium brown hair was down to his shoulders, and he wore baggy pants slung low on his slim hips and a chain that attached his wallet to a belt loop. But then we grew up. He had to be professional, and I had to stop admitting I liked grungy boys, because old ladies like me can't like bad boys in a band. Now he prefers to keep his hair perfectly coiffed in a short pompadour style.

Sammy's hair is almost black and super thick. It curls when we let it go too long between haircuts. His eyes are hazel, like mine, but lighter, with a tendency to be greener rather than brown.

"Come on, guys. Time to get up. Now, Jake!" My husband jumps a little as he realizes he's reached that point when he really needs to get moving.

"Do I have to go to school today?" I like to refer to Sammy as inert. He's not great at changing direction. If he's in bed, he wants to stay there. If he's at school, he wants to stay there. A Sammy in motion stays in motion; a Sammy at rest stays at rest.

"Um, yup. It's a school day. Get. Up. Now."

He groans as he forces himself out of our bed and down the hall to his own room where he slams the door, hopefully to get himself dressed. I always heard how much easier boys were to raise than girls. Maybe that only applies when they don't have three older sisters from whom they learn how to act.

As I walk down the hall, I hear arguing behind the closed bathroom door.

"No, Phoebe. You can't borrow it." As the oldest, Jessie has always been my rule follower and most responsible kid, as long as the rules and responsibilities are logical. There is no room for nonsense in Jessie's mind.

"Why not?" Phoebe whines. There is plenty of room for nonsense in her mind. She's brilliant but much less rigid than her big sister.

"Well for starters, you'll ruin it. Plus, I don't know when I'll ever see it again—if I ever see it again. Don't look at me like that!" Jessie tries to be unyielding with her little siblings, but she usually ends up giving in to them, and she often ends up regretting the concession.

I continue down the hall, and Natalie's door is still closed. My nine-year-old is my late riser. She is the most like me in personality, to be honest. Although she has outgrown sleepwalking into our bedroom every night, she still prefers to have me wake her up with a morning snuggle for a couple minutes. I tilt her blinds open a bit so the morning sunlight filters into the room. I climb into her bed, and she doesn't open her eyes before snuggling into me.

"Good morning, love bug. Five minutes of snuggles, then time to get out of bed. Okay?"

While she is always ready to get up when our time together ends, I have to pry myself away. I know from her sisters that this year is likely the last she will insist on any kind of snuggles. Maybe it is the last she will even permit them. By next year, who knows if I will even get a good-bye hug as she races out the door. So, I hold her and stroke her silky golden hair. When my alarm chimes, I kiss the top of her head. She smiles at me as she opens her eyes, mostly blue with specks of green. I smile at her and then head downstairs.

Once again, our day starts with a typical stress-filled morning. I mean, such is life with four kids. I take breakfast orders on my way to the stairs and have eggs scrambling, bagels toasting, and frozen pancakes microwaving when Jessie and Phoebe walk into the kitchen, arguing, as usual.

Phoebe is pleading with her big sister. "No! They're obviously mine. They're way more my style than yours."

I take in Phoebe's bright tie dye top and gauzy floral skirt to try to figure out what she's stolen and hopes to pass off as her own. I assume it's the earrings. I remember when I bought them...for Jessie.

As does Jessie. "That's so not true, Phoebs! I went through a flower power stage two years ago, and that's when I got them. Mom, tell her. You bought them for me."

Phoebe crosses her arms and juts her hips to one side, indignant. "Okay, but even if that were true, you're only into black and rage now, so...isn't it better someone owns them who will actually wear them?"

I remember how happy I had been when Phoebe finally outgrew whining. But now that she's replaced whining with logical arguments that make saying no hard, I'm not sure which era I prefer.

"Nope. They're still mine."

Phoebe throws her arms up in the air. "Oh my god! Why are you so against letting anything bring me joy? I didn't wear the stupid sweater you told me I couldn't borrow!"

"Gee, I dunno." Jessie pauses with a hand on her chin looking like The Thinker. "Maybe because you're a thief and liar and I hate you?" Her hand drops so both are fists balled at her sides.

"Okay, girls. Enough! Sit. Down." They do and then: sweet silence. It may be a far cry from the sisterly bonding I secretly wished for them, but it's still a rung higher on the ladder of parental joy we perpetually climb—only to soon slide down again, like Sisyphus and his damn boulder. Push the rock up; watch it roll down. Push the rock up; watch it roll down.

From across the kitchen table, they glare at one another. I roll my tired eyes as I put a plate down in front of each. I'm shocked no one complains about what I gave them. They must be too annoyed at each other to change their minds from what they asked to eat ten minutes ago. Still, it's a win for me.

Natalie comes in next. She's dressed in jeans and a faded T-shirt, but not the cool kind of faded. It's the, "I'm the third daughter, and all my clothes are at least four years old by the time they get to me," faded. At one point, the shirt was white, but now it's kind of gray, and I can't really make out the kitten and butterflies anymore. She takes her usual post at the end of the table and closest to her sisters, watching over them like a referee. I put her plate of eggs in front of her and kiss the top of her head. She looks up at me and smiles. Her bright eyes are my moment of solace in our crazy as usual morning. I take a deep, clarifying breath.

When Sammy stumbles into his seat at the opposite end of the table, I'm pulled from my moment of zen. He's still rubbing the sleep from his dark brown eyes, and his hair is mussed, which looks adorable, but of course I don't tell him that. He starts in on his bagel as soon as I give it to him.

While they're eating, I double check that I signed Phoebe's art club permission slip for her field trip and stuff it in her folder, drop Natalie's overdue library novel in her bag, and make sure Sammy's homework log is checked off.

They've all finished breakfast and are finding their shoes when Jake finally makes his appearance.

"Everyone ready to go? Oh, Miranda, can you please make sure to run a load of socks and underwear today so I have enough for my trip tomorrow?" Jake seems to have more and more work trips lately. Either talent managers are in hot demand, or they are competing so fiercely that he has to be everywhere at once to not miss an opportunity. I have a hard time following what exactly he does, so I can't be certain which situation he's dealing with right now.

"Yup. Thank you for not waiting until half an hour before you leave for the airport to tell me this time." My eyes sparkle at him. This is how we flirt now.

He tilts his head and squints his eyes a bit to acknowledge my dig. Then he laughs, grabs the breakfast wrap I made him and gives me a quick thank you kiss, and they all head for the door. Jessie and Phoebe are once again engrossed in their bickering. Natalie gives me a quick hug and "Love you," and Sammy momentarily melts into my arms before rumbling "I love you" into my belly and running off to join the rest.

And I'm left in the calm after the storm. I ask our digital assistant to play one of the albums that no one but me enjoys, and I begin to clean up the kitchen, as I do every morning, while shaking my head at the monotony our chaos has taken on.

With a cup of coffee in one hand, I check my to-do list for the day: a PTA meeting, groceries, the post office, meeting a friend for lunch...For now, I'm going to enjoy the quiet.

I slowly make my way up the stairs, clutching my coffee and breathing a little heavier by the time I reach the top. I head to my room, with every intention to find some real clothes and begin my own day. But then I spy my empty, beautiful bed. I just need to lay down for five minutes...

As I give in to the mattress's siren song, I hold the coffee mug to my chest. It's warmth somehow sends a chill through me. Setting it down on my nightstand, I lie down, close my eyes, and smile. I know one day I'll miss this brand of insanity.

Chapter 2

Miranda

An hour and a half later, I head back downstairs with only twenty-five minutes until my PTA meeting at the elementary school. Oops. It's okay. I needed that hour-long nap.

The coffee is still hot as I pour myself a second mugful. I can't help thinking about how this double-walled carafe turned out to be a great Mother's Day gift from Jake, despite all the pouting I did at the time because he had bought me a kitchen gadget to celebrate me birthing our children. But to him, he selected an accessory for one of my biggest interests. Silly, oblivious husbands not knowing the arbitrary rules we have ingrained in us.

Sadly, I can't savor this cup as I did my first today. This cup is strictly for survival. I drink it while standing at the sink and staring absentmindedly out the window at our wooded backyard. A neighborhood fox bats around a ball the kids must have left outside, and it pounces on the ball and rolls in the grass like domesticated dogs would. Since I often catch foxes playing with the balls we forget to put away, I've come to learn foxes are just as playful as dogs.

I smile until the fox turns its back to me, and I count not one but three fluffy, swishing tails, as fiery and active as licks of flame. I look down at my now empty mug and sniff the remaining drops to determine if my half and half turned and made me hallucinate. When I look back up, the fox is gone.

I shake my head and pour myself a travel mug to take to the meeting, because apparently a nap and two cups of coffee is still not enough to keep me from sleepwalking through today.

***

When I arrive at the elementary school, I walk over to the blacktop where a circle of chairs has been set up and wave to my friend Nadia, who is our PTA president. Her long, straight black hair shines in the sun, and her eyes twinkle with their usual kindness as she waves back. Halfway there, a sort of low, chuckling whisper to my left catches my attention. I chance a look and glimpse a red bird zooming away. At least I think it's a bird. It's wings are flapping more like a bat, and I don't think I saw a beak. Shaking my head once again, I gulp down more coffee and then collapse onto the empty chair beside Nadia's.

"What's going on?" She furrows her brow and can tell I have something on my mind. But, given she's always nervous before she has to speak, now's not the best time to tell her I'm either hallucinating or a three-tailed fox played in my yard this morning. That might distract her a little too much right now.

"Nothing. I'm good. No really, I am." I give her a shaky smile and attempt to wave her concern away with a flip of my hand.

She gives me an incredulous look but raises her eyebrows and shakes her head to get her focus back on the meeting she's about to lead.

The day is sunny and bright, with a clear blue sky, thankfully. Brisk, but still relatively warm for this point in fall. It sucks that all our meetings must take place outside since the conference room had to be commandeered for use as another classroom. Obviously, the kids' needs are more important; I just wish we could have space for everything.

More parents arrive now. Being good friends with the president, I try to be early so I can support her with whatever she needs. Therefore, I am usually the second one here. But I don't feel like such a great friend during the meeting.

Nadia's voice fades away. Even as I try harder to listen to her, another conversation replaces her words, starting with the low chuckle I heard in the parking lot. Then another, slightly higher whisper joins the first. Then another. And another. I can't understand the breathy murmurs, but they sound like a conversation. I look around but don't see any of those birds. Then again, I can't tell which direction the sounds are coming from. They seem to be multiplying by the second, as well as moving in on me from all sides. My heart races as I turn my head back and forth, up and down, trying to figure out what is making this noise.

Then Nadia's hand is on my shoulder, and the whispers quiet down. "Miranda, you okay?"

Everyone at the meeting is looking at me with their faces full of concern. I consciously and slowly pull in a deep breath and let it go again. I nod.

Nadia nods back to me and after a moment asks, "Could you give us the report on the bake sale?"

"Oh! Shit, yes! I'm sorry." I sit straighter in my chair and pull a slip of paper out of my notebook to make sure I give the accurate numbers. "Okay, at our October bake sale—Halloween themed, of course—we had sixteen parent bakers. This was our first time setting up the separate table for the allergy aware students, and I think it really helped them. We should keep track of which bakers have which allergen-free kitchens for the kiddos. We sold about five hundred items in thirteen minutes. And, our total revenue for the sale was, drumroll please, $1308. So, we can definitely get at least one or two more sets of the foam blocks the office asked us to get the kids for recess."

"That's fabulous, Miranda! Thank you. Okay everyone, I think that wraps everything up. Thank you so much for coming today. We'll see you next on December 14, same place and time, so dress warm."

Everyone gets up and gives me sideways glances that make me feel like they're questioning my sanity. Not that I can blame them. I am too.

"Hey, really. Are you okay?" Nadia looks at me with concern. "You looked like you had a particularly large mosquito buzzing all around your head for a minute there."

"Yeah." I force a smile. "Just a weird day. I honestly couldn't explain it if I wanted to. I need to figure out what's going on in my head."

This doesn't seem to reassure her. She arches one eyebrow and purses her mouth the way only a mom who knows her kids are lying can. "I wish I could say I'm not worried, but I can't."

"Really. I'm okay. I just need more sleep. Or more coffee. Or both." I flash her a nervous smile. Maybe my freakout was only an aura before a migraine. I'd never hoped for a migraine before. We share a quick hug, and then I sprint across the parking lot so I don't have to linger where I first encountered that bird, and so I can get the hell out of here.

***

Ten minutes later, I pull into the Shop Rite parking lot, breathing a sigh of relief. At least I managed to drop off the mail at the post office with no strange experiences.

I park and gather my purse, list, and shopping bags. I groan a little at the thought of going in. Generally speaking, I do not like people, which I know contradicts my constant involvement in my kids' PTAs and my other volunteer groups in town.

Footsteps rhythmically tap on the pavement behind me as I head into the store. I glance behind me to see if I know the person behind me and should say hi, but no one is there, except for a brilliantly blue butterfly that landed on the windshield of my minivan. Normally, I love butterflies. But after the bird at the PTA meeting, I'm not getting too close to this one. I walk through the automatic doors, grateful for the lack of fresh air and wildlife.

As I go about my shopping, I keep feeling as though someone is behind me, but there never is. I fill my cart with fresh produce for my kids and processed junk I don't have to lift a finger to prepare for myself, regardless of my body's best interests. As I approach the end of the aisle, someone behind me chuckles. I freeze in place because this chuckle is not the airy illusive sound I heard in the school parking lot. This chuckle belongs to a man amused by his quarry. As my adrenaline kicks in, I spin around to catch whoever is behind me before they can disappear. As I twist, my knee groans and pops; still, no one is there, and now my knee is throbbing. Awesome.

I turn back to my cart and shriek. A young man wearing a grocery apron grips the front of my cart, his knuckles white. His shiny brown hair is barely longer than a buzz cut, and his jade green eyes appear to be...yup, they're glowing. His teeth are straight and white, but something about his smile is off. The corners of his mouth are too high and at the wrong angle. The center of his bottom lip is too low, making his smile too...deep. He resembles a caricature more than an actual person.

"Finding everything you're looking for?" His mouth is the only part of him that moves when he speaks, and even then, just barely, but he over annunciates his words.

"Y-yes. Thank you." I make eye contact as I speak in an attempt to show dominance over my situation. But when I try to pull my cart free, he keeps it in his hands. As his eyes study me closely, his smile becomes a little less impossible looking, but it's still quite menacing. "Please let go of my cart."

He lets go and brings his hands to below his face, fingers splayed. But that deranged smile never leaves. I back up quickly, not sure if I should go around him or backward. I don't want to give him the satisfaction of either, but I push my cart to the far side of the produce section so I can resume my route without getting too close to him. He watches me until I turn the corner, still glancing back at him to make sure he doesn't follow me.

I don't see the man the rest of the time I'm shopping, but I hold my keys in my fist like claws as I walk to my car. The butterfly hasn't left my windshield. At least I think it's the same butterfly. It's hard to tell because now a whole flock of them covers the glass. "Are you serious right now!"

A slightly hunched-over grandmother with a shawl wrapped around her shoulders loads the car next to me. She looks at me sharply as she moves her last bag from the cart to her trunk. She must not find a gaggle of butterflies as strange as I do. But then again they're not on her car. I give a friendly head nod and quick wave and mutter an apology. The butterflies flutter away and land on a nearby cart corral so I can get to my car. Well, maybe that's assigning too much intention to them. I mean, they are insects.

As I drive home and unpack my bags, my mind keeps jumping back to all the inexplicable things that happened today, in spite of trying to focus on the podcast playing. Not just inexplicable. Creepy. Even haunting. The fox, the laughing bird (or birds), the eerie man, and the butterflies... So. Fucking. Weird.

I hope our food is going where it's supposed to because my mind is somewhere else while I shove my groceries into my overstuffed cabinets (I really need to clean out this kitchen). As soon as I'm done, I collapse onto the couch to take a nap. Unfortunately, I can't stop thinking about that freaky grocery store dude's grotesque smile. His leer made him look like a hyena or something. Beyond bizarre. Just as I finally am able to push the image of him out of my mind, my alarm buzzes. Shit, my lunch date with Eliza.

"Oh no. That's not going to happen…" I pull my phone to my face and send her a quick text:

> Having the absolute weirdest day imaginable, or not even imaginable tbh. Anyway, can we meet for coffee tomorrow instead? How's 9:30 at The Tulip?

Not a minute goes by before she responds:

> O Thank GOD. Yes. T just spit up all over the inside of the diaper bag. Raincheck til tomorrow!!!

I stare at the ceiling until my alarm tells me to start my afternoon rat race. I groan and rub my eyes. On my way out the door, I pour the last, and now cold, cup of coffee and swallow it fast. It's pretty nasty, but I need the caffeine boost to get through a few more hours.

I pick up Sammy and Natalie first and then race to get Phoebe. Jessie will get a ride with a friend as usual, since I cannot get to that many places in the short amount of time I have to do it all. As I grab my purse, I stop for a beat in the mudroom and look at the peg board. I grab a baseball cap and pull it down low over my forehead. Maybe if I hide, any other weirdos will stay away for the rest of the day. Any more encounters will leave me curled in the fetal position, sobbing.

As I walk from my car to the school in the baseball cap and a pair of oversized sunglasses I found in my glove compartment, everyone looks at me funny. Actually, they probably don't, but I feel like they do. Nadia puts her hands out questioningly and mouths, "What the fuck?" when she sees me.

I look at her and shrug as I pass her. "Don't. Ask. I don't even know. But I promise I will tell you when I figure it out." *If. If* I figure it out. I don't know if I'll ever understand this day, but I can't tell her that right now.

My kids raise an eyebrow and shake their heads when they see my accessories, and they didn't even see me freak out at the PTA meeting or grocery store. They just know I'm their mom, and therefore I'm automatically weird and not cool, regardless of what I'm wearing on my face and head.

Jessie doesn't get home in time to spot my makeshift disguise, but I keep glancing out the window and scanning the backyard often enough that she notices.

"What is UP with you?" she finally asks, as I open the curtains for the eighth time.

"Nothing." I close the curtains, faster and snappier than I intended. Whoops. She stares at me for several seconds.

"You're so weird!" She huffs and leaves the kitchen.

She's not wrong. I don't know if I even want to know what's going on at this point. It's fine, though. I'm fine. Everything is totally fine.

***

When Jake makes it into our bedroom, it's close to midnight. Even though I have been lying in bed and trying to fall asleep for forty-five minutes, I'm no closer to sleep now than when I was at the grocery store. When he comes in, he loosens his tie and walks up to my side of the bed to see if I'm awake. I'm not sure why he's surprised that I am.

"Hey there." His voice is raspy from the lateness in the night. He leans in and kisses me lightly, his hands on either side of my shoulders. Then he pushes off, drops his tie by my feet, and walks around the bed toward the hamper while shedding his navy-blue khakis and light blue, pinstripe, button-down shirt.

"Hey yourself. Why are you home so late?"

"Sorry. Ryan and I had to clean up our presentation. We're both pretty nervous about this pitch." He's down to his boxer briefs as he walks to the bathroom. I love those boxer briefs. They hug his thighs just right, and they have this little pouch that...never mind.

"Oh, shit! That's right. You're leaving tomorrow. Where are you going again?" I call loud enough for him to hear me but not so loud that I'll wake the kids. I say a quick thank you to the laundry gods that I remembered to run his underwear this afternoon.

I used to know all his trips, down to his flight numbers and hotels. That was at least eleven years and three kids ago. Now I have enough other schedules in my mind that I struggle to keep track of when he'll be home and when he'll be away. I hear the toilet flush and water run, and a moment later, he's standing in the doorway and brushing his teeth.

"Vegas, meeting with that new pop group Chris wants us to woo. Callie and the somethings..."

"Oh right. Well, don't woo them *too* much."

The corner of his mouth quirks up in a smirk. "You worried?"

I yawn, desperate for sleep that is still a very long way off. "Yup. Always."

He rolls his eyes and walks back into the bathroom to go rinse.

I'm not lying. I may have shrouded my words in sarcasm, but I do worry when he goes away, even when it's not to Las Vegas. His body may not be exactly the same as it was when we got together, but it's a hell of a lot closer to its original condition than mine is, maybe even better. I have seen how women look at him when he's dressed sharp for work. And I see how they look at me next to him. I don't like it.

He walks around to his side of the bed, and I feel a slight shift on the mattress as he sits. But instead of lying down, he looks at me with a devilish smile. "Well, I guess you better make sure I don't go thinking of anyone else while I'm away." He shifts to his hands and knees and crawls toward me like a tiger impressing his mate, or perhaps intimidating his prey.

When he gets to my side, he swings one knee gracefully over my hips so he straddles me. He leans back on his heels, sitting up and regaining the use of his arms, while also taking in the sight of me. I can't imagine I'm particularly attractive right now with my mind all over the place, sure I'm losing it, and exhausted from the day I'm still ruminating about.

But he looks at me as if I'm the sexiest person he's ever seen, regardless of my oversized T-shirt that replaced teddys over a decade ago. My hands are folded across my breasts, and in one deft move that he has practiced over our years together, he takes both of my wrists in one hand and raises them above my head, pinning them there, gently. As he lowers his mouth to mine, drinking in my moans, his other hand slips down between us and begins to rub me through my thin cotton panties. A wet patch quickly spreads there, and he moans in anticipation.

He reaches lower, still holding my wrists, and as he makes his way back up my body, he's clutching the tie he left by my feet.

"Hmmmm. Wrists..." He trails his fingertips down my arm, across my collarbone, and along my face, and my breaths deepen and hitch the longer he debates what to do with me. "Or eyes. Decisions. Decisions." He clicks his tongue pensively while staring into me, seeing everything I am, everything I have ever been. His dark eyes are penetrating. I feel them probing for a tell of my greatest desires in this moment. I bite my lip. The corner of his mouth quirks up and I am putty for him to manipulate however he pleases. He slowly wraps my wrists together with his silk tie. I gasp a little, and he plugs my mouth with his finger. My hips begin to writhe beyond my control as I start to suck on him. Then he leans down so his mouth brushes my ear.

"Shhhhhh. We have to stay quiet, or I'll have to find a way to keep you quiet. Understand?"

I nod.

"Good." He presses his lips to my mouth. His kiss is hard and deep and delicious and makes my back arch in desire. He then gently kisses my chest and belly as he makes his way down to where I want him most. He pulls my panties down and off. When he spreads my legs, he looks at me as if I'm a feast he's been looking forward to indulging in for far too long. I know I am dripping, waiting for him to partake. I press myself towards him, I need him to make me forget the insanity of my day.

Then his mouth is on me, sucking and licking. I arch my back, grateful to lose myself in this pleasure. I easily free my wrists from their bonds (he's too nervous to tie me up for real), and I weave my fingers into his hair. I'm finally getting out of my head and into the moment when he stops. He shifts his position so his cock is at my entrance and slips in. I close my eyes and try to latch onto my own satisfaction, but after having four kids, I don't get much pleasure from this position anymore. However, since I'm not the one leaving on a business trip to the city of sin in the morning, I'll let him have it his way tonight.

He finishes, and as he rolls away from me to check his email, I'm left with an orgasm that never came. The sex felt good, but the older I get, the weight isn't the only thing that's hard to get off. Normally, I'd be pissy afterward, at him as well as at my own body for letting me down. But I honestly have too much on my mind to worry about not being properly pleasured right now.

I have one quick thought before I finally fall into what ends up being a ridiculously restless sleep: I'm sure when I wake up tomorrow, everything will be totally normal, and all the strange events from today will feel like a far-off dream.

Chapter 3

Miranda

While I never enjoy having to wake up, today I'm absolutely terrified to open my eyes when the alarm on my phone sounds at 6:15 a.m., as usual. I scrunch my eyes tighter for a second, thinking about everything weird from yesterday. How much weirder can it get though, right? Okay. Let's do this.

I turn off the alarm and sit up, looking around suspiciously. The house seems pretty normal. Sammy and Jake are snuggled together next to me, as usual. I slide silently out of bed and take a lap to peek in at my sleeping children before I go into the bathroom to get ready for the unknown day ahead.

Once I am done brushing my teeth, I flip on the light.

"Time to get up!" My voice is a little shakier and less cheerful than usual, although I'm fairly certain Jake and Sammy won't notice, considering they're both still seventy-five percent asleep.

On my second walk down the hall, I see Jessie and Phoebe already up and fighting in the bathroom, per usual. In Natalie's room, I settle in for our morning snuggles, knowing I need them more than she does this morning.

"Good morning, love bug. Five minutes of snuggles, then time to get out of bed. Okay?"

She nods sleepily and snuggles in.

Normally, I melt around her, but today I stay rigid, my eyes open and darting around her room. When my timer goes off, I kiss her head and give her a final, "Time to wake up, Sweets," and then I head back to my room. Maybe Jake and Sammy did notice that something was different in my demeanor this morning because they're awake and getting ready before I return to my room.

Damn straight. I nod to myself and head down to the kitchen.

***

As soon as breakfast is on the table, I pull back the curtain and stare out the window, silently willing the fox to come back. I need to see it again, to see that I was mistaken. Surely, it didn't have three tails. There must be an explanation for what I saw. Maybe it had one super fluffy tail. One supercalifragilisticexpealidociously fluffy tail. Or maybe the fox was just waving its tail so fast that it looked like three tails.

"Um, Mom...what are you doing?" Jessie's voice pulls me out of my daze, for now. Usually, the only similarity between them is their light brown hair color, but now she and Phoebe stand inside the doorway and stare as if they caught me kissing Santa Claus.

"Oh, I was just looking outside. Looks like another beautiful day!" I pull the curtain all the way open.

"Oooookay.... Ouch. Phoebe!" Jessie hops around on one foot, nursing the toes her sister just stomped.

Phoebe's arms are outstretched towards me in a dramatic gesture while her stick straight hair swings back and forth to accentuate her point. "Give the poor woman a break! Maybe she just needed a mental vacation for a moment!"

I shake my head to bring myself back to now. I'm not sure if Phoebe meant to be kind, or to roast me, but I don't have the time or energy to spend analyzing which scenario was more probable, so I push it out of my mind.

"Okie dokie then. Pheebs, don't forget your cello. You have orchestra today. Jessie, did you finish your book report?"

"Yes, ma'am."

"Okay, great. But please don't ma'am me."

I am not in my normal flow this morning and keep forgetting what it is I should be doing. While I grab bowls and spoons instead of plates and forks, Natalie and Sammy come in together.

Sammy is noticeably frazzled. His fingers are tangled in his curls, holding on to keep from smacking his sister. "Oh my god, Nat! She is not my girlfriend!"

All other sound in the room cuts off abruptly, and for Jessie and Phoebe to put aside their fighting to listen in on their siblings is really showing how the topic at hand is surprising us all. We all freeze, A Tableau of a Family at Breakfast.

Natalie turns her bright blue eyes into spotlights as she stares down her brother. "So then why were you holding hands on the way to art?"

"Nat, I have known Jackie since we were two. Is she sweet and funny? Yes. Is she super pretty. You betcha! But she is not my girlfriend, and you are not allowed to say that to anyone. Understand?" His little foot stomps to punctuate the nots.

I'm so confused. "Whoa. What now?" Nope. It is not acceptable for my baby to be growing up like this right now. I am not okay with this. This week is weird enough.

My son's curly haired head snaps toward me. "Ugh, Mom! Just don't, okay?"

Natalie sits down with a smug look on her face, her blond hair creating a halo behind her, while Sammy frowns so deeply that even his dimples turn into scowls. I go back to the window.

And there it is. That adorable little red canine. And its three plush tails. There is no doubt. There is no illusion. And I wonder what this means about my sanity.

"Boo!"

"Ah! Damnit Jessie!" She had snuck up behind me and placed her chin above my shoulder before startling me.

"Sorry. But seriously, Mom, what are you doing?"

I decide to find out just how crazy I am. "Do you see a fox in the yard?"

She squeezes by so she is in front of me now.

"Yes. What kind of quiz is this?"

"Shush. Is there anything weird about the fox?"

The silence lasts for three of my rapid inhales and exhales, which is long enough for me to begin thinking I'm delusional.

"Does it.... Why does it have three tails?" Jessie shrieks her question into my ear.

"Thank you!" The tension I've been holding in my entire body evaporates at the realization that I'm not insane.

A commotion breaks out at the breakfast table, plates and silverware rattling, as all of my children stampede over to see the mysterious beast. The kids shove me further and further back during the riot, and I can't make out the details of anyone's stunned utterances. Until....

Phoebe pushes to the front of the pack and jumps up and down on her toes while flailing her arms. "Oh! It looks like a kitsune."

I grab Phoebe's arm and pull her to me, quickly but not roughly. Her deep brown eyes are still wide with excitement from our discovery. "What? It has a name?"

"Um, yes...I mean, no. That is just a mutated fox or something weird like that. Kitsune aren't real."

My interest is peaked, even though she says the animal I so clearly saw right before my eyes is not actually the animal I so clearly saw right before my eyes. I blink rapidly.

"Please...explain."

She takes a deep, exasperated breath. It appears I'm below her for not knowing kitsune foxes exist and yet don't.

"Kitsune are from Japanese folklore. They're powerful spiritual beings that appear as foxes, and as they get older and wiser, they gain more tails."

I look back at the fuzzy object of our discussion, which has curled up in a patch of sunlight, napping.

"How are you so smart?" I ask in genuine amazement.

She rolls her eyes. "I think you gave me a big chunk of your brains when you made me. Do you miss them?" She playfully pushes my shoulder and walks back to the table.

She's probably right. But even so, one question still bothers me: If this is an animal of Japanese legend, how and why is it in my New Jersey backyard?

Just then Jake walks in. "Why are you all standing around the window?"

"There's a crazy mutated fox!" Sammy blurts out, making Jake's brow furrow as he comes to join us.

"What in god's name.... Miranda, promise me you will not go near that thing! I know you think it's cute, but no." Jake's eyes bounce between the fox and me frantically.

I roll my eyes. "Oh my god, Jake. This is totally different from that time with the feral kittens. Don't worry."

"Okay, but don't you think we should call someone to take care of it?"

"I'll try animal control, but I'm not really sure how much help they'll be."

Because of the distraction of our new four-legged friend, the kids are almost late for school, and the chaos around the front door becomes even more frenetic than usual as they gather everything they need and get their socks and shoes.

In the chaos, Jake almost forgets to kiss me good-bye before he leaves with them, only instead of carrying a backpack, he's towing his luggage behind him. Because of open-ended trips like this one, I have no idea when he'll get to kiss me next. Luckily, he returns, wrapping one arm around my waist and the other around my shoulders, and pulls me close.

"Ewwwwwwwww! Are you serious? We're all right here."

"Hey Jessie, I am very much in love with your mother and not afraid to show it. Need I remind you, none of you would be here if I wasn't?"

Groans from all of them. I have to admit, tormenting them at this stage of our lives is a little fun. Jake and I have been together for more than twenty-years, and the fact that we still have enough passion to make our kids sick is nice, in a way. But once upon a time, their sweet little faces would look up at us in awe when we showed each other affection; they would ask us to kiss over and over again, giggling every time. They've grown so much, so fast. One day, I'll miss having them around to groan at our love.

"Sorry, guys. But he's flying out as soon as he drops you off, and believe it or not, we still miss each other when we're apart for a few days." I don't know why I feel the need to chime in as well. Maybe to show a united front. Maybe because part of me feels like if I don't say anything, I'm letting my man speak for me.

And then, once again, they are out the door and onto their own adventures for the day. I pour myself my first cup of coffee for the morning and glance out the window. The mutated fox is gone, and I try to remember what Phoebe called it. I pull out my phone, open a browser, and type "fox k" in the search bar, but I don't see anything that is even close to what I'm trying to learn about. But knowing something like this is in the world somewhere, I try being more direct: "Japanese fox with three tails."

Bingo. First, I scroll past images of sketches and cartoons, and then I see: "People also ask: What is a fox with three tails called?"

Am I not the only one to have seen such a creature? I click on a link to a website about folklore and consume everything the page can tell me about my backyard visitor.

The more tails a kitsune has - they may have as many as nine - the older, wiser, and more powerful it is.

More powerful? I wonder what kinds of powers we are talking about here.

Certain mental disorders have been attributed to possession by kitsune.

Yeah, I can see that happening...

Kitsune often have powerful magic, and are known for their charm, illusions, possession, and mind manipulation.

Sounds like a blast. So glad one has decided to frequent my yard. Really. I wonder if a normal exterminator or wildlife expert know how to get rid of them. I assume not, because kitsune aren't indigenous. Do I need someone Japanese? Or a priest? Do I need a Japanese priest? I shake my head. It's gone for now. I won't worry...too much.

It's hard to go through your day knowing a mythical beast may be chilling in your yard. It's pretty distracting, like not knowing if you left the oven on, only times a billion. But I can't ignore my life to stare out the window all day, especially if I'm not going to do anything about it even if I do see the furball return. Besides, I can't ask Eliza for another raincheck two days in a row, and she's probably the only person I could disclose my new psychoses to who would not only defend me from being committed but also shrug and say, "Okay. So how do I help?" She is a professional author, so no matter how weird my life is right now, she's guaranteed to have written weirder shit.

Eliza, or Aunt Eliza as my kids know her, is my ultimate bestie. She is almost a decade younger than I am, but that just makes our friendship stronger. I can give her parental like advice, and she can help me relate to my kids a little better. Now she's a mom herself, and I get to be Auntie to her little squish.

When I walk into our favorite little coffee shop, I spy Eliza and hear Tabitha's happy squeals. I don't even place my order before I walk over to tickle her chunky little toes. I don't have to order anyway. The barista brings a honey caramel latte over to me a couple of minutes later. We're here a lot.

Eliza is dressed to impress as usual. Her hair has a magenta hue and a gentle curl to it, reminiscent of 1930's Hollywood glamour. Only someone who has been her best friend for over a decade would recognize the slight dull to her made-up eyes that indicates her new mom exhaustion.

"How are you doing, Lize?"

"Oh, we're great! I did have a couple questions about her poop though. When I babysat your kiddos, I sort of remember their poop changing when they started solids, but does this look normal?" She flips through photos on her phone before tilting her head and squinting her eyes, nodding, and handing it to me. I zoom in, squint even with the closer crop, then nod as I hand the phone back.

"Yup. Looks normal to me."

"Okay, but can we talk about the smell? It's much worse now."

"Yep, because she's eating actual food and not just milk."

"I know that, but my god! I swear my next villain is going to be my daughter's digestive tract!"

In her stroller, Tabitha lets out a full belly laugh. I smile at her and coochie-coo her toes again. We often bond over teasing Eliza.

I hesitate before slamming my foot on the gas. "So, I need your advice on something." I almost lose my nerve when her eyebrows shoot up. Normally, she's the one coming to me for help. "Yeah, yeah. Shut up. This is serious. I think...I think I'm losing it."

"Oh, honey. You lost it years ago. Are you just figuring this out?"

"Ha! No. Seriously. I think I'm hallucinating or something." I look around to make sure no one is at the tables closest to ours, then lower my voice to just above a whisper. "I swear a, a kitsune has been hanging out in my yard."

A moment of silence. Then Eliza's face splits open as she lets out a deep laugh that even has some intermittent snorts.

"Oh, that's amazing! There's a nine-tailed fox living in your yard?"

"Well, only three tails, but yes!" I nod along as she laughs. Then I look up at the ceiling, asking some invisible force I don't even believe in for patience. "Okay, okay. You had your laugh. But I'm serious. Shhh!"

She needs two full minutes to stop laughing. "Oh, I'm sorry. I needed that. It's been a long few months...You know Rory works long hours and I don't really get real adult interaction aside from ours." She blots the tears from her eyes, being careful not to smudge that perfect liner and mascara. "Okay, so tell me about your mythical fox."

I pull my coffee mug in closer and intertwine my fingers around the back of it while staring into the petals the barista created in the foam. "I don't know that you deserve to hear now."

"No, no, no. I promise to be good. Please, just tell me."

I take a deep breath. "Fine. I first noticed this weird fox yesterday morning, but it was back today. For the record, the kids all saw it too, and Phoebe said it looks like a kitsune. I saw these weird red birds, and I heard this whispering that drowned out the PTA meeting. Oh, and a horde of blue butterflies covered my car at the grocery store. Oh my god! The guy! This man at the grocery store grabbed my cart and—"

Eliza holds up her hand while closing her eyes. "Jesus, Mary, and Joseph, give me strength...." After a pause to inhale deeply and exhale slowly, she reaches into her bag and pulls out the steno pad she always has handy. Her eyes lock with mine momentarily, but then she flips her pad open to a new page and speaks with measured patience. "Okay. You told me about the fox. Now, tell me about the birds first."

She takes fast notes in her experienced shorthand. I'm not sure if she's interested in helping me or collecting fodder for her next book, but at least I have a confidant. I know how insane she must think I am, but she shows no indication on her placid face. After I finish telling her everything, she continues taking notes for several minutes, even turning the page once or twice, all the while holding up her left index finger to signal "one minute" to me. She finishes, places her pen diagonally across the pad, and looks up at me with a smile. "Okay."

I lean toward her until the table is pushing between my ribs, waiting for more of a response than her smile. "Okay? Do you have any insight or questions or anything?"

She pats my hand in what is supposed to be a calming gesture. "Yes, I do have a question actually. Have you been drinking your water?"

My head shakes quickly in disbelief of her casual attitude. "My what? What could this possibly have to do with my water intake?"

She shakes her head back at me and her shiny hair falls behind her shoulders. "I don't know, but that's my gut reaction to everything with you because I know how shitty you are about drinking your water."

I roll my eyes. Like not drinking enough water would cause me to hallucinate or something. Could it? I make a mental note to look up the possible effects of chronic dehydration...just in case. "Any other, non-gut reactions? Something that may actually be helpful?"

"I have to think about it." She stares off for a second, and a look of confusion crumples her face. "Describe the red bird thing again?"

"I didn't see it well, but I swear it was chuckling and whispering."

She nods along. "Okay.... Um, did it look anything like that thing?"

She points behind me. I am afraid to turn around, but I know I have no choice. I steel myself with a deep breath and pivot slowly in my seat. Hovering outside the high window at the front of the coffeeshop are two red...not birds. Based on the wings, maybe dragon wings is more accurate? Then again, from where I sit, the creatures look like little red people with little red bat wings. I can't make out the details, but they definitely have two pointy somethings on their heads. When they see me looking at them, they start jumping up and down with excitement. Thankfully the coffeehouse is largely empty, as can be expected late on a weekday morning. The only other people in the restaurant are some businessmen with their noses buried in their phones and the baristas trying to assist them.

I turn back to Eliza, who is practically cross-eyed with confusion.

"Yup. Pretty sure that's what the bird was. Hey, Eliza?" She still looks completely lost and confused. "Eliza?" She finally looks at me, but her face is still scrunched. "What the fuck are those?"

"Miranda, I have absolutely no idea. But I promise you, I will research as hard as I've ever researched anything in my life, as soon as I can devote the proper time to the task. I want to know what's going on too."

We finish our coffees in silence but for Tabitha's coos. When we walk out together, I hear a chuckle. And another. And then the whispering back and forth. I hope I'm just imagining it, but I know I'm not, and I can't help but look all around us to find the source of that whispering. Eliza also darts her eyes left and right over and over again. "Wait. Lize, do you...do you hear them?"

"No, sorry. Seeing you look all about like that got me nervous, but I don't hear anything. Is it the same sounds you heard at the PTA meeting?"

Even if she can't hear them, I'm so happy someone else knows what's going on. I could actually cry. "Yes! It is exactly what drowned out the PTA meeting yesterday. So now I know it's these little red things."

"Oh, wow. Can you make out what they're saying?"

"Nope. They were way louder yesterday, but I couldn't understand them then either."

"This is bizarre." She shudders with her entire body, as if trying to force away a skeevey feeling. "I'm taking my baby and getting out of here. You going to be okay? I promise I'll get researching as soon as humanly possible."

"I'm good. I'm just glad I'm not crazy."

"Yeah, well, you have plenty of other reasons you're crazy. This would just be a bonus. Okay, love you!" She wraps her left arm around my neck for a hug while keeping her other hand tightly on Tabitha's stroller. I bend down and give the baby one more kiss, this time on her forehead.

Then I head to my car. I'm practically strutting. I'm not crazy! This weird shit is for real. Still, I'm no closer to finding an answer than I was yesterday, and with this sobering thought, I slump my shoulders. But I now have a friend who will find anything she possibly can to help me. And she knows I'm not imagining it. That's the best I've got, and I have to be okay with it. For now.

Chapter 4

Miranda

Once I'm in my car, I pull my phone out to check my to-do list. I'd rather go home and take a nap, but instead I'm off to the pharmacy to pick up my anxiety medication. Yawning, I walk to the back counter and get in the line that is strangely long, considering it's 10:30 am on a weekday. I'm absentmindedly scrolling through my social media feeds when I hear a whisper. But this whisper doesn't sound like a person. This voice rumbles like the whispers I heard yesterday, only I can understand the high-pitched and cutting words.

Is this a great warrior or a weak fraud? This Chosen One is a joke. The Chosen One...

The words dissolve into a dry cackle. Is there a witch somewhere? I whirl in a circle, examining the room and expecting to find some strange-looking creature nearby. But I just see people. Normal people. Normal people looking at me like I'm not normal because of the way I'm looking at them. And I can't blame them. If I were them, I would think I'm crazy too. I mean, I think I'm crazy too, and I'm me, so...yeah.

The blond guy, about college age, standing three people behind me in line continues to scrutinize the label on the vitamins in his hand. Then he glances up, and his blue eyes focus on me. His brow is wrinkled but I'm not sure if that is from reading the tiny print or my crazed expression. "You okay, ma'am?"

I nod, hopefully reassuringly. His calm presence is reminding me to slow my breathing and I feel my blood pressure lower in response. "Yup. I'm good. Sorry, just...thought I heard something."

I turn back to face the pharmacy counter, and the small, older man in front of me finishes his transaction. A little hunched over, he turns to leave, and his smile makes me jump. It's the same wrong smile as the guy at the grocery store. The same glowing green eyes. They make his weathered face look barely human. And he looks right at me.

The pharmacy assistant impatiently declares, "Um, next?" while giving me the stink eye.

But I am rooted to my spot in line. Neither the old man nor me move. Then I hear the young man's voice in my ear, telling me, "You can do this. It's okay. He's not going to hurt you." I turn around to tell this college kid that he can go in front of me, only he's still in his same spot, three people back. He watches me intently though, encouragingly, unlike the rest of the people in line who huff and puff, tap their feet, and roll their eyes at me. So I move forward, slowly. One step at a time.

The smiling old man keeps his face toward me as he backs away from the counter. Putting on imaginary blinders, I focus on the pharmacy worker and ask for my medication. I go through the motions of normal human interaction until I can get the hell out of here. I'm barely able to stay contained in my skin. Once I've paid, I use my peripheral vision to glance at the college kid. He's still watching me, now with a surprised smile on his face. He nods proudly at me as I pass by.

When I get in my car and lock my doors, I take a deep shaky breath. "What. The. Actual. Fuck!" To my credit, the first two words were calm. But then I sob. I shake. I wipe ugly tears from my eyes and snot from my nose. I send a quick text to Eliza.

Oh. My. God. I am so losing it! We need to chat later. I can't
even explain what just happen in a text...

I sit in my car, waiting for my shaking to subside, when small shadows flitter over my dashboard. I don't see anything casting them when I look up, and I don't know if that makes me feel safer or in more danger. I no longer try to talk myself out of what I think I'm seeing, because I clearly am.

The college student walks out and looks around as though he forgot where he parked. When he sees me looking at him, he gives a nod of acknowledgement as we lock eyes from a distance. For a moment, I think he may come to my window, but he doesn't, thank god. I don't need to explain my situation to him, although I'm not really sure I could if I wanted to. But part of me wants to know what he saw standing at that pharmacy counter. When Eliza witnessed the bird-men-dragon things, I felt reassured that I'm not insane. Maybe if someone else confirmed that old man wasn't quite human, I'd be able to calm down. But the blond is at his own silver hatchback now.

Finally, I stop shaking enough to drive. On my way home, I think about the last few minutes, the eerie whispers and shrill words, the blond, the old man, the chosen one, the cackle. The chosen one? What the fuck was that about?

Once back inside my home, I take a scalding hot shower and wrap my hair in a towel, before pulling on my comfiest sweats and passing out for an hour. I wake up only because my doorbell is ringing. A lot.

At first, I drag my pillow over my head and try to go back to sleep, but then my phone keeps buzzing with alerts that someone is at my front door. Stupid video doorbells. My eyes aren't even focusing yet when I open the app, but they focus damn fast when I see the college kid from the pharmacy looking around nervously and pressing and pressing and pressing the doorbell.

Grateful I napped in my sweats instead of my underwear, I bolt out of bed and down the stairs, not knowing what I'm going to say to this kid beyond asking who the hell is he, why the hell is he here, and how the hell does he know where here is.

Instead, when I pull the door open, I find myself unable to speak as I continue panting from my run down the stairs. I'm lucky I didn't miss a step and somersault down the rest of the flight. Having made it to the bottom relatively unscathed, I stretch my shoulders to try to get the spasming in my back to subside.

While I struggle to catch my breath, the college kid holds himself very still, very tense. Standing so close now, I see he's a little older than I originally guessed, and in spite of his frantic arrival, not a strand of his long, platinum blond hair is out of place. Loosely combed over, his hair falls to the corner of his right eye and ends just under his prominent cheek bone. Thankfully, his brilliant blue eyes are normal, everyday human eyes. Although he's not smiling, his mouth looks perfectly proportioned to the rest of his face. He's rather handsome, if you like that clean-cut, all-American kind of look.

He quickly scans my entire body, as if inspecting it for any obvious damage. When he is satisfied I'm unharmed, his tension visibly eases.

"Hi, Miranda. I'm George Keating. Can I come in?" Though young, he speaks confidently. He looks over his shoulder quickly, the longer hair behind his ear gently swinging.

Although all I see behind him are shadows dancing in the grass, I can't help but sympathize with the poor guy's anxiety. Still, I'm not okay that he knows me, but I don't know him. "Why do you know my name? Or where I live? Who the—?"

He pulls out a folder that he's been holding behind his back until now and taps it against his hand. The edges are battered. He's obviously been carrying it around for a long time. Every couple of seconds, he looks around us nervously. "I can explain. But can we please have this conversation inside? I do not like being out here. Not right now."

It is my turn to look him up and down, and I decide he can't be more than a hundred and twenty pounds. I can knock him out if I need to, especially given that my adrenaline has been consistently pumping for the last day. So, I move back a step and let him in. He nods gratefully as he practically runs past me. I give the door a shove so it swings closed, and then I lock the deadbolt, looking out the window on the side while I do so. Just in case.

I lead George into my kitchen. I need a cup of coffee. Right the hell now. "Can I get you anything? George, was it?"

"No, I'm good, thank you. And yes, my name's George."

I nod as I pull down a giant mug and pick up my carafe. Once my coffee is ready and I take a long, long, long swallow, I look up at this guy.

"So George, how old are you?"

"Twenty-four."

"Cool. Cool. Cool." I take another sip. I close my eyes and slowly move the creamy caffeinated perfection around inside my mouth before allowing myself to swallow. I breathe in. And out. I open my eyes and look into George's. "And George, what, and I mean this with all due respect, what the fuck is happening to me? I have a feeling you know, and I would very much like to stop from feeling as though I'm losing my mind."

Now it's his turn to take a deep breath.

"Okay, Miranda. I can explain. Just try to stick with me until I'm done, okay?"

I raise my eyebrows and nod, tightly and quickly. It's all I can manage to do without screaming.

He gestures toward the kitchen table. "Do you want to sit down or something? This may be a hard to hear."

I shake my head, but my muscles have tightened up so much that my head makes basically the same motion as a nod.

"Okay." He breathes in and out again, then clears his throat. "On second thought, can I have a glass of water?"

"Spit it out, George."

"Right. Okay. So...first of all, you are not losing your mind. Are you familiar with the idea of 'The Chosen One'?"

A chill hits me as I remember that shrill voice from the pharmacy, whispering, *This chosen one is a joke. The chosen one...*

"The Chosen...what, exactly?"

He begins to pace, taking a couple of steps before turning around and retracing his steps, back and forth, all while he continues his explanation. "Every generation, a girl is born who's destined to be the Chosen One, the Guardian. Basically, there are all sorts of baddies and creatures—beings that no one thinks are real. And we need someone to keep it that way, to keep these creatures under wraps."

"Ummm, okay. So, Chosen One. Guardian. Creatures... Got it. Please, go on."

"Okay. When a Guardian's born, she obviously can't fight because she's a baby, right? So, the powers that be, the League of Docents, identify the next one long before the previous Chosen One is...done." He stops pacing across from me and brings his hands to rest on my counter top.

"Wait, what do you mean, when she's done?" The look he gives me sends chills up my spine while rooting me where I stand. "What do you mean 'when she's done,' George? When she dies? What is she chosen to *do*, George?" I don't enjoy the shrillness coming from my vocal cords, but I'm having a hard time keeping my tone under control

George stares down at his hands, one of which is picking at the other's thumbnail. "Yes, when she dies. She's chosen to protect humanity from those creatures I mentioned, because people en masse are not supposed to know they exist. Sometimes, the Guardian needs to just remind the beings to stay better hidden. Sometimes, she has to fight them. Sometimes, she has to kill them."

I feel like the room is closing in, the air being cut off from my lungs. "What kinds of creatures are we talking about here?"

He shifts uncomfortably on his feet. "Well, lots of different ones, from different regions, cultures, religions." He stops and stares into my eyes for a second, or I have him glued to the spot with my own gaze. He swallows hard, then continues. "Miranda...you're The Guardian. You're The Chosen One."

I stand still and stare at him, unable to blink. I can't seem to look away from him, so I close my eyes and drink the rest of my coffee before my heart can beat again. I put the mug in the sink basin and walk over to face him. I lift my chin and look him in the eyes. Then, I burst out laughing.

"This is amazing! The Chosen One! Me?" I wipe the tears from my eyes. "Did Eliza put you up to this?"

"Of course not. She has no idea about any of this."

"Then, how do you even know who Eliza is?"

He plops the folder onto the counter between us. Before I pick it up, I read the clean page pasted to the front of the otherwise tattered folder.

CLASSIFIED

Property of the League of Docents

Guardian #417: Miranda Jones Gold

Predecessor: Joanna Beaufort

Docent: George Keating

I look from the folder to George. "Twenty-four, you say?"

He doesn't respond with more than a beseeching look.

"I haven't been Miranda Jones in about seventeen years, so did you start this file when you were seven? And what the fuck is a docent?"

"Basically, I'm your trainer, your guide on this path. We're spiritually bound to each other. But...I wasn't your original docent. He unfortunately died of COVID three years ago. I'm his replacement." His Adam's apple bobs as he swallows those last words, leading me to speculate that he had some kind of relationship with my former docent.

I nod slowly because I don't know what else to do. "I'm sorry for your loss."

His eyes flick up to meet mine briefly. Then he looks around the room, uncomfortable in these surroundings, or maybe just around me. His eyes stop for a few moments on the bulletin board full of my kids' drawings and his shoulders drop a fragment of an inch, enough to be perceptible, but barely. I am suddenly very aware that he is looking at the items that most show my children's personalities, although I'm not sure why they are making his shoulders slump. Does he not like my kids or something?

"So, I'm spiritually bound...to Captain America...Junior. Great. So, how did I even get picked? I'm obviously not a baby."

"No, but you were chosen when you were born, like all Guardians. Creatures haven't been out as much as they were in past generations. Joanna barely ever had to fight, so she wasn't in as much danger as previous guardians. So, you never had to be called up. Until now."

I feel my pulse kick up, my arms and legs tense. I am beginning to panic. "Danger? What kind of danger are you implying I'm in, George?" He was just looking at my children's art. He should know the stakes if I'm in danger.

"You're not in danger *now*. It could be coming though. Things are waking up, becoming real again. That's why we need to start your training. I want you to be ready for anything."

"So the previous Guardian, she's dead now?"

He looks confused. "Oh! No! Not at all. She just had her sixtieth birthday, so the League of Docents decided she deserved to officially retire."

"Okay, but if they're—I mean, we're—chosen at birth, shouldn't there be another...one of us? Some teen or twenty-year-old who was picked for after me and maybe is in slightly better fighting condition than I am? Who doesn't have a family to take care of? Why isn't she being trained?"

George is quiet for a moment. Something heavy is going on in his mind, and he's trying to find the pieces that are light enough for him to share. Finally, he does. "A successor was chosen for you. Suzanne. She had started her training, but she also died a couple years ago, just before her eighteenth birthday."

This kid is surrounded by misery. I pinch the bridge of my nose and feel a headache coming on. "I'm sorry, George, I really think you have the wrong person here. I mean, is my family going to be in danger?"

He slowly draws a breath in and locks his eyes on me. "Your family should be in no greater danger than the world at large if you train hard and follow your destiny."

I furrow my brow at such an obviously rehearsed line. I choose my words carefully but still they shake. "These are my children I am talking about. They are more important to me than the world at large." We stare into each other's eyes for a few moments but I know I'm running out of time to have this conversation. I look down at my hands gripped tightly to the edge of my counter of their own volition. "I'm going to need a little time to process all of this."

"So, I get that. I do. But, I don't know how much time you have to process this. That was a Jinn in the pharmacy today." His words are fast. He is panicking as well.

"There was gin at the pharmacy? Did you have any of that gin? Are you drunk now, George?"

He rolls his eyes. "No, not gin. A Jinn, as in a genie."

"Oh! A Jinn. Of course." I would laugh at the absurdity of it all if it wasn't happening to me.

"He looked right at you, Miranda. He knew who you were. That's...not good."

"And...why is a Jinn knowing who I am not good?" I cross my arms awaiting his response. Absolute silence fills my kitchen for a beat, until my alarm goes off, telling me to start my school pickup routine. We both look at my chiming phone, then to each other. "Well George, looks like our time is up for today. We're going to have to pick this up next time."

"Right, of course. Well, that folder is for you. Look through it when you can. I have it memorized."

"Of course you do."

We walk to the door together.

"Miranda, I know this is shocking, but it's real. And it's important. I know it seems completely crazy, but you are The Guardian. You need to look out for yourself. You need to be careful. You're obviously behind in your training, so we need to get started right away." He crosses the threshold and turns back to me, holding out a scrap of paper with an address on it. "Meet me here tomorrow morning after you drop the kids off. We need to get to work."

I take the paper, not sure yet what I think of everything I just heard, but I'm fairly certain I will not be meeting this strange kid at a random address in the morning. However, I also need him to leave, so I nod.

"Okay, George. It was really, really strange to meet you. See ya."

I close the door behind him, make sure it's double locked (wouldn't want any Jinn sneaking in) and shake my head, a lot. I can't make sense of this now. I lock the folder in the file cabinet that is part of my kitchen command center. I don't need any of my kids finding it.

I grab my phone and try to call Jake. When it goes straight to voicemail, I remember he's flying right now, so I send a text instead. I delete and retype my message six times before I finally send it:

> I really need to talk to you later. Potential job opportunity/higher calling situation. Call when you can.

Then to Eliza:

> Do me a favor? Add "Jinn" to this search you're doing? Thanks, Love.

I'm looking through my bag for my keys when the phone chimes.

> Ummmm, Jinn? Did you rub a lamp? I can't wait to hear the latest. CALL ME WHEN THE KIDS ARE ASLEEP!

I definitely cannot commit to making that call right now, so I throw the phone in my bag with my keys, pause and grab a bottle of water, just in case Eliza is onto something with this dehydration theory.

I mumble to myself as I head out the door to pick everyone up. "Sorry George. The only monsters I have time to deal with today are the ones I created."

Chapter 5

George

When I get to my car, I'm exhausted. This was never supposed to be my life. This was my father's calling, not mine. All I wanted was a boring life. But here I am, hopefully not leading this woman to her demise. I know the odds of that happening are far greater than I could possibly hope. And especially with this Guardian. I'm sure she's a fantastic person. In fact, I know she is first hand. But she's still forty-two. It's just never been done before.

Most Guardians are fifteen or sixteen when they begin training. And not just because that's when their predecessor is reaching an age when fighting off monsters is harder. Being a Guardian is an important role, and it's draining in every way imaginable. Physically, they need to be able to fight. Hard. Against large, powerful, unbelievable foes. Mentally, they need to research, learn, and remember the ways to confront, fight, and defeat everything. While I know Miranda is brilliant, I also know from observing my own mother over the years that being one can be a big distraction when it comes to cognitive function. Being a Guardian is also emotionally draining. When it comes right down to it, if Miranda has to pick between saving the world or saving one of her kids, will she be strong enough to make the right call?

To say I was not happy when the League of Docents came to my father's funeral and assigned me this position is quite an understatement. It was the height of the pandemic, and no one was going to funerals in person. But there they were. I tried to argue with them. I tried to fight their decision, for both myself and Miranda.

They asked me to accompany them into the library, although I didn't have much of an option. There were six of them, and they directed me to sit down in one of the big leather armchairs by the windows. Then they surrounded me, making me feel outnumbered and trapped.

The Arch Docent, Perry Philips, is the most intimidating, the most powerful. So, if they wanted to scare me into compliance, it made sense to have him do the talking.

"George, you know why we're here. This pandemic has people scared and returning to belief systems they had abandoned over recent years. We've heard grumblings that gods and creatures are beginning to stir. Joanna is fifty-seven and hasn't had to fight in years, although Benjamin keeps her in good shape, as much as he can. Still, she deserves something no guardian before her has ever achieved: retirement, and soon. Benjamin and Joanna want to live out their lives together in peace. This means someone has to take up the mantle and train Miranda." He talked to me like a boarding school headmaster would explain the rules to a transfer student with an unacceptable past.

"Miranda? Isn't she too old to become Guardian? She's pretty much the age they normally... Can't you just move on to the next one?"

"No. We can't. We tried. Suzanne...Suzanne was special. Even more so than Guardians are to begin with. Your father was not assigned to her, so you probably never even knew she existed, but she was a natural protector. At fifteen, before we'd ever talked to her, she signed up for the junior rescue squad at the police department. That's when we decided to call her up instead of Miranda, when the time came."

I looked at his face, full of regret and sadness. I wasn't used to seeing the old curmudgeon feel so much. I was almost afraid to hear the rest of the story. But I had to know. "So, what happened to her?"

He smiled weakly, with no joy. It was more of a grimace of pain. He looked into the distance while pulling the memory to the front of his mind. "It was a freak car accident. It had rained briefly but very hard. She couldn't tell how wet the road was, and she hadn't had her license for even a year. Her car hydroplaned into a tree. She died instantly." He gave himself a full minute to compose himself before forcing his eyes to look into mine. Back in his usual emotionless voice, he told me, "Miranda was chosen, and the time is coming for her to fulfill her destiny."

He had to be joking. How could he possibly think Miranda Gold could do this still?

I was outraged on her behalf. "But she's a wife. She's a mom. We've never had a Guardian with her lifestyle before. We can't expect her to just abandon her family to start the training."

"No, you're right. And we don't expect that at all. You can run her training while her children are at school and her husband is at work." He remained calm throughout his explanation, as if this obviously was just the way things would be. Forget that no one had handled things this way before, in the history of the Guardian.

"So, what? She'll be a part-time Guardian? Doesn't make much sense. Guardian isn't a part-time job. We don't have another one to cover her night shifts."

"Not at all. You will train her during the days. When there are times necessary for her to leave her children, we will provide childcare. But who knows how old her children will even be when the time comes for us to call upon her? This entire conversation may be for naught, for all we know."

Once again, there was no question. This was how it was going to be, and nothing I could say or do would change their minds. This was going to be my life.

It took them three more years to decide Joanna should retire. And they only did so when the grumblings they had been hearing turned into sporadic sightings. Before the pandemic, people had begun to worship consumerism in place of myths and religions, and as a result, the creatures associated with those beliefs began to fade away. When the pandemic hit, the entire world fell into chaos. Over the years, more and more people returned to those myths and religions, and their renewed belief has enabled the creatures of old to begin reclaiming their place in this world.

The League didn't want to force Joanna to fight something big and bad, not now, not at her age, and not when she hadn't fought in decades. The time had come for her to retire.

And Miranda's time had come to step up. And I had to tell her.

I think it went as well as could be expected. Sure, she's in a bit of disbelief, but who wouldn't be? She's long passed the age where fairytales still hold the vaguest sense of possibility. I've been following her story my entire life, first through my father's stories and now through my own spiritual bond with her. I know her, much better than she knows I do. I know the rationality her mind needs to work at its peak, and this new slant on her world view must have her in a tail spin right now. And, once again, I can do nothing about it.

On the other hand, I'm excited for the chance to train her. She's stronger than she knows. She's endured a lot in her life. In fact, I think she survived her childhood only because she's so strong.

Her biggest weakness she'll need to overcome is her trouble believing in herself.

Chapter 6

Miranda

'm about to finish cooking dinner when I get a text from Jake.

> Hey, landed a couple hours ago, but it's been a whirlwind since we got off the plane. I'll try to call tonight, but why do you need to go back to work? What are you even qualified to do now? Our kids need you more than any place that would hire you, don't you think? Love you.

I had almost felt bad for not calling him, until I got his response. I'd been so consumed with creepy whispers, glowing eyes, and blond boys supposedly connected spiritually to me all afternoon that I hadn't thought to check in with Jake. But now, I'm just pissed.

What am I even qualified to do? Are you fucking kidding me? Well, Jake, apparently I'm qualified to save the world. Dipshit. But no way he'd believe that, obviously. He couldn't even bring himself to believe I could get a job working retail! It's okay. It's not like running a household with four actual children and one proverbial one counted for anything. So, does this random George kid have more faith in me than my own husband of seventeen years? I ruminate for a long time before I finally respond:

Okay, well, we'll discuss it later. I think it would be good for me to have something to do outside the home, and this employer seems very interested in hiring me, surprising as that may be. In fact, it may be something I don't have a choice but to accept...

I wish this was the first time we'd had fights like this. He definitely feels that being "Mom" should be enough for me, whereas I feel I've been nothing but "Mom" for thirteen years, and I'm desperate to get back to being Miranda first. I watch the three dots in their little gray bubble throbbing for a few seconds before they disappear. I grunt and resist the urge to throw my phone across the room before shaking myself back into the moment and shouting, "Kids! Dinner!"

***

Aside from the usual fighting between Jessie and Phoebe, and the occasional glare between Natalie and Sammy, dinner is pretty quiet. I ask all the kids how their days were. They all evade giving answers with any kind of substance.

The only one that still wants me to read bedtime stories is Sammy, but I still go into all their rooms individually to talk to them one on one for a few minutes each and every night. I have to keep the lines of communication open between us, so they know I'm here if they ever need me—something I did not have growing up.

For example, tonight Sammy confides in me that he may be in love with his long-time friend, Jackie, but he has no idea how she feels about him. He doesn't want to scare her off. He'd rather be her friend than not have her in his life at all. He is so wise for a little boy.

Granted, all my kids are wise beyond their years. It makes it really hard to parent them. This is for many reasons, one of which is that I am quite certain, at least in many regards, I am less mature than they are... Sam's almost asleep, so I kiss my sweet boy on his soft hair and whisper my nightly prayer to him. "Sweet dreams. Sleep tight. Don't let the bed bugs bite."

I move onto Natalie's room. She's lying in her bed, cradling her koala babies, and reading when I walk in.

"Please stop torturing your brother about Jackie."

She stretches and yawns and places her book on her nightstand. "Did it really bother him that much? I'm sorry."

"Don't tell me you're sorry, tell him... Actually, don't. Just let it go. Okay?"

"Yeah, okay... He's okay?" Her blue eyes twinkle with concern.

"He's fine. You're a good sister for asking." I perch on the edge of her bed and brush her silky hair out of her eyes. "Anything new going on with you? Anything you want to chat about?"

"Nah, same old, same old." She's content snuggled into her marsupial collection. "Okay. You know I love you, right?"

"Of course, I do. I love you, too. How's Daddy's trip going?" Natalie has always been a daddy's girl.

"Good, I think. He sent me a text a couple hours ago. He's just really busy."

"That's good then." She yawns again. "I'm good, Mom. I'm ready to go to sleep."

"Okay, love bug. I love you."

"Love you too. Goodnight, Mom."

"Sweet dreams. Sleep tight. Don't let the bed bugs bite."

Phoebe's listening to The Beatles and laying out her outfit for the morning when I knock on her door frame. She smiles at me while singing to herself about a fireman rushing in from the rain. I'm drained from the day, so I lie in her bed to wait for her.

"Mom, you okay? You seem a little...off?" She places a striped shirt and polka-dot pants on her dresser, and I suppress my grin. Even at eleven, she matches only by accident, but she always looks adorable. Coordination and conformation are overrated anyway.

I roll my eyes. Even her concern is sassy. "Thanks, hon. Love you too. I'm okay. Just have a lot going on. A lot to think about."

She quirks an eyebrow as she looks over her shoulder at me. "Like the weird fox?"

I smile. "Yeah, like the weird fox."

"I'm sure there's a reasonable explanation. All folklore and myths have to start somewhere. Maybe it's a relatively common occurrence, and that's where the myth about kitsune started."

"I'm sure you're right. You usually are." I puff my chest out in pride at how brilliant my kids are.

She beams at me from the acknowledgement and shuts her light. Then she skips over and hops into her bed.

I cuddle up next to her, tucking her head under my chin. "Anything you want to talk about?"

She shakes her head. "I'm good. But can you just snuggle me for a few minutes? It's harder for me to fall asleep when Daddy's away."

"I'm happy to, Sweets." She doesn't often ask for me to snuggle her anymore, so I'm definitely not going to pass up this opportunity. She is my most empathetic child. Whenever something is off with one of us, she feels that imbalance, and it affects her.

We lie in quiet for a few minutes. Then she announces, "Okay, there's no way I'm falling asleep like this anymore. Sorry!"

We both crack up laughing. I kiss her head and say, "Goodnight, sleep tight. Don't let the bed bugs bite," into her hair.

She gives me one last tight hug. "Night, mom."

I pause outside Jessie's door, steeling myself with a deep breath for my strongest child. I'm not sure I can handle her strength right now. I open her squeaky door. She sits on her bed, her headphones and video game discarded beside her. She's erased all traces of her childhood obsession with kittens from her room. Instead, posters of rock bands cover her walls. I poke my head in through the narrow opening I allow myself. "Hey, Sweetie."

"Hey, Mom." She looks up and closes her laptop so we can actually communicate. "Are you okay?"

I'm taken aback by her question. "Umm, yes? Why?"

"I mean, remote encounter with a very real three-tailed fox aside, you just seem to be distracted and not quite your normal self." Her hazel eyes look stormy as she locks them on mine. She must pay more attention to me than I thought.

I raise my eyebrows. "I'm okay. Just lots going on, ya know?"

She nods quietly. She hardly ever does anything quietly.

"Are *you* okay?" I ask, fighting the sudden urge to comb her long, mermaid-like brown curls the way she used to let me when she was six, and hasn't since.

"Yeah. I think I'm just getting my period. A little weepy, you know?" And then her tears well up. And then mine well up, because that's what happens when your strong first born shows their vulnerability. And then we're sitting on the edge of her bed, hugging and crying about everything and nothing because we have to do that once in a while.

Sometimes you find out you're supposed to be fighting mythological beasts and life just builds up to the point when you need to cry. But your husband is out of town, and your best friend is on a crazy schedule with her baby, and you don't know who else you could tell this bullshit to who wouldn't have you committed. So, you hold your girl and cry.

After a few minutes, she gently pushes back, wipes her cheeks, and looks me in the eye. "I'm good, Mom. You can go." She smiles at the end, so I know she's okay.

"Okay, baby. Just, come find me if you need me." I don't really want to leave, but I know it's important to give her space when she wants it.

"Okay, Mom. Goodnight." She still has her slight smile on her face.

"Sweet dreams. Sleep tight. Don't let the bed bugs bite." I tuck her in like she's still six and kiss her forehead.

Once I close her door, I head to my bathroom. Mascara has gathered in my already prominent bags, making me look haggardly. Thank god Jake is away. He'd have something clever to say about this look, I'm sure.

Two make-up remover wipes later, I'm bare faced. I find a comfy pair of pjs and take off the sweats I never changed out of when a certain someone so rudely interrupted my nap.

George Keating. Ugh.

I grab my phone from its charger on my nightstand, note that it's nine thirty, then I head back downstairs. On my way down, I get a text from Jake.

> Hey, sorry. I know it's late there. Things are really insane here. I should be able to call for a couple minutes in about an hour, if you'll still be up. Love you.

I text him back while I sigh to myself.

> Yup. I'll be here. Call whenever. I really do need to talk to you.

For a minute, I consider calling Eliza. She told me to call her. But I don't want to get stuck in the middle of filling her in and miss my chance to talk to Jake, so I lose myself in some trashy TV instead. Two and a half episodes later, my phone vibrates my pocket.

When I answer, I can barely hear anything over the music booming in the background. Then my husband's slightly frantic voice comes through. "Miranda?" He shouts so loudly that I have to pull the phone away from my ear.

"Jake? Jake? Are you there?"

After a few seconds, the music drops a few decibels.

"Can you hear me now?" he yells.

"Umm, a little better. Where are you?"

"Oh, Callie and her band took us to this club. It's so loud. I don't really like it. But you know, we're supposed to woo her and all. I didn't even like this kind of place when I was twenty-one. Now? Forget it."

I smile to myself. At least I don't need to worry about him falling in love with the Las Vegas scene.

"I really need to talk to you about that...job offer. Now, actually. Things have been really crazy here, and—" I stop because I hear Ryan's voice. I can't make out what he's saying, but I know what's coming anyway.

"Hey, I have to go, Miranda. I'll call you tomorrow when I can. Don't take any job offers until we can hash out the pros and cons, okay? Love you!"

Then both the music and my husband cut off. The phone is silent. I look at the built-in bookshelves surrounding our television and see the globe we bought when we visited the world's largest globe in Maine on our babymoon when I was pregnant with Jessie. I go over and turn the world until the United States is facing me. I put my thumb on Las Vegas and my pinky on New Jersey, measuring the distance. Then I trace the line between us back and forth before I kiss my finger tips and place them

on Las Vegas. "Sweet dreams. Sleep tight. Don't let the bed bugs bite...,
you dick."

Past midnight, I drag myself upstairs. I may as well attempt to sleep, I
guess. Who knows when destiny will ring my doorbell again.

***

Not having had the most conducive sleep conditions, the next morning
is a blur. I manage to get everyone up, fed, and in my car without anyone
being late for school. My only other stop is to pick up a giant latte before
going home to do some laundry and crash on the couch. With coffee in
one hand, I switch my first load to the dryer and am throwing in my
second when my phone rings.

"Hey, Eliza."

"You didn't call last night! I need to hear the latest. Why am I looking
up Jinn, Miranda Gold?"

"Oh, right. So, are you familiar with the concept of The Chosen One?"
Silence. Then, "Go on..."

Surprisingly, Eliza remains quiet while I tell her all about the pharmacy
and then the college kid showing up at my front door and how I'm
supposedly a Guardian and how he expected me to go meet him at
a random address today and how I blew it off because there's just
no fucking way that was going to happen. "Maybe there's a statute of
limitations or something, and I can get out of this?"

"God, I hope so. I don't want you to pop a hip out fighting a sphinx or
something. No offense, but you're kind of I-slept-on-it-wrong years old. I
mean, remember the time you slept on an extra pillow and couldn't turn
your head for three days. How exactly are you going to be fighting, like,
Cerberus?"

"Um, I mean, thanks for that... Well, I'm going to go. Maybe if I look through this folder, I can find a customer service number or something. You know I hate to be a Karen, but I think I'm going to need to speak with this kid's manager."

"Ok, Honey. Good luck finding a loop hole in your destiny." She's so cheery about all of this, but I'm not super encouraged.

I plop my phone down on the kitchen table and collapse into a chair to read my file. Whoever these League of Docent fuckers are, they really have followed me closely my entire life. The file includes my newborn picture with my birth announcement, and my school photos from kinder-garten through senior year of college are stapled to photocopies of my report cards and my annual physicals.

Passing my medical history, I find typed reports on everyone I have ever been close to—family, friends, boyfriends, and roommates. Even though my entire life is in this folder, there is no form I can file with a complaint department. No Return My Birthright Authorization Request. No customer service line. I can't even find a piece of company letterhead indicating who collected this information.

If most pages weren't clearly older than George, I would have won-dered if he had collected it all himself somehow.

Speaking of George, he obviously thinks there's been some kind of horrible mistake as well. Some pages have notes in the margins. The handwriting looks way too neat for a twenty-four-year-old, but they all end with the initials G.K.

My adolescent poetry includes comments like, "Is this girl stable enough to take this on?" And I roll my eyes when I see, "After reading this, I'm a little concerned she'll sacrifice herself unnecessarily." Oh, George, you try being a thirteen-year-old girl sometime. Jerk.

Then, on photocopies of my junior high yearbooks' activities pages, George wrote, "One year of softball. One year of basketball. One year of track. Not a lot of perseverance."

Oh, fuck this asshole. I have always hated sports. That has nothing to do with my perseverance. At least I kept trying new ones when it turned out I hated the last one.

Focus. This is not the point, Miranda. He's actually proving your point with his stupid, immature commentary. "I am so not the Chosen One. No way! No how!"

Only, saying that aloud makes me sound like Jake. I decide to try calling him again. Even if my so-called destiny is obviously a mistake, I need to win this fight. Both fights, actually. But first, I need Jake to admit I'm desirable, as an employee... I need him to see I'm more than his kids' mom.

The phone rings and rings and rings before going to voicemail. So, I call back. This time, he picks up on the second ring. "Jesus, Miranda! Don't you know what time it is here?"

I look at the clock, and do some math. "It's 7:30. You'd have been up for an hour already here. Get over it. We need to talk."

"Really? Yeah, if I was home, I'd have been up at 6:30, but I'm not home. I'm in Vegas, Baby! I went to bed only three hours ago." His voice is gravely and his words slur a bit.

"Are you fucking kidding me? I'm here taking care of our four kids, and you're staying up until 4:30 a.m.? What were you doing? You know what, I don't think I want to know. I need to talk to you about—"

"Yeah, right, your job opportunity. What kind of awful pyramid scheme do you want to get into?"

"Ex...Excuse me?" I feel like he punched me in the stomach.

"Isn't that the employer you're talking about? What else could you possibly be qualified for that someone would be so insistent on hiring you to do? You haven't been in the work force in well over a decade."

"You know what? Go to hell." Silence divides us, but I can hear his angry tired breathing. "You've made it clear many times that you think being a mom should be enough for me, but you've never been such a flat-out dick about it before! Enjoy Vegas. Let me know when you book your return trip so I can let the kids know."

I hang up before he can say anything else. I hate that so many of his trips are open ended. I never know when I can depend on him and when I can't.

I stand up and begin to pace. I'm fuming. How dare he think so little of me, of what I'm capable of. How dare he stay out partying and doing god knows what with god knows who while I'm dealing with Jinn and little dragon man birds and blond guys and our children! I mean, not that dealing with our children is the same as the rest, but they definitely have their own set of challenges that exhaust me.

I return to the folder. My folder. George's folder. What did I do with that address he gave me? I wasn't going to go, but I must have thrown it out by mistake. So now I have no way to contact the weirdo if I even wanted to. That may be for the best, really. I definitely shouldn't reach out to him now, when I'm so angry at Jake. I might do something I'll regret, like agree to be this Chosen One.

Instead, I shove the folder into my oversized purse, grab my keys, and jump in my car. I need to go shopping, so I drive to the mall, but not the everyday reasonable mall. Nope. I'm going to the super posh mall where I always feel uncomfortable in my own skin. How's that for us not needing anymore income, Jake!

I'm pulling out of my driveway when my phone rings. I push the button on my steering wheel and hear Bluetooth pick up. "Hey, Eliza. What's up?"

"Did you find anything out from your folder?" She sounds like she's chewing.

"Just that George also thinks this is a horrible mistake." I hear the anger in my own voice.

"Oh, okay. I found our red bat birds." She sounds totally calm, as if this is an everyday research mission I sent her on.

I am obviously not as calm. "What? You could have led with that! What are they?"

"Imps."

"Imps?" I don't realize I've effectively parked at a stop sign until a honk behind me startles me back to the real world.

"Yup. Imps."

"Okay. You have anything else for me there, Oracle?"

She pauses before asking, "Matrix Oracle or Batman Oracle?"

"Um, Batman Oracle?"

"Okay, thank god. So, imps are generally considered to be more mischievous than dangerous." She's in writer mode, all business.

"Well, that's a good thing. Yay, some good news!" I am all emotion.

"Right, but they rarely appear on their own. They're usually running errands for a greater being. Like...a god."

"Come again? What the hell? A god? I'm going to have to deal with gods now?" I'm grateful the mall parking lot is so empty since I just swerved across two lanes of parking spots.

"Keep in mind this is all folklore I'm looking at. It's far from scientifically proven facts." A baby starts crying in the background.

My heart melts. "Awww, Tabby. Go get your baby. I'm good. I'm going shopping."

"Of course, as one does in a moment such as this... Be safe!" Her mom voice is getting good! She must be practicing.

"Yup. Talk to you later."

Running errands for a god... What the hell?

***

Twenty minutes later, I'm sipping a Frappuccino and walking toward Williams Sonoma to shop for some new bakeware. The hairs on my neck stand up a little.

"Oh, you've got to be kidding." I stop and look around, but I see no red batlike things, no butterflies, and no creepy smiling guys with glowing eyes. So, what will it be now?

"You didn't meet me."

Fuck. I turn slowly on the spot, and there he is, about ten feet away from me. George. Fucking. Keating.

He ambles slowly to his left and so I follow in kind. Thus, we do this little dance around one another.

"So, what kind of mythological creature are you, George?"

"What are you talking about? I'm just your docent. I told you."

I pause where I am. "So why are you the only thing I've come across that makes my hair stand on end?"

The corner of his mouth lifts into a smile, in a charming way. Unlike the deranged Jinn, George is quite handsome. Granted, that could be the massive fight with my husband talking. But then his piercing blue eyes lock on mine. No, he's definitely handsome. I mean, if you're into that blond surfer-boy kind of look... Too bad he's a fetus. Or good thing he's a fetus. Depends on your angle, I guess. I'm okay to continue the circling until I hear it. That voice. Again.

The Chosen One...

The shrill whisper pounds inside my skull. I grab my head with both hands and double over.

I look up at George. Is this his mind talking to mine? Is this part of our connection, because if it is, he can keep it.

"I don't need this bullshit! I have a good life. I don't want this!" I scream over the wordless screeching cackle that has replaced the whisper in my head. Falling to my knees, I pull my head down to try to block out the laughter, but I can't turn it off. I can't make it go away.

George runs and slides across the floor towards me feet first, landing in a lying down position such that he quickly wraps his entire body around me. He brings his face as close to my ear as I'll allow and yells so I can hear him over the hellishness in my own head. "You need to come with me, Miranda. You need to train. This is only going to get worse if you don't accept it."

The sound starts to dissipate. I look at George, and he wipes away the tears I didn't know I had shed. "You don't believe it should be me either. I read your notes. I know what you think of me. I have no perseverance. I'm not stable. I. Don't. Want. This."

A look of confusion casts a shadow across his face. I pull the folder out of my bag and thrust it into his lap.

He opens it and leafs through the pages until he sees the notes in the margins. "Oh, these? These are by my dad. He was the one originally assigned to be your docent." Suddenly quiet, George disappears into his memories. "When he died, the league asked me to take his place. That's when I started to learn more about you. He studied you for thirty-nine years. I've had three to catch up. I'm sorry if you're afraid I'm not ready, but I truly am." He pauses and looks at me, this time with a tear in the corner of his eye. "I think you are too."

I shudder.

Damnit. Damn *this*. This moment. Because this is when everything changes. Not when I saw the stupid fox, or the dragon bird, or even the creepy guy at the grocery store. This right here. This is the one. This is when I decide to go with George Keating and change my life forever.

Shit.

Chapter 7

Miranda

"**F**uckfuckfuckfuckfuckfuckfuck." I cannot believe I am going along with this. What was I thinking? This kid shows me one moment of emotion at the mall yesterday, and I cave and let him blindfold and drive me to who the hell knows where?

"Will you please calm down? You can handle it. I know you can. That's why we're doing this! You need to prove to yourself that you can do this, and you are The Guardian. Because I'm sorry to say it, Sweetheart, but you are." I can hear the smirk in his voice.

"Sweetheart? Really? I could be your mother!"

He releases a deep throaty laugh. "Nope. You couldn't. No way."

"Whatever. You seem to be driving very fast."

"It just feels that way because you're blindfolded. I promise you, I'm being perfectly safe."

"Fine. Whatever." I literally begin to twiddle my thumbs because what else can I do?

I don't bother trying to keep track of the turns, and I have no idea how much time has gone by when he finally slides the car into park and turns off the engine. My heart is racing, and I think I'm definitely going to throw up. I hear him take a deep, shaky breath next to me.

This admittedly makes me freak out. "Hold on…Are you nervous? You're not allowed to be nervous! You're the one who brought me here. You're the one saying I can do this. If you're nervous, I'm fucked!"

"I'm not nervous. I know you're the one. I know you can do this. I'm just… It's still a new experience for me, okay?"

"Oh. Okay. Sure. That puts me totally at ease, George!"

I hear a chuckle before, "Let's get this done so we can get some coffee."

"Coffee? There's coffee after this?" I would never have complained if I knew there was the promise of coffee. "Now you're talking. Why didn't you say so! Let's go!"

"You know, I bet if a serial killer showed up to lure you into his van,, he'd have no problem so long as he had a pot of fresh coffee inside." I can hear him shake his head right before I hear his car door open and close a moment later.

Alone in the car, I give myself a pep talk. "It's cool, Miranda. You are amazing. You made four amazing little people. You can do anything. You can. You are definitely not going to die wherever we are and leave those four amazing people to get themselves home from school this afternoon. Not an option."

And then my door is pulled open. I knew it was coming, but I still jump and give a little yip from the startle.

"You okay there?"

"Yup, yup. I'm grand." My voice is shaking, but his is too. "Hey, George? Why is everything so…loud?"

"Is it? I guess when I blindfolded you, it awakened your super hearing."

"Super hearing?"

But he's done talking, and I am lifted to my feet. I hear my door close, and he is walking me into…something. Somewhere. I don't hear a door open, but the atmosphere changes around me. The air feels a little colder and smells a little stale. The sound of my feet dragging against the smooth floor creates a bit of an echo with every step. I hear a big door being dragged closed behind me.

George walks me forward for a couple more minutes. I say a couple minutes, but I have no idea how long we're walking. Time has no meaning, and we're making so many turns, left and right and right and left, that I wouldn't be able to keep track if I'd wanted to. Maybe your average young lady Chosen One could. But not me!

He puts something in my hand, something heavy and awkward and dangerous. I swallow hard.

"Okay. There's your protection. I'm going to walk away now." With his hands on my shoulders, he speaks into my ear quietly from behind. "Count to one hundred, and then you can take off your blindfold."

I swallow hard again and nod. I count out loud but quietly, because if I try to do it in my head, I'll lose count. Once at one hundred my empty, shaking hand raises to remove my blindfold. I struggle with the knot for a few seconds before getting frustrated and just pulling the whole thing up and off my head.

I'm inside what looks like a dark warehouse, but I can still see as if I am outside on a bright summer day. It's a strange feeling, and I wonder if this enhanced vision is something I just have now, like my new super hearing. If it is, will I ever get used to it? Of course, all I can see anyway are boxes stacked to twice my height. Paths on both sides of me twist around corners to who knows where. I can sense someone running on the far side of the space to my left. I stand still and close my eyes, tracing their path around the room with my hearing, like some freakish bat lady. Whoever, or whatever, that is, they have entered the maze.

Damn it! Enhanced hearing is not something I need with the way my kids whine…

Quite frankly, this entire situation is utter bullshit, but if I need to listen to my kids fighting on eleven now too, I'd rather just use this machete thing to stab myself right here and be done with it. Machete thing? Is that what this is? Why do I know that, and why do I have this? What am I doing in here that I need a fucking machete?

I can make out the ragged breathing of whatever is in here with me. It's somewhere behind me and sounds like it holds a whole lotta breath. I'm not ready to turn around, but I can tell it's getting closer.

What the hell did he put in here with me?

Why did I do the one thing that I, as a woman, have learned not to do from the time I could comprehend personal safety: trust a totally random guy I just met? Big mistake.

I look to the ceiling, hoping I can get my bearings and figure out where in this maze of boxes I am. Kind of near the center maybe? At least it looks that way to me. A path open to my left leads to a right turn about ten feet ahead. Behind me, I see a sharp right, followed by a left. That's where the breathing is coming from, but I can't see anything, aside from the boxes.

No way am I getting out of here until I face whatever that thing is, so I can either run until it finds me, or I can put on my big girl panties and go find it first. That's not much of a choice; fight it exhausted from running away, or go looking for it (granted, also exhausted, because what the fuck is even happening right now). As I move quickly (for me) through the path to the right, I realize I may be heading toward the sound of breathing a little too enthusiastically.

I turn the corner and slam face first into a wall. But this wall isn't made of boxes; it's made of flesh and bone with a baseball-sized belly button right below my eye level. Up close, that ragged breathing sounds much more like snorting. I let my gaze drift upward. The musky smell of a farm on a hot summer day bombards me, as hot air puffs onto my face from the giant bull looking down at me. Well, not really a bull... A bull head on a human body. Why is that so familiar?

Holy. Shit. That's a minotaur.

"Holy shit. You're a minotaur!" (Hey, you try to keep your internal monologue internal when you're face to navel with a motherfucking minotaur.) Immediately, I spin on my heel and run back along the path I just came from, toward the center of wherever the fuck I am.

Oh! It's a labyrinth! I probably could have pieced together that I'd be fighting a minotaur, if only I'd thought about the fact that I'm clearly in a maze and George and I have been talking about how I have to learn to fight various mythological creatures. Total mom-brain moment. But, in all fairness, I never once considered the possibility that a minotaur could be real.

I reach the spot where I first uncovered my eyes in this strange maze of certain death and continue to follow the path to the right, right, left, left...right into a dead end. In a small space, about the size of a standard walk-in closet, I look up at the ceiling high above. It looks like I'm dead center in the room. Although, I definitely could have thought of a different way to describe it... Dead. Center.

Guess this is where I fight or die. Let's see if this guy is right about me or full of shit. I turn to face the only entrance into the space, holding up my machete, as if I know how to use it.

The minotaur enters. Slowly. He's not in a rush. He tilts his giant head, as if he's confused to find me here. As if he didn't just follow my scent or my breathing or whatever minotaurs use to track their prey, to this exact location, for this exact purpose. He licks his lips; grins the most sinister, gruesome looking grin I've ever had the privilege of seeing; and rubs his hands together like he's sharpening a pair of kitchen knives. The snorting breath comes faster now, probably because he realizes what a tasty morsel I'll be. Okay, a full course meal. Whatever.

"Fuck." It's more a breath than an utterance, but it has to be said.

The behemoth stumbles toward me, all brawn with no grace. Unfortunately, I possess neither of those myself. Also, I have no idea how to leverage to my advantage the knowledge that he's not graceful. Instinctively, I crouch down and somersault between his legs.

What the fuck was that? I haven't done a somersault in thirty years. What in God's name made me think that was a good idea? Holy shit, I could have decapitated myself with this machete. Definitely not the smartest thing I've ever done. But also, that was awesome. Go, girl! Eeek! Minotaur! Head in the game, Miranda!

As surprised as I am, I manage to jump effortlessly to my feet. At that same moment, he swings his fist into the side of my head. It isn't really a punch so much as a push, but it still hurts like a sonofabitch and knocks me off of my feet and into a wall of boxes. They and I topple over. I'm literally stunned. I've never been hit before, much less by a minotaur. With my ear ringing from the impact, I can't hear him approach. So, I'm unprepared when his face is suddenly right up in front of mine. I wish I had a pair of billiard balls because I could use them to stop up those nostrils that are only inches from my face when

SNOOOOOORRRRRTTTTTTTTTTTTT.

Another swampy puff of air accosts what is left of my senses. My face is left damp, but I refuse to think about which of his bodily fluids it is. We freeze staring at each other, him at my face, me at his snout. Then he starts to grunt in a way that makes his abdomen shake up and down, and I realize he's actually laughing at me.

My shoulders collapse. I've been laughed at like this before, though not by a minotaur. I am suddenly so much smaller. I hear his laughter echoing through my childhood bedroom, my childhood mind, my entire childhood really. I was always the butt of his jokes. I feel myself give up. My fingers loosen their grip on my only weapon. The edges of my vision turn black and the darkness encroaches inward.

George was wrong, and now I'm not going to get out of this. I'm going to die here. I knew I couldn't do this Guardian thing. Oh my God, my kids... Will they ever know what happened to me? What do they say to family of the Chosen One when she's killed in the line of duty? Do they stage a car accident or something? And who even are *they*?

As I wallow in my self-doubt, the minotaur suddenly crouches to the ground, grabbing my ankles and yanking, flipping me to hang upside down. I hear the ocean as all the blood rushes to my head. The machete lies on the ground beneath me. My head is once again level with the creature's abdomen, only this time my feet aren't under me to carry me away.

Being upside down makes my body tingle and my senses wake back up. My first thought is, of course, my kids. Right now, they're in school, being kids, their only concerns being their orchestra lessons, or algebra test, or whether that cute girl likes them back. And that is what it should be. There is enough bullshit in this world that they shouldn't have to worry about a fucking minotaur killing their mom. I need to get home to them. I need to embarrass them with hugs when they walk out the doors of their schools. I need to feed them ice cream for dinner and let them finish a movie before tucking them in for bed tonight. I need to hear their laughter. Their laughter can heal anything broken in me.

The thought of my babies hones my determination to survive. My pulse is strong and steady. I look that beast right in the belly and inhale his smelly body odor deeply before I let out my own, "SNOOOOOOOOOOR-RRRRTTTTTT." Then I take the only chance I can think of and reach out toward him. I hold my breath and mentally cross my fingers as I channel my thirteen years of parenting experience into my finger tips and tickle that beast's belly as if my life depends on it, because it literally does.

His abdomen shudders once. Then a single giggle creates a ripple effect that strengthens until the beast wriggles and twists to escape my assault, but I latch onto his fur with one hand while I tickle up and down his sides until he sinks to his knees, his body convulsing with laughter. He drops his arms to guard his stomach, leaving me in a heap on the floor but still free. The machete is in front of him and I am by his feet. I have to get around him to get it.

As I quietly approach he spins to face me, one knee still on the ground, and I launch myself at him with a fresh batch of tickles. He falls backwards and kicks at me, but I use his chest hair as hand holds to climb him and that sensation is starting to wear him down. Finally, a kick connects with my stomach and sends me right over to the machete.

I allow myself to feel the pain for one second then, scrambling, I grab the machete and spin back. He's shuddering on his side in the aftershocks of his first tickle torture.

I have only one option in this situation, as far as I can tell. I'm clearly no expert. With every ounce of resolve I can muster I swing the machete above my head and come down with as much force as I can into the side of his neck.

The damn blade gets stuck.

"Are you fucking kidding me!" With one foot on his shoulder, I pull my blade out and try again. And again. And again. Either the tickling really incapacitated him, or the first stroke, though not fatal, sent him into some kind of shock, because he's not fighting back. He just lies there with his head angled away from me, allowing me to try again and again, while he kind of looks at me. Each strike makes little progress cutting through his thick skin and the muscles of the creature's neck.

"Didn't."

Swing.

"Your."

Swing.

"Mother."

Swing.

"Ever."

Swing.

"Tell you."

Swing.

"Not to play with your food."

This time, I clear the hide. The machete slices through the beast's neck with such surprising ease that I spin to the side with the force of my swing, almost falling into another wall of boxes. In the same moment, something warm and thick splashes across my face and hands. I'm glad I don't own any good clothes, because I'm pretty sure when I look down, I'll find every inch of my body covered in blood. I take a deep breath and use the inside of the collar of my shirt to wipe my face so I can at least see.

As the adrenaline fades, my arms and legs start shaking. I drop the machete and fall backward, tears silently streaming down my face. I roll to my side just in time to be sick without choking myself on it.

Holy shit. I'm alive. I killed something. I killed a minotaur! Ohmygodohmygodohmygod.

Behind me, I hear clapping. I spin to face the entrance of the dead end, only to see George Keating, the man child that got me into this mess, grinning from ear to ear.

He rakes his eyes over the decapitated monster on the ground, before raising his eyebrows and looking my blood-soaked body up and down. This man, in his pleated khakis and crisp polo shirt, has the audacity to cross his arms in pride and announce, "Told you so! Now, do you believe you can do this?" Then, without even waiting for an answer, he adds, "Okay, let's go get you cleaned up."

***

In the car, we sit in silence for a few minutes. Well, except for plastic that crinkles with my every breath.

"I cannot believe you wrapped me in a contractor bag."

"Really? This is a new car, and you're covered in minotaur blood." His voice cracks a little on the word "you're." His head is angled to the window but I see the hint of a smirk on the side of his face.

I'd almost find that adorable if he wasn't so irritating. "I'm covered in minotaur blood...because of you, George!"

He shrugs. He can't argue that point.

Crinkle, crinkle, crinkle.

Now he's irritated. "What are you doing?"

"I can't exactly check my watch or pull out my phone. I'm trying to find the clock in this new car."

He smirks and taps a spot on the very busy control display in the center of the dashboard. "It's 10:47."

"Wow, I am good. That was fast! I still have so much time before I have to pick up my kids." This must be adrenaline talking because I feel like I was in there a month.

"Well, that's good, because you really need to get cleaned up first. In fact, it's probably a good idea for you to get cleaned up before you go to your house. Unless you want to cover your own car in minotaur blood, or for your neighbors to see you hopping in in a trash bag."

"Ugh. Fine. Where are we going? I believe I was promised coffee."

"My place. And I'll brew a pot while you clean up. I definitely need some caffeine as well."

"You're place? That's kind of weird."

"Nope. Not weird. It's fine. It's your new headquarters after all."

Whatever I expected George's bachelor pad to look like, this is not it. We turn down a perfect treelined street and stop at a huge iron gate with stone lions on either side. He types a code into a little key pad sticking up from the ground, and the gate swings open. Further down the driveway, we approach what I can only describe as a castle. Its rectangular blocks of stone in shades of red and gray loom ahead. My jaw drops.

"What is that?"

"That's...headquarters." He slides the gear shift into park.

"George... I have a very serious question." He turns to look at me and once our eyes are locked, I ask, "Are you Batman?"

His laugh is deep and rich, from his chest. He pulls his face into a serious expression and drops his voice an octave or two. "No, Miranda. I promise. You're the only superhero in this relationship."

I swallow hard as his clear blue eyes lock on mine.

He's young enough to be your son, Miranda... Keep it together.

He clears his throat to break the awkward silence. "Seriously though, this property has been in my mom's family for years. It's not some docent estate or anything. Okay. Let's get you cleaned up!" He slaps his knees for emphasis and gets out of the car. When he comes to my door and opens it, he looks at me cocooned in my contractor bag and thinks out loud, "What are we going to do with you..." Then he snaps his fingers as an idea hits him.

I do not like the smirk on his lips.

***

Ten minutes later, I'm still wrapped in plastic and cursing him out as I lie on the floor of one of his guest bathrooms while he gets the shower ready and goes to find some clothes that can replace the ones I need to throw away.

I cannot believe he carried me here in this garbage bag. How could he possibly be so strong? I must be twice his size! And I didn't even get a good view of the inside of the house because he threw me over his shoulder like a sack of potatoes. I can at least say the house does have beautiful old oak hardwood floors though. But still! I let out a primal scream.

He calls to me from another room. "I wasn't going to let you drip minotaur blood all over my house."

"Once again, the blood...your fault!" I quiet down as a terrifying thought hits me. "Wait, am I going to be covered in blood often now?"

He comes back in with a stack of fluffy towels and clean clothes, a ponderous look on his face. "That's a good question. I want to say no? There will be lots of times you don't need to kill anyone, and even when you do, it won't always need to be so...yeah. Gross."

"George, did it need to be so gross this time? Was there another way I should have gone about killing that thing? Or *not* killing it?"

"Probably. I have so many books we'll read, together. We'll get it all figured out next time. I don't know the right way to handle every situation. I've spent the last three years studying *you*. I haven't really had time to research the rest. I guess I've been thinking you'd just know about everything on your own when the time came. But today was about your instincts, about proving to you that this is who you are meant to be."

I nod. "I get that. Thank you for showing me what I am capable of. Never in a million years would I have expected that I could save myself with my mad tickle skills." I pause to let this moment hold its space. But I still have shit to do, so I don't pause too long before I continue. "Hey George, can you get me out of this garbage bag now?"

"Oh, shit. Yes! On it." He takes a pocket knife and cuts the bag free in one smooth motion, then helps me to my feet. He looks at me for a minute until I raise my eyebrows. When he realizes I still need to undress and get in the shower, a blush reddens his cheeks, and he stumbles over his words as he rushes out the door.

I smile to myself and lock it. Right, onward then. I strip my clothes, standing on the cut open bag, and then wrap them in it in such a way that there is no exposed blood to make a mess. Then I get in the hot shower and make the water hotter. After seeing this "house," I'm sure his hot water tank is big enough to accommodate. The shower is too big to both lean against the wall and stay under the water, so I collapse in a heap in the middle of the floor. The hot water washes away not only the blood of the minotaur but also the sins of my prior life. It's baptizing me, the new Guardian.

Now I know I can do this.

Now I know I will do this.

Now I know who I am.

And I'm all in.

As soon as I can get myself up and off this floor.

Chapter 8

George

I am thoroughly impressed with Miranda. She was actually able to kill the minotaur...I put in a maze with her. I know her success shouldn't surprise me; she is a Guardian after all. But it did surprise me. I was really worried about her. I still am, actually. As she showers, I am afraid of what is going through her head and how she is going to react to those thoughts.

All docents worry about their charges; it comes with the territory. But no other docent has ever been in my position, with a Guardian like Miranda. I'm struggling to wrap my head around how many lives will be destroyed if something happens to her. Miranda has kids, a family, something no other Guardian in history has had the privilege, or lifespan, of experiencing. Those four kids need her. Her husband needs her too. Even her friends need her; she has seriously meaningful relationships with those women. Women who would miss her, and mourn her, and though I'm certain they would step in to help Jake with those four little humans...I can't go there.

The thing that has always struck me about Miranda, the thing that helped me realize she could not only succeed as the Guardian, but would absolutely kick ass as long as she believed in herself, is knowing she built this life full of love and connection out of the ashes of her past. She escaped; from her parents, from that house, from that life where she was made to believe she was unworthy of love. When she left, there was no safety net. If she failed, her options would have been to return, defeated, to the beasts who remained inside her childhood home, or a life doing Gods knows what on the streets. But when Miranda sets her mind to something, there is no option to fail. She would never accept that. So she succeeded, with quite a lot of grit and determination, to build a life filled with everything she had never known; safety, comfort, support, love. That woman's ability to love with so much of herself, unconditionally, and without having had an example of how that could be done, is a superpower all on its own. I can't help but feel she is meant for more than even this.

And yet I can't deny the world needs her. Although I resented having this role forced onto me too, I am glad to be assigned as her docent. I want to give her every chance I can to succeed and every opportunity to live as full a life as she can possibly hope to live now that her life has been altered beyond her control. I need to be a better docent for her. More studying, more research, more creativity in training. Miranda needs to be prepared for all the inevitabilities, and it's my job to ensure that happens. So George, you need to step up.

And in that vein, I'm going to do some reconnaissance work this weekend to get ahead of this Jinn problem we seem to have. Maybe I can even take care of the whole issue without Miranda needing to get involved at all. She can just focus on training for the next big bad we need to handle. Well, she needs to handle.

Chapter 9

Miranda

As soon as I'm dressed in clean clothes, George agrees to give me the weekend off. We plan to meet Monday to start reading through his library of reference books so I can be better prepared for my next mythological encounter.

Then, after we each consume two giant cups of coffee, he drives me home so I can change into my own clothes before I pick up the kids. By now, my muscles have let the day's activities sink in, and they are aching. I move at the slowest pace I have ever moved as I make my way up the front steps.

Behind me, George yells, "Go take some ibuprofen!"

I turn to flip him off, but it's a very slow turn, so he's already driving away by the time I face the street.

Once I'm in my own house, I lean against my locked door and breathe. Now that I'm home I hear my stomach growling. In fact, in this silent house it sounds uncannily similar to the minotaur's snorts. I down a yogurt, take two painkillers, and pass out on the couch. I have to leave in an hour, so I don't even try to make it to my bed because by the time I hobble up the stairs, I'll already have to come back down.

My alarm goes off too soon for my liking, and, for a moment, I wonder what would happen if I didn't show up to pick up my kids... Dumping that thought into the trash, I force myself to my aching feet and head to the car.

***

My children watch me with varying degrees of concern as I move slowly around the kitchen. As I open the cabinet to look at my pots and pans, I stop. This is not going to happen.

"Okay. Pizza or Chinese? No way am I cooking." I'm not moving, bent over to look in the cabinet, not sure I can stand back up.

"Um, Mom, what is up with you?" asked Jessie, ever the tactful one.

"I ...joined a new gym. New exercise routine. I'm just a little sore is all. I'll be fine tomorrow."

I don't think any of my offspring actually believe me.

On the plus side, the evening is pretty uneventful, or maybe it just feels that way because I want to take more pain killers and climb in to bed by six o'clock. I am so drained I don't know how I make it through getting everyone to bed. I tell myself I've done enough for today and give myself permission to leave cleaning up downstairs for tomorrow. I mean, I did kill a minotaur and all. I deserve to turn in early tonight.

I check my phone. I haven't heard from Jake all day. I decide I don't want to talk to him anyway. We'll talk when he gets home. I can't tell him about all this on the phone when he's hundreds of miles away. We'll talk when he's back. Whenever that turns out to be. For now, I just need sleep. Lots and lots of sleep.

As I change into my pjs and brush my teeth, I can't stop thinking about how I haven't heard from him at all. Not even a quick good night text. That's unlike him. I grab my phone and walk to my bed. Trying to be the bigger person, I text him:

Hey. Sorry for fighting. I hope you're having a good trip. Let
me know when you'll be home. Love you.

I climb into bed and plug my phone in on my nightstand. As I turn off
my bedside lamp, I hear a buzz.

Sorry too. Just busy here. I should be home Sunday. Wrapping up tomorrow. Love you, too.

I fall asleep smiling to myself. Then I remember what he said about me
getting a job, and I still have a whole prophecy type thing to somehow
explain to him when he gets home. So maybe the smile is a little
premature.

***

When I open my eyes Saturday morning, I'm grateful my kids are finally
old enough that they let me sleep in sometimes. 9:30 a.m. That was
practically unheard of a few short years ago. I stretch, well, attempt to.
My body craves it, but as soon as my arms are over my head, "Aaaaarrrr-
rrrrrgggggggggg" escapes at such a volume that Phoebe and Natalie run
in seconds later.

"Mom! Are you okay?"

I'm honestly not even sure which one of them asked because I'm still
seeing stars from the pain coursing through my entire body. I can barely
respond through gritted teeth. "Yes. I'm fine. Just...still sore from my new
gym, I guess. Actually, I'm not entirely sure how I'm going to get out of
bed."

"Oh, poor Mommy! We'll get you some breakfast so you can take a pain killer!"

I can't turn my head, but I know this is Phoebe. She's the most nurturing one of my children and the only one who would have thought to do anything like that for me.

While she runs back downstairs to gather sustenance for me, Natalie rummages through the linen closet for the heating pad. Of course, since it won't cover my entire body at once, I'm not sure how much help it will be. Natalie finds the pad and brings it to me, plugging it into the power strip I keep tucked underneath my bed. "Where does it hurt worst, Mommy?"

"Good question." Everything is throbbing and it's hard to tease out what hurts worse than what. So, my response is mainly a groan, and then I ask her to put the heating pad across the back of my shoulders while I lay on my stomach. The spasming going on there is some of the worst pain I've ever experienced.

Phoebe brings me a tray loaded with waffles, fruit, and hard-boiled eggs, and Natalie helps me roll over and sit up so I can eat. Then she puts the heating pad back on my shoulders.

While I'm eating, Phoebe fetches the bottle of ibuprofen from my medicine cabinet. Eleven years old, and she's still respectful of not opening the bottle. I love my kids! Wow, I am really in some pain... I finish my meal, swallow two pills, thank my girls, and settle back into my pillows to try to minimize the amount of pain coursing through me. Napping is likely not going to be a possibility. I'm just attempting to achieve a level of pain that doesn't tell me I'm going to die right here.

Thank goodness it's Saturday! This way it isn't a big deal when the pain killers kick in and I do drift back off to get a couple more hours of sleep.

But I'm woken up sooner than I'm ready when my phone starts buzzing with a call. I try shoving it under Jake's pillow so I can ignore it but that just makes the entire bed vibrate, and not in a fun kind of way. I ignore it, assuming it's Jake (and therefore he can wait), and I try to fall back asleep. But when the call repeats three more times and I'm more and more desperate for rest, I check who's calling. I don't recognize the number, so I'm hoping it is someone I can tell off for calling so many times.

Answering, I lay the phone against my cheek so I don't have to keep my muscles engaged. "Hello?"

"Hey, Miranda. It's George."

"Oh...hi?" My voice raises an octave but that's all the energy I can muster.

"I just realized you don't have my number if you need to reach me, or if I need to reach you. Now you know it's me... So, here I am."

"Umm. Okay, but you could have left me a message, you know, instead of calling me four times."

"Oh. I... Sorry. I also got a little worried when you didn't answer. How are you feeling?"

I yawn. "Kind of like a giant minotaur beat the hell out of me. Thanks for asking. I'm going to go try to sleep now, until my body feels less broken."

And I hang up. What a weird moppet of a man he's turning out to be. This entire experience has been nothing but bizarre. I'm just about asleep when my phone buzzes again but with a much shorter alert. A text instead of a call. Jake.

Taking the Red Eye tonight. See you all soon. I truly cannot
wait to show you how I have missed you. Love you.

Okay, whatever weirdo. It even hurts when I roll my eyes. I lean back into the nest of pillows Natalie set up for me and drift into blissful unconsciousness.

I pass the day in a cycle of sleeping, waking up sore, taking more pain relievers, and going back to sleep. The kids take turns checking on me, feeding me, and assuring me they're all fine. The good news is every time I wake up, I feel a little less sore and more myself. When I wake up at 2 a.m., all traces of my pain have subsided.

"That's so weird," I say aloud, but softly, and only to myself.

I stretch and get out of bed, unable to comprehend how the pain could completely vanish. Jake must be in the air now, I assume. Considering he didn't bother to send me his usual pre-flight text telling me he loves me and will be shutting off his phone, I can't be sure.

My stomach growls interrupt my thoughts, so I head for the stairs, noticing how loud the squeaky parts of the floor are when the rest of the house is silent. Hopefully, that's just my new bat-like hearing. The lights are off, but rays of moonlight shine through the windows, illuminating enough of the house that I can tell the rooms are pretty immaculate, considering it's been Lord of Flies here for the last day. My children have impressed me.

But of course, they are impressive. Their mama is a full-fledged super-hero! I pull a quart of ice cream out of the freezer, a spoon from the drawer, and sit at the table to go through my missed emails (and, of course, missed social media). So much junk email. I pause on an email with a comedy and tragedy mask at the top. A local theater is holding auditions. It makes me nostalgic for my adolescent days when I would try out for all the plays. I rarely got an actual role, but just getting to be in the background or the chorus and pretend to not be me for a couple hours was a nice break. To have a place to go outside of my house. Outside of myself. Outside of his reach.

Soon, I'm mindlessly scrolling without absorbing anything. My eyes give up on trying to focus, and my ice cream melts. Quickly healed or not, my body wants more sleep. I clean up and go back to my bed. At least Jake will be home in a few hours, and I'll be able to lean on him a little for emotional support as well as help with the kids.

***

I'm running around an affluent California suburb with my favorite teenagers, getting a crash course in hunting monsters, when I feel something tickling my side. I think it's a spider, swat it away, and go back to my lesson on stabbing with the pointy end. I am mid smart ass retort when I feel the sensation again, only this time it is along the inside of my thigh. And there's a wet sensation on my neck? As the graveyard fades around me, I open my eyes to find Jake lying in bed beside me, his fingers tracing around my body while his tongue swirls along my neck, eliciting a moan from my barely awake lips.

The kids are still asleep. It would have been wiser for him to let me sleep, but apparently he's not feeling wise...or patient...or calm. He's feeling something though. And I'm feeling the proof pressing into me through the covers. I gently push him away so I can breathe and look at him.

"Umm, hi. How was your flight?"

He has a look on his face that tells me he has zero interest in talking. "It was fine. Now I want to lay with my wife." He kisses me again. Again, I push him back.

Where did he learn that line? "Lay with your wife? Okay, but your wife is still mad at you for how you spoke to her the other day."

His brow furrows for a split second, and I wonder if he even remembers the disagreement. Maybe it was nothing to him at all.

"Don't you remember? You were at some loud club? You could barely spare a moment to talk to me about the job opportunity I was offered and then insulted my abilities to do anything but housework?"

He smiles at me, well, at my lips. He can't seem to stop watching my mouth.

"I'm sorry. I was drunk a lot of my time away. I don't think I can be held accountable for anything I may have said under the influence of that city. But I guess I need to make it up to you then." Before I can respond, he is under the blanket.

"I'm sorry, did you just say you were drunk a lot of the time? And do you think I want you to make it up to me this way? This is not what I need, Jake!" But then, I can't bring myself to protest anymore.

He kisses my inner thighs, one and then the other, and runs the tip of his tongue up to where my legs meet my hips, licking firmly along the line they make. I try to keep my resolve to be angry, but holy shit, this feels good! I didn't even realize how badly I needed this. I moan quietly, expecting him to chastise me. But when his only response is to suck my clit into his warm mouth while slipping his fingers deep inside me, I get louder.

I feel him smile against me, proud of what he is accomplishing. "That's a good girl. Let it out."

I slip my fingers through his hair, using my right hand to hold him against me, and use my knuckle as a gag to keep myself from screaming. Maybe it's all my new heightened senses, but sex hasn't felt like this in years. When he realizes I've put a damper on my sounds, he reaches up and grabs my left wrist, tight. He roughly pulls it to my side and keeps it pinned there. Then he does the same with my right, not because he plans to stop what he's doing, just because he wants to have me completely under his control.

"I don't want to wake the kids!" I hiss, before I can't.

When he looks up at me, there is fire behind his eyes. "The door is locked. It's fine. They're all old enough to know their parents still fuck. Now shut up and moan." It's impossible for me not to follow that command as he pins both my wrists in one of his hands so he can slide his fingers back inside me, pulling them forwards to hit the spot he knows will make me writhe, as he sucks my clit into his mouth and uses his tongue to gently stroke me.

An intense heat is growing deep in my belly. I arch my back to try to keep it from exploding right away. I don't ever want this feeling to end.

But then it does end. He lifts his head away, leaving me on the precipice of the highest mountain I have ever climbed. If I could speak, I would ask him what the hell he thinks he's doing, but right when I can form words again, he grabs my waist and flips me over. He presses one hand between my shoulders while lifting my hips with the other.

And then he's inside me. He moves his hand to rub me while he grinds into me from behind, and within moments, I can't hold back any longer. I cry out while I orgasm against him, pushing him further inside me. He lets out a guttural moan as he climaxes, too, and we collapse in a heap on the bed.

I only have a moment before he flips me over and kisses me hard, laying himself on me to pin me in place.

"Well, that was quite a welcome home," he grins as if he's the devil himself. Then I notice he's still hard against me, and he seems to think he's going to be using it, again.

"You're joking, right? If we didn't wake up the kids this time, we got lucky. I'm not pushing that luck. Now get off me. I need to go to the bathroom."

He presses me down harder as his eyes lock onto mine. "I never joke about this," and his hand moves quickly to caress between my folds again.

I consider giving in once more but shake some sense into myself. "Nope. Sorry. Off!" I use almost no effort to flip him over to his side of the bed, the dry side. I grumble as I head to the bathroom to clean up.

When I get back, he's sulking at the giant tent pitched in my bed.

I point to his groin. "Um, are you going to do something about that before the kids get up?"

He rolls his eyes. "I was trying to when you stormed off. This is not my fault. If you want this to go away, you do something about it."

I'm taken aback by how obnoxious he's being. I stomp around the room as I get dressed, accentuating my words to him. "Or you can go to hell." I feel his eyes on me. "You know, I have barely heard from you since you went away. Then you pull that bullshit about how I couldn't possibly be qualified for a job that is worth doing. Really, Jake? Really? What exactly is the litmus test for if something is 'worth it'? Is there a certain amount of money I need to be making, or could it ever be possible that feeling like I'm worth something more than just Mom could make it worthwhile?" I stop and look at him. Again, I see fire behind his eyes, but this time I think the feeling might be rage. At least, I'm hoping it is. I just want him to give me some kind of emotional response that's more mature than a fourteen-year-old boy.

But when he stands up from the bed to approach me, his erection is still almost comically pronounced. Standing before me, he runs his fingers through the hair on either side of my face and then locks his thumb under my jaw to turn my face up to his. In spite of the force, his touch feels surprisingly gentle. "I'm sorry. I didn't realize how important this is to you. Of course, I want you to feel you have as much worth as I already feel you have. Do you want to tell me more about this...opportunity?"

And in this moment, I realize I have no idea how to tell him about any of it. "Well, it doesn't really pay...at all. It's more of a volunteer position.

It's sort of a community outreach...neighborhood watch kind of thing." I watch his face carefully. I have no idea how he will react.

That fire flashes brighter for a second, and then the corners of his mouth quirk up a touch. He moves his hands to meet behind my neck and rests his forearms on my shoulders. "I think that sounds like a wonderful opportunity for you. I can't wait to hear more."

Why was that such an easy conversation?

"Ok...thanks. I don't think I have a choice at this point anyway, to be honest. It feels almost like, like I was born to do this."

"Sure, it does. I understand." Suddenly, he presses down on my shoulders, gently but insistently. "And now you need to understand this problem you want taken care of isn't going to take care of itself." He doesn't stop pushing until I'm on my knees.

I look up at him, way more aroused by this turn of events than I want to admit. He looks at me with such intense passion that I almost burst into flames.

"You know what to do," he says.

And I do.

Chapter 10

George

Over the weekend, I take it upon myself to do some reconnaissance work. I will still need to call on her in the case of an emergency, but I think we're missing something important so I don't want to sit around, thinking about the potential pitfalls Miranda's unknowingly walking into while doing un-Guardian-like things with her family. I'm anxious to start her training this week, and I'll feel much better once she knows how to fight some foes.

I head to a local dive bar where creatures masking as humans tend to congregate. I need to find out about this Jinn that has been around town. I can't let it hurt Miranda. I would be the worst docent ever if something happened to her so fast. Miranda's birthright is to protect the world. Mine is to protect Miranda. And I take that responsibility seriously.

Twenty minutes later, I pull into an unpaved parking lot. The gravel has eroded away, and the lot is mainly dirt. At three o'clock in the afternoon, quite a few cars fill the lot—mostly beat up, rusty piles that don't look like they would move on their own, much less transport someone without falling apart. The bar, if you can call it that, is built entirely of cracked and faded wooden beams. The whole building appears to be leaning to one side and as if nothing's holding it together besides old chewing gum and demon spit.

I walk in, and I'm kind of surprised the music doesn't screech to a stop like the scene of a movie when the hip city dweller enters the local yokel bar. Not that I'm cool or hip, but I am human, and that's still out of place here.

At one of the dark wood tables, two humanoid demons and a cyclops play a game of cards. The other three tables have their mismatched chairs filled with mismatched friends. A satyr is drinking with a siren and a pixie. Two gargoyles are chatting up a harpy. And at the far table, I spy a Jinn, but not the one from the pharmacy. At least, I don't think he's the same. He could have shape shifted into a different grotesque human-like resemblance, but my gut tells me that's not likely. This Jinn is younger, with short curly brass-colored hair, and still has the telltale glowing green eyes. Beside him sits a similarly aged female Jinn who looks nervous. In front of them, six imps crouch on the table, trying to look scary while talking to the Jinns and failing miserably because they're only about as tall as pint glasses. I head to that table.

I walk up behind the imps, with the Jinn facing me. The male has his arm around the female whose arms are crossed in front of her, shielding her protectively. The imps can't see me from where I stand, and as I catch the male Jinn's eye he flashes me a look that begs me to rescue him and his female. That must be the reason he's holding her that way. Imps do have enough power in their little bodies to cause some bodily damage, but mostly they're just self-important nuisances.

The closer I get, the better I can hear the low gravely voices of the imps. "You know what they want from you. It can be one of you, or your uncle, but it needs to get done. Or else." The one talking slams his fist on the table and the group starts to fly off.

I jump in cheerfully. "Hey there! So sorry to interrupt. I was wondering, do any of you folks know anything about a Jinn who would have been at a pharmacy in Nutley this past Wednesday?"

The Jinn exchange a look, her brow is furrowed, he is stroking her shoulder with the hand he has wrapped around her. When the male Jinn speaks his voice is quiet and quaking. "No, I'm really sorry." Then after a pause, "Are you human? How? How do you know about us?"

I probably should have been more low-key, considering this is my first real case. Oh well, too late now.

I look around the room and then bend down closer, talking in a hushed voice. "Haven't you heard of H.A.A.M.? Humans All About Mythicals? We're a collective that knows all about you. We even have pins and a secret handshake!" I start to do a few weird gestures, then stop abruptly. "Oh, no. I can't show you that.... Well, I just wanted to give you a heads up. I should be going. Thanks for your time!"

As I'm crossing the dirt lot back to my car, I hear the male Jinn call to me. "Hey, ham guy! Wait!" I stop in my tracks and turn to him. He catches up to me, panting a bit. "I think you were asking about my uncle. Is he okay?"

"He's fine. But what was he doing? He made quite a scene with gua—a girl. Most people wouldn't have noticed, but ya know. I'm a H.A.A.M., so I did."

"Oh, we were summoned by those imps back there. They want one of us to—" I must have looked too eager because he stops and begins to back away. "Ya know what? It won't affect you. Don't worry. Sorry you had to witness that. See you!" With a single wave, he turns and runs back into the bar.

And I have gleaned the slightest bit of intel to work with, which is better than absolutely nothing, I suppose.

Chapter 11

Miranda

I've been downstairs for twenty minutes, brewed a pot of coffee, and been staring out the window, hoping for a glimpse of the fluffy kitsune, while pondering what the fuck is going on in my life right now, when the first of my kids shows his groggy face. It's only 8 a.m., but I feel as if I've had a thousand new experiences within the hour and half my husband has been back from his trip.

"Hey, Sammy!" I think I said that with a little too much enthusiasm when he stops in his tracks and raises one eyebrow. I clear my throat and try again. "What can I get for you?"

He still has that one eyebrow raised, trying to decide what is going on with me, but he asks for eggs and toast. "Did Dad get home yet?"

"Ummm, yup. He's pretty tired from his flight, so he's sleeping."

Sammy plops into his seat, his black curls appear as if he is living inside one of those static balls. "Okay. I'll go get Dad in a little while."

I nod. Luckily, I was prepared to make multiple servings of eggs because Phoebe comes in next, still in her pjs (which do match, ironically) and asks for "some of whatever smells so yummy."

I start to whistle while I plate their breakfasts and when I turn around, they're both looking at me like something is seriously wrong with me. "What?"

"Why are you whistling?" Jessie stands in the doorframe with her brown hair in a bird nest behind her and her eyes barely opened.

"I...guess I'm just happy Dad is home." Avoiding Jessie's stare, I hand full plates and forks to my little ones.

Jessie drags her feet to the table. "Really? You've never seemed so happy to see him before. Ew. Mom. You're blushing! Ew!"

I smile to myself as I fix her a plate. Teenagers can be so much fun to torment. I swear. And she's just at the beginning of her teenage years, so I have lots of years to mess with her. If I survive them, that is.

"So, what are everyone's plans for today?" I'm met with silence while they are busy eating. "Okay, then. Good talk. I'm going to go check on your sister."

I plop my apron on the counter and head to the stairs. I start up at the same time Jake is heading down. He smiles at me and when we pass each other half way, he turns quickly and presses me to the wall with one hand on my hip and the other at my neck. He kisses me deeply, then says, "Good morning, again," before he turns and continues on his way.

Seriously, what has gotten into that man? I'm still shaking my head when I get to Natalie's room. She's half awake and in no rush to get all the way there. She stares out the window at the tree a few feet beyond, watching the birds flutter from branch to branch.

"Good morning, sleepy head." I smile at her, and she smiles back, her blue eyes sparkling.

"Hey, Mom." She stretches her arms above her head, accidentally knocking three koala stuffies onto the floor. "I'll be down soon. I just wanted to sleep in today."

"Okay, Sweetie. No problem. See you in a few."

As I approach the kitchen, it is suspiciously quiet. I stand in the doorway and see Jake regaling the kids with some story from his trip. He's telling them about Callie and her band, the Celestials, and the crazy life they lead, which makes me wonder if that's what this morning was all about, that he thinks our lives are too boring now. Another possibility hits me, and I suddenly feel ill.

I try to stop my mind from going there, but images of what might have happened in Las Vegas bombard me, of him getting carried away at one of those clubs or parties and cheating on me, and now he's had a taste for some kind of more wild intimacy, and brought it home.

Look, I'm not complaining about the sex itself. If that's how things are going to be from now on, I'm totally okay with it. But if he cheated on me, that's a different story.

I feel hot and cold and sweaty all at once, so I run to the nearest bathroom where I throw up. I wash my face and grab the toothbrush I keep in the powder room. While I finger comb my hair, I talk to myself in the mirror. "Get it together, Miranda. You killed a Minotaur. You are a badass. You are also imagining shit that would never happen. Then again, you thought you were imagining a fox with three tails and creepy guys with glowing eyes..."

It's probably best I don't closely examine the odds of anything right now, because if I do, I'm pretty sure the odds that my sexy-as-hell, hot-blooded-male, already-admitted-he-was-drunk-most-of-his-time-away husband cheated on me in Las Vegas are way higher than the odds of there being a Chosen One, not to mention the odds of that Chosen One being me.

I am sick again.

A few minutes later, after I finish puking and cleaning up, I head back to the kitchen. Natalie has joined everyone else, and the kids hang on Jake's every word. I move around to the sink and empty the dishwasher while listening.

"And even though her voice is beautiful, her lyrics..." He gives a low whistle. "They are completely out of this realm. She carries this really cool digital writing tablet with her, so whenever she thinks of something or hears something, she writes it down, and it gets sent straight to the cloud so she can see the notes later, but they just disappear in the moment so no one can steal them."

I cock an eyebrow. The kids have all had tablets since they were five years old. Why is this so unbelievable to them? I chalk my dissidence up to jealously and continue with the dishes. Whatever. Let them have their musician hero. I'm a real-life mother-fucking superhero!

"Ouch!" I jump back from the dishwasher and cradle my finger.

Pheobe is the first to look at me. "Mom! Are you okay?"

"Miranda, you're bleeding!" Jake starts toward me, but I put up a hand to stop him and head for the door.

"Yeah, I'm fine. I just grabbed a knife wrong. I'll go clean this up. Be right down."

Your Guardian, ladies and gentlemen...

I'm made no less suspicious over the course of the day, which I have to spend listening to Jake tell the kids, in absolutely insane detail, the events of his trip. Unsurprisingly, he's close to signing the group for his agency. I've just never seen him care so much about any trip, or client, before. This girl must be some great performer...ick. I don't want to think about all the implications of that statement, so I take a mental vacation and text Eliza.

> Hey. I'm definitely going to need to debrief later. Jake is home. And...weird.

Her response takes a couple minutes, but it's still faster than I expect.

> Can't wait to hear about his trip! Coffee tomorrow?

I start to agree but then remember the other side my life now has.

Can't…starting my training with George…

This time, she responds almost instantaneously.

Oh, that's right! I cannot wait to meet this kid!

I roll my eyes.

Haha. Too bad that's never gonna happen…

A brief pause.

Yeah right. That's what you think. Go spend time with your family. Talk to you later.

But I don't really want to spend time with my family. They're giving me all sorts of weird vibes. And given my recent experiences, that's saying something. So, I go up to my room to fold laundry and watch TV.

I'm three episodes and four baskets of laundry into my tasks when Jake walks in. He automatically closes and locks the door behind him.

"Hey, you. You disappeared."

"Nope. I'm right here. I just figured that since you had the kids entertained, I could get some laundry done without being missed." That probably had more of an edge than I meant it to. Or I did mean it to. Whatever. But it doesn't seem to bother him either way as he saunters toward me.

"Well, I missed you." He slides his hand under the collar of my shirt, pushing it and my bra strap off my shoulder, while he starts to nibble my earlobe. I might give in, except I still feel queasy about everything that could have happened in Las Vegas. So, I quickly find an excuse.

"I don't think so. Look at all the freshly folded laundry. No room on the bed. And if you even think of knocking over these perfect stacks so help me—"

He silences me with a kiss. Then, with his mouth still pressed to mine, he whispers, "The floor doesn't have any stacks of clean laundry." His tone doesn't have any question to it. He's telling me we're going to have sex on the floor, and that's it. Before I have a chance to decide if I want that to be it, he lifts me up with his hands, firmly grabbing my ass, and lowers us both, so we are sitting up intertwined on the patch of floor beside the bed.

But I can't keep going with all the doubts running through my head. All the questions and possibilities of what went on in Vegas.

"Jake?"

He doesn't even pause kissing my neck. "Mm?"

"Did something happen that I should know about while you were away?"

He stops abruptly and leans away from me.

"What do you mean? What do you think happened?" His mouth hangs open and his eyebrows raise at the notion that I might not trust him.

"I don't know. You're just acting very...amorous?"

He thinks for a minute. "Amorous? And I'm not normally?"

"I mean, I always know you love me, but no. You're definitely not normally like this."

He stares off to the side, his whole face pensive, as he thinks about the meaning behind my every word.

"I'm sorry. Well, I'm not sorry for being more amorous, as you say, now. But I am sorry I let everyday-life get in the way of showing you how intense my passion for you still is. I'm sorry if I haven't truly fucked you enough lately. I plan to correct that mistake..." He kisses right under my ear. "And correct that mistake..." He kisses a little lower on my neck "And correct that mistake...over and over and over..." He continues kissing lower with every word. When he gets to my collar bone, he stretches the collar of my T-shirt down and pulls one of my breasts out. "For the rest of my life." Then he takes my nipple into his mouth, and I dissolve into a puddle of unawareness and contentment.

I can't remember ever making love while the kids were home and awake. But the few times I get anxious, he assures me they won't come up. I don't know why I don't care why, but I just don't. I let myself be taken by this incredible man.

Over and over and over.

Chapter 12

Miranda

When my alarm goes off Monday morning, I'm almost as sore as I was after fighting the minotaur. I'm also incredibly confused. I would think I'm hungover, except I know I didn't drink. I don't notice any of my new super powers, but maybe they only emerge when I need them. I wake up and go through the normal routine, and when I get to Natalie, she asks if I'm feeling better. Apparently, Jake had told them I needed to sleep off a headache while he had taken care of their dinner and got everything ready for bed.

My brain has a layer of fog over the memories from last night, but I let it go. I probably passed out after all the sex, and he didn't want them to find me naked and drooling on the floor. Everything is par for the course at breakfast. The only notable happening is the particularly deep good-bye kiss Jake gives me on his way out the door. It actually leaves me a little weak in the knees. And steaming in my very core. (Holy shit is that cliché! What is this man doing to me?)

But I cannot dwell on my libido, because I start my training today. As soon as they are out the door, I have my first cup of coffee and go shower. Noting some intense bruises when I undress, I wonder if they're from the minotaur, or Jake.

***

"Okay, so where do I start? Do you have a pamphlet for me, 'So, You Just Found Out You're the Chosen One!'?" As I sit down at the shiny oak table in his library, I think I see amusement in his eyes, but I can't tell for sure. For someone so young, he's very serious. Obviously, he's disciplined. More so than I ever was anyway, especially at his age. Or I might not be that funny, but I don't think that could be it.

"Not exactly." The tome he drops in front of me makes a thud that echoes through his mansion's cavernous library. I have never used the word "tome" before, but this is way more than a book. I can't guess how many golden-edged pages are between the soft black leather covers. A metallic purple and gold swirl is the only adornment on the front.

I hold my hands out, wanting to open the book but also not wanting to touch it in case it falls apart. "You just throw this thing around? How old is this?"

"Um, I think it was printed in 1997? Yup, see. There's the date." He had nonchalantly flipped to a page, not quite a copyright page, but still one with information of when and where this marvel was printed and assembled.

"Wait, what? Why does it look ancient? I am so confused." I flip through the pages now that I'm less intimidated, and the text is clearly modern.

"When you were born, my dad found out he was your docent. He was twenty-one at the time. He had a lot of time to kill before you would be called up, and he wanted to be ready for you. So, he started to research. He found all of the journals of past docents, but he couldn't always make out what they had written. The books were so old, and many of the docents were from other countries. So, he made it his goal in life to decipher all the journals and get the information printed in an easier-to-read format. The notes are still chronological... Oh, but you can use the index in the back to find exactly where to look for whatever information you need. See?" He was giddy with excitement, showing me this amazing project his dad had put together for himself. For me, I realize.

"He must have been incredible, George. I'm sorry I never got to meet him."

"He was, thanks. You did meet him though, and he loved you."

"What? How?"

George looks at me like I am so naive and then smiles. "Think about it. I'm George Keating. My father was also G. Keating."

My eyes widen. "Wait, not Dr. Grant?" George nods. "So, wait a minute, your father, my...docent was my...pediatrician?" A million memories flood my mind.

I loved Dr. Grant! He was my favorite grown-up when I was a kid. He never spoke to me like I was just a little kid. He talked to me like I was his peer, his equal. That means a lot to a little girl, particularly if she doesn't get that kind of encouragement elsewhere in her world. My parents would try to rush through my appointments, anxious to move on to the next thing they needed to do for themselves. But Dr. Grant never let them. He let them pace, or tap their feet impatiently, while giving me the attention he somehow always knew I needed.

I don't know what I would have done with my life if it hadn't been for Dr. Grant. I don't know if I even would have survived childhood. He was quietly encouraging, the same way George is to me now. Well, maybe George isn't quite as quiet. Now that I know the connection, I can't believe I didn't see it! But I didn't use Dr. Grant's last name very much, if at all.

George's sweet smile cracks into genuine mirth. But a less than wholesome thought pops into my head. "That seems like something he should have had to disclose to my parents or something, don't you think?"

"It's not like he was using your medical information for nefarious purposes."

"No, no, of course not. Just to plan out my future training as a guardian."

His blue eyes warm as they lock on mine. "No, Miranda. You're not A guardian. You're *The* Guardian."

Chills. Chills right down my spine. Goosebumps everywhere. I stop breathing for a few seconds.

"Oh...I'm going to need some more coffee."

We retreat to his professional-grade, gorgeous, amazing, jealousy-inducing kitchen for the coffee, because liquids cannot be allowed in the library. As he fixes the mugs, I watch him work. I love watching a man make coffee...a woman too, really. As long as I get a mugful at the end.

"Okay, so, how did this all come to be? How did The Guardian start? How did I become one? I mean, okay, I was picked at birth, but isn't there some kind of age or weight limit or something that should preclude me now?"

He shakes his head but doesn't look at me. "You're supposed to know this already."

"Yeah well, I was also supposed to get this news when I was a lot younger, with a lot less kids and a lot more time, so spill it."

"Touche." He carefully places my mug in front of me and stares into his own.

"Every culture and civilization has its own folktales, myths, and monsters. Right?"

I take a long sip from my mug before speaking. "Right. They usually get started because someone would rather scare their kids than just talk to them, so they make up a tale to keep their kids on the straight and narrow."

George bobs his head back and forth in a yes-and-no kind of way. "Technically, that's accurate."

"You're not telling me that these myths are based on real creatures?"

"No, not at all. *Technically*, the creatures are based on the myths."

"I'm sorry, what?"

"The tales that were most compelling, that were passed down the most, that the people believed in the most—their belief over time made the creatures come to life."

I stare blankly to the count of five. Then, "Come again?"

"Monsters, demons, fairies, gods… They all came to exist in our world when the people who believed in them willed them to be."

"Okay, we'll come back to that later. And…the…Guardian?"

He raises one eyebrow. "Growing up, did you ever believe in a guardian angel that would protect you from the monster under your bed?"

With no hesitation, I answer. "I didn't have a monster under my bed. I had a monster down the hall. And no. I never believed anyone would protect me. I knew that was up to me. I was always my only great protector."

George smiles. "Exactly."

***

Two full cups of coffee later, one made a little bit Irish, we're back in the Keating family library. While I read through the giant book of docents' notes, George peruses a shelf of books to my right, searching for some more anthology-style reads to give me a general background of knowledge. I watch him, giving my eyes something farther away to focus on because the words have started to blur. His fingers trace the book spines. Watching him I realize don't know anything about this random guy that walked into my life without giving me an option. Not that he had much of an option himself.

"Hey George?"

"Hmm?"

"What's your story?"

He stops and furrows his brow before he straightens his shoulders and neck and turns to me. "What do you mean my story?"

I slide down in my chair a bit so my shoulders meet the backrest. "I mean, what's your story? You have a file you've committed to memory of every detail of my life, down to which Girl Scouts badges I earned in Brownies. But when it comes to you," I use my fingers to enumerate the few facts I've learned, "I know your name is George Keating, you live here, and you're my docent. Does that seem fair to you? It doesn't to me. If we're going to spend all this time together, I think I should get to know more about you."

George walks toward me hesitantly, hands in his pockets. He collapses into the chair across from me and rests his elbows on the table, steepling his fingers that he presses to his lips. His pupils are dilated, leaving just a ring of bright blue around them. Being he's one of the most beautiful people I've ever been so close to, I begin to feel physically uncomfortable staring into his eyes like this. Maybe this is his version of playing chicken. Maybe he's trying to make me squirm, so I give up my quest for knowledge about him and try to skim the open pages in front of me.

Finally, he speaks. "What do you want to know?"

I swallow, not sure anymore. "Um, you know, whatever you want to tell me, I guess."

He doesn't change his posture or position, but his eyes drift to the side as he thinks.

I'm not sure how much longer I can take this silence, so I try to speed things along. "How did you become my docent? I know your dad was supposed to be, but how did you end up getting the gig? Does it always run in families?"

"Excellent question. It doesn't run in families. Just like the Guardianship does not. But my father was always open with me, wanting me to be prepared if I ever had to deal with anything. Thus, when he passed, the League decided I should be the one to train you."

I nod along. "That must have been hard. Where's your mom? And have you been local this whole time, or did you need to come back?"

He sighs. His shoulders drop and he slouches down in his chair. He no longer looks like my sturdy docent; he looks like a little boy. "My mom moved to Florida about a year ago. She has family there and wanted to be closer to them. She was never a fan of the docent lifestyle, but she loved my dad and put up with it for him. She would have moved sooner, but she didn't want to leave the house vacant. When she knew for sure I would be coming home, she took the out."

"So, you weren't living local?"

He shakes his head and lower his hands, and eyes, to the table. He studies his thumbnail as he talks, avoiding eye contact with me. "Nope. I was in California. I went to school out there. Lived out there." He keeps his eyes downcast.

And then there is silence. I need to know what he's not saying. "Ok...So you were living out in California. And now you're back home. Was that a hard transition for you? Can you go back?"

His answer is abrupt. "There is no going back." I keep my gaze on his face. I hope he will continue but I don't want to push him too much. His eyes flick up to mine. "I was living with the love of my life. We were planning our wedding when COVID hit. He was not happy when the League told me I would be your docent. He wanted me to tell them no. He didn't understand it wasn't a question."

His eyes turn glossy. I reach out my arm and am about to put my hand on his, but he retracts his arms and wipes the tears away before they can fall. "Anyway, we spent two years trying to pretend everything was okay, hoping I'd never get the call. But then I did. He told me if I left, that was it. I haven't seen or heard from him since."

I let the silence hang in the air for a minute before I dare speak again. It's my turn to stare down at the table. "I'm so sorry, George. I feel responsible."

He grabs my hands. "Miranda, you are as much a victim in all this bullshit as I am. As Evan is. Do not blame yourself. Okay?"

I nod, wanting to cry for him, but I keep it together because he doesn't seem the type to want pity. He nods back, then stands up and returns to his post across the room. We resume our respective research for a few minutes until another question pops into my head.

"George? I have one more question."

He drops his head only a fraction of an inch in exasperation, which is much better than I have done when faced with a barrage of questions. "Yes, Miranda?"

"Should I be concentrating on studying Jinn? You made it sound like they're exceptionally bad for me."

He stops moving but continues to stare at the books on the shelf, until he sucks in a deep breath exhales forcefully. Then he looks at me, apologetically.

Without a word, he walks past me to the shelves on the other side of the aisle. He traces the row of books, long fingers playing a silent piano made of leather, paper, and ink, until he pulls a navy-blue cloth bound book with silver embossed writing from the shelf. He flips through the almost sheer pages as he walks to me. Finally satisfied he's found the right passage, he puts the book down in front of me and places the tip of his finger at the indentation where he wants me to begin reading.

He still won't look at me, so I begin reading out loud.

> Jinn, later referred to as genies: Like people, Jinn in general
> are not all good or all bad. They can change form at will
> because they have less matter than humans. They generally
> prefer to appear as snakes, lizards, and scorpions; however,
> over the years, they have come to enjoy masquerading as
> humans as well. This is believed to be because they can
> then seduce human women. Jinn were often called upon
> for protection; however, they are easy to anger and spite.
> They are mortal and as frail as humans, but because of their
> semi-corporeal form, they can also invade a human body
> through possession if they feel they have been wronged.

As I read, I'm freaked out, not so much on a personal level, but on a holy-shit-these-things-are-real level, once again. I wonder if that will just be my baseline state going forward.

"Okay, but what does this have to do with me specifically? Why is it so bad they know who I am?"

"Turn the page."

I obediently do so.

> Jinn are known to be summoned by sorcerers to possess
> and afflict their enemies. These afflictions often manifest
> as epilepsy, apoplexy, and hallucination, as well as many
> other mental illnesses.

"Oh good, more mental illness. How will I know if it is the fox, the Jinn, or just me?"

"Fox?"

"Didn't I tell you about the kitsune in my yard?"

"Um, nope. You failed to mention that."

"Oh, well, I've seen one with three tails a few times now. But I want to figure out this Jinn thing before we worry about that. Any more insight for me, or are you just going to tell me to keep reading?" I fight the urge to curse him out as he arches an eyebrow in response. "Keep reading it is, I guess."

> More than one Guardian has been incapacitated by Jinn summoned to remove them from power for the sake of a sorcerer or a god or angel, both fallen and heavenly.

"Oh, shit."

"Yeah, exactly. Now you know why I came to your house that day. When I saw him, I knew it was time you found out and started training. Since then, I've found out imps summoned him. I just don't know why or to what end."

"Well, that's all scary as hell. Now, about the training... What is that, exactly? Us sitting around your massive library, reading old books, and hoping I get lucky that the next creature I encounter is one I've already studied?" My tone is harsher than I intend, but the stakes keep rising, and my knowledge and skills are still subpar.

"That's only part of it. We also need to start physical training."

I laugh. "Okay, so when's that starting, so I know when to call in sick?"

He doesn't look amused. "We need to start soon. It's a miracle you beat that minotaur. You must have some memories from the karate you took when you were young."

"Whoa there. You pit me against that minotaur, knowing fully well how behind in my training I am. It's not like you can't see how out of shape I am by looking at me. If I had died in there, that would have been completely on you." Sometime during my diatribe I finally hear the other part of what he said. "Wait, what karate?"

George closes the book on Jinn and slides a different one in front of me. "My dad wanted to start training you when you were a child. He talked your parents into signing you up for karate, but I don't think it lasted long. But you need to know this isn't about your size. It's about your mind. You need to know what you are capable of, because it's a lot."

This makes me roll my eyes.

His eyes open wide in response. "Really? I mean, aside from the fact you created four little humans, you did kill that minotaur. Without any help. All by yourself. Haven't you notice your heightened senses? Your hearing and sight? Your reflexes? How can you still not see how amazing you are, the amazing things you can do?"

I don't know how to respond to this. I've never been able to take a compliment or see the good things about myself. My parents didn't exactly teach me how to. Suddenly I'm back in that house...

I was just a little girl. Eight? Nine? Too young to understand and yet I did, too clearly. He smelled sour, again. He slurred his words, unable to annunciate them fast enough to keep up with his anger. She sat at the kitchen table, her eyes swollen and red, again. And he couldn't handle seeing the effects of his own actions. His face turned crimson as he screamed about how weak we were as he smashed Mom's dishes on the floor. I think he specifically meant her, but he included me in his tirade. Because I wasn't good enough for him either. She was weak, and I was...I don't know what.

He stormed out. He came back. He stormed out again. She blamed me each time. When the house was thick with sudden silence but for her sniffles, she told me it was my fault, that I shouldn't have been such a bitch to him. But, I was nine. I was just trying to survive in a house where

I wasn't wanted. A house where words hurt the same as hands, and love was as elusive as Santa Claus. Even affection hurt in that house.

So, I took in the pain, in silence. The blame was all I knew. I was at fault. I wasn't good enough to save us, to keep him happy. It never occurred to me until I was in therapy, years later, his happiness never should have been my responsibility. But by then, it'd become my driving belief: I'm not good; I'm not enough. And I never will be. Even if I'm perfect, I'm not good enough. And I'm far from perfect. So, I keep trying to be better.

"Miranda, where did you go?" George's voice cuts through my memories, his tone soft with concern, and maybe fear.

I blink and then look into his eyes. They're blue, like my mother's, but his contain a kindness and compassion hers never had.

"Are you okay?" he asks.

I push my chair back and bounce onto the balls of my feet to bring me back to the here and now. "Yeah, I think I'm good. But I think I should go. It's a lot to absorb, ya know? Can we pick it all up again tomorrow?" I head for the door before he can respond.

He calls after me, "He knew, you know."

I stop short but don't turn around.

George sighs. "He wanted to report your dad, but he had no proof. He noticed when you became withdrawn, and he followed up with your parents. He tried to get you help when you became depressed, but they didn't want the stigma of a kid with mental health issues. He couldn't do more. He couldn't risk his medical license or, more importantly, his cover. He hated himself as he watched you get quieter. Sadder. He hated your parents as he watched the brilliant light inside you fade."

I walk out of the oak paneled library, taking deep breaths as I hurry through the sitting room big enough to be its own social club, across the marble floored foyer, and past the heavy double doors complete with brass door knockers set into relief carvings of open scrolls. When I get into my car, I lock my doors and sob so violently I can barely pause to breathe.

Four minutes later, my phone chimes with a new text from the number George used the other night. I guess I forgot to program it into my phone, but I still immediately know it's him.

> I'm sorry for upsetting you. Rest up. And tomorrow, wear something you can exercise in. And no calling in sick.

I smile, strangely grateful to have George on my side. I add his number to my contact list under "Docent George." Looking in the mirror, I manage to somewhat erase the raccoon eyes my teary mascara left in its wake. Then I pull away from the stone mansion and drive off to begin my afternoon pickups.

***

The evening goes as well as it can. While the kids are in their rooms doing homework, I'm in the mudroom, throwing in a load of laundry, hoping no more childhood memories resurface. I open the little detergent drawer with the same amount of effort as always, or so I think, but the drawer flies across the room, and the pieces from inside it scatter around the floor. I get on my hands and knees and start collecting them all when Jake comes home.

I'm not sure how long he's been watching me, but as soon as I stand up to slide the drawer back into place, he's against my ass, and once again hard. His hot breath caresses my neck.

"Heya, Sexy."

"Um, hi. What the hell is with you? Have you been taking Viagra instead of your vitamins or something? Why are you always raring to go?" I turn around to face him and he is pressed up against me the entire time. He looks insulted, but jokingly so, I think.

He places his hands on my hips and pushes himself backwards a bit to speak to me. "How dare you insinuate that I cannot be naturally this excited to see you! You are a strong, beautiful woman. I'm so lucky to have you for myself. I don't need any help to want to please you. I want that all on my own."

"Okay. Okay. Sheesh." I give him the side eye because, quite frankly, he deserves it. "Why are you talking like that? You've been so weird since you got home from Vegas."

I slip past him and don't stop moving to hear his response. I have four kids to feed and a house to run, not to mention that I'm also preoccupied with my new calling to save the world. I can't dwell on his weirdness right now. I head to the kitchen to finish dinner, hesitating only when I'm forced to alter the familiar choreography when I encounter Jake standing where I need to be.

He tries to pull me back into conversation. "Where are the kids?"

"In their rooms, doing homework."

He nods. "When are they coming back down?" On the last word, one eyebrow goes up, and he looks at me calmly but expectantly.

I pause. "When I call them down for dinner."

"They won't come down before then?"

"No. They won't."

He stares into my very soul. Before I know what's happening, he wraps his arm around my waist and pulls me to him. He does kiss me, but it's more ravenous than passionate. He wraps his fingers in my thick curls, tilts my head back, and then kisses down my neck, nibbling with his teeth. Occasionally, he bites. I'm not sure I like this, but I'm captivated all the same. He wraps a leg around my ankle and knocks me off balance, but he catches me so that I don't fall and don't have a choice but to allow him to lower me to the floor at his own convenience.

I'm a little uneasy, but all of his attention is also making me wet. I close my eyes to figure out exactly what I'm feeling in this moment, besides horny as hell. But what I feel is Jake tugging off my pants. This time, he doesn't bother with foreplay. By the time my eyes are open again, he is against my opening, pressing inside. I gasp, and he grabs my face so I have no choice but to look at him.

"No gasps. No moans. I want you to scream with pleasure this time."

And with that, he rolls his hips into me again and again, and I can't help but scream out as wave after wave of pleasure washes over me. Right there. On the kitchen floor. So many emotions have been reawakened in me lately.

Chapter 13

Miranda

My body is so sore and weak from Jake pounding me on the kitchen floor last night that when I wake up, I'm not exactly sure how I'm going to train with George. Granted, I never knew how I was going to train, given my primary form of exercise for the last thirteen years has been chasing my kids around, and, let's face it, even that hasn't happened in about three years.

I use the code George gave me to open and drive through his wrought iron gate. Before I'm out of my car, he opens the front door and stands on the top step, barefoot and wearing black warmup pants and a tight T-shirt. Really tight, in fact. I actually am a bit embarrassed at how tight because as I get closer, I can see how well defined his muscles are, and it hits me that they obviously have been this whole time. Meanwhile, I'd been thinking he was a scrawny little nothing and wondering how the hell he was going to train me to fight. Now I'm debating heading home before he has the chance to kick my ass.

"You ready for today?" He confidently grins at me.

I cower. "Um, I guess?"

"Nah. Remember, you're amazing. You can do this! Let's go."

I hang back for a second, my brow furrowed. I'm not used to this cheery version of him. I'm not sure what's coming, but I'm terrified to find out.

I hurry to catch up before he lets the giant oak door close in my face. Inside, I follow him to the right, through a dining room furnished with the longest table I've seen outside of Versailles and past the kitchen where we had our coffees yesterday. I try adding to the mental map I've been attempting to make of this place. Past the dining room, he opens a door on the far end of the hall and stands in front like a castle guard, his body holding it open. He's crossed his arms behind his back, hands on elbows.

Beyond the door, my jaw drops as I enter a full dojo, straight from a martial arts movie. The high ceilings of the house add to my awe. Aside from the perimeter of the room, woven mats of bamboo cover the majority of the dark ash hardwood floor. I try to remember from my geisha obsession phase what those mats are called...tsunami mats? No, that's not right....

The walls consist of large panels of clean white paper with a cross work of black wooden frames. At the far end of the room, a three-panel work of art comprises the majority of the backwall and dominates the room with its gold leaf and colors so rich they must be enamel. The panels depict a large blue dragon on the left and a warrior on the right, much smaller by comparison.

No, I'm wrong. As I get closer, I know she's not a warrior. She's a Guardian.

Her long black hair flows behind her, loosed from the intricate hair style still pinned atop the crown of her head. A few strands blow across her white face. Dark red lips bloom, a small, sad rosebud. I'm scared for her and in awe of her. Even more awe than I have for this room. Her finely detailed teal kimono includes whisps of white and purple birds. No, not birds, but swirls that match the one on the cover of that docent book. The pattern is perfect on her. She is perfect. Her red sash, her obi I remember from my reading, looks like it's holding her upright, and yet it could also be a bleeding wound. She is my predecessor. Her legacy is mine now. This is my burden to bear, and I will use her as my muse as I train.

I tear my eyes away from her to look at the smaller figure behind her. The recessed hairline and high dramatic bun clearly identify this figure as a man. He wears full armor even though he stands behind her. In one hand, he holds a large scroll and in the other, a brush. Is he a scribe? No. He's her docent. I smile. I turn to make a smart-ass comment to George, but he's still on the far end of the room, and I'm right up against the beautiful painting. He smiles to himself with deep satisfaction, as if I passed some sort of test by being drawn to this work of art.

"What?" I call sheepishly across to him.

Still smiling, he bows and walks onto the mats. (Tatami! That's the mats!)

I perch a hand on my hip and cock my head to the side. "Why are you smiling like that? I have an art background. Is it so surprising that I would be interested in this?"

"Not at all. On the contrary. My dad couldn't wait for this moment. All the docents wrote about the moment their Guardians felt the connection to their lineage. This was your moment." He stops directly in front of me, revealing that today, in this room, his blue eyes are more stormy than bright. "You may have accepted your destiny when you fought the minotaur, but today, now, you believe in it."

His confidence makes me very aware of myself, my clumsiness, my age. All of my disadvantages. I clear my throat, trying to fake feeling that confident in myself. "What are the swirls on her kimono? I saw one on a book in the library yesterday, too."

He steps closer to the painting, and to me, to look closely. "Oh, that is the symbol of the Guardian. It is a swirl of protective wind to symbolize that Guardians are protectors, not aggressors." On his last sentence, his eyes are back on me. I curl in on myself.

Not letting me shrink further, he puts his hands on my shoulders and pushes them back, so I stand straighter than I usually do.

"Be confident in who you are. Right?"

I nod, even though I'm not feeling it. He knows this, but he lets it go.

"Ok, so you've seen the dojo, and the Shomen." He indicates the painting behind him. "Now, shall we get started?"

He moves me to the mats and positions me to face the work of art, the Shomen, which he stands in front of and faces me. For the first time, I notice the black strip of fabric around his waist.

"You're a black belt?" I ask it rhetorically, but he nods. "Huh. That explains the muscles, I guess."

"What?"

"Nothing...."

He looks up to the ceiling, as if asking God herself for strength, a smirk on his lips. Then he begins to pace as he talks. Regardless of his words of confidence for me, he doesn't appear completely confident in himself.

"So, your physical training will largely be karate based. That's what I have my black belt in. That's what generations of docents have based the training of their Guardians in. The reasoning behind this, besides the fact that the first Guardian was from Japan," he waves his hand to point to the woman in the painting, "is that karate is a largely defensive martial art. Regardless of what certain movies will have you believing, you should not strike first. The word karate means 'empty hand,' and since you will not be armed in your daily life, it's good technique for you to have. Remember, you are the Guardian. Not the huntress, not the attacker. You use defense whenever you can and offense only as a last resort. Any questions?"

I shake my head.

"Okay, so I don't think we need to get too technical since it's just the two of us. That being said, I will make you follow all the customs if I don't think you're taking our training seriously. Got it?"

"Got it." I nod tightly. I think one corner of his mouth twitches in a smile, which he tries his hardest to suppress.

"Okay, we're going to start with a warm up. Let's do fifty jumping jacks."

I can't help but laugh out loud.

He rolls his eyes. "Fine. Let's start with ten. Ten jumping jacks. Okay?"

"Sure. Let's give that a shot!"

Every time I land, I feel a familiar sensation of warm liquid dripping out. Luckily, I came prepared for this. When I told Eliza I would be doing physical training with George, all she had to say was, "Just remember the day we met...." And I knew to don the incontinence undies I invested in after my first gym experience as a mom.

"Okay! You made it to ten. Let's do ten more."

Unfortunately, I don't think the undies were made for this level of leakage. By the end of the fourth set of ten, I'm soaked. Luckily, I'm also prepared for this since I packed three more pairs in my purse. I raise my hand again.

"Yes, Miranda?"

"Um, slight issue. Could I please go to the bathroom?"

He frowns but agrees and leads me to a bathroom down the hall. When I start to change, I pull off the wet undies...and my soaked pants. "Shit."

"Everything okay in there?"

"Um, yeah...." I open the door a crack because I don't think this is a conversation I should have through a door. "I, um, had some...woman...mom related...physical issues...during that warm up. And I don't have any spare pants. I think we may have to call it a day?"

After a moment, recognition lifts his furrowed brow. "Oh! Um...hang on one second."

He disappears into the next door and comes back a moment later. "I promise I had been planning to present this to you with a little more...ceremony. But I guess now will have to do." From behind his back, he produces a perfectly folded white garment.

I look at him, confused.

"It's your gi." Tucking the bottom piece under his arm, he unfolds the cotton top. On the back of my gi, in beautiful embroidery, is the woman from the painting.

I put my hand on my mouth. "Thank you," my words barely more than a breath.

"Try it on. We can be done with the jumping jacks," he winks.

I let out a chuckle and disappear into the bathroom to change. A sense of power washes over me as I tie the gi top and look in the mirror. Never in a million years did I ever expect to see myself in one of these. Martial arts always seemed an elite club I never thought to join, or ever cared to try. But now that I am here, wearing this, it all feels so right. I'm going to learn karate!

Before I head back in to train, I smooth the bottom edge of the top against my thighs. When I arrive in the dojo, George is standing where he had been before and holds something behind his back, but I can't make out what. I run, eh, walk briskly, back to my spot and face him. I have no doubt that the corners of his mouth quirk up this time. He has true joy in that sly little smile. I can't help but smile back, a little more confidently than I ever have before.

"That gi suits you." He smiles widely. "Before we continue, I have one more thing to give you. I wasn't sure when I should present this to you, but since I gave you the gi, it's only fitting you have this as well." He pulls his hands around to where I can see them, and in them he holds a white belt. "This is your first obi, your white belt. I was going to tell you that once this is on you, you will not be the same person. But honestly, between the painting and the gi, I think you've already felt that today."

As he wraps the belt around my waist, I'm trembling, buzzing from the energy in the room. I definitely cannot follow how he twists the obi so deftly, leaving a little arrow in the knot that becomes more apparent when he tugs tightly on the ends.

"You're going to need to teach me how to do that." My words are shaky from my nerves. I feel his silent laugh pulse through him as his hands finish straightening my belt. Then he takes a large step back, slaps his hands to the sides of his legs, and bows to me. I mimic what I see, bowing back.

He claps for me, genuine applause. But because it's only one pair of hands, it sounds sarcastic to my ears.

"Now, let's get started…for real. I'll consider you warmed up already. The first thing you'll need to know before anything else is how to fall." He throws himself backward, smacking the floor with his hands by his waist, while yelling "Hiya!" He stops moving only when he has rolled halfway onto his side, knee bent in the air, foot poised to kick, hands in some positions in front of him.

I can only imagine what my face must look like because he breaks out laughing.

"Okay, Miranda. That might look hard, but you can definitely do it. Oh! But I should probably teach you some stances first. Sorry, you're new to learning, and I'm new to teaching." He blushes a little.

I first learn neutral position, when my legs are tight and my hands slap my outer thighs. Then I learn to stand strong with my feet hip-width apart and my fists kept down but in front of my waist. I'm supposed to default to this Yoi Dachi Stance when just standing around. Okay sure, that's definitely a comfortable, natural position. I also learn guard stance, the position I need to assume before throwing punches or kicks.

After that, we move on to the fall he first showed me. Again, I laugh and shake my head. There's just no way I'm going to be able to do that. He breaks it down into steps, has me squat down low, roll backwards, slap the ground.

"No! Watch your elbows! They shouldn't hit the ground."

"None of me should hit the ground, George!"

"Well, you're going to, and when you do, you need to be able to control your fall so you can jump back up and keep going."

"I couldn't jump back up and keep going even if I landed on a trampoline, George!"

Eventually, he convinces me to pretend I'm an egg and rock back gently. Lo and behold, I actually get the fall somewhat correct. "Okay, good. I got that. Can I be done for the day now?"

He rolls his eyes. "Fine. You have to get the kids soon anyway, and you need extra time to go home and change."

I thank him, and he walks me out. At my car, he holds my door open to talk to me. "You did good in there."

"Thanks...."

"I'm not done. You did good. But you're the Guardian, and good isn't good enough. You have to be outstanding. Incredible. Top notch. I took it easy today because it was your first. You're going to come back tomorrow, and we're going to fight. And I'm not going to take it easy on you. This isn't something I should ease you into. The minotaur didn't. No one else will. I want to be your friend. You're fun to be with, but I need to be your teacher first. This is too important, no matter how badly you make me want to forget that."

I feel my cheeks redden, not really sure what that's all about.

"How do I make you want to forget that?"

He smiles and looks away, thinking. "You're just not a typical Guardian."

"Have you met many? I mean, you're younger than I am, and if I was already the Guardian when you were born—"

"First, you weren't the guardian when I was born. You were only now called up. When I was born, you were still in line. And second, no, I haven't met many. I've only met you. But I've read all the docents' notes. You're all born into this, and so you're all special in your own rite. But none of the Guardians had a chance to live their own lives and become their own people. They never had a chance to develop their own natural strengths and power. You have."

I laugh full out. "Sure, okay. That sounds exactly like me."

"There you go, doubting yourself again. I don't get it. Birthright aside, you are probably the most amazing woman I have ever met. Don't doubt yourself."

"Okay, George. You're how old again? Like, sixteen? Give yourself a chance to grow up and get out more. When you've actually met a few more women, you can come back and tell me that."

"I'm twenty-four, remember? I've met plenty of women. Believe me, you are as incredible as they come."

***

Jake comes home early, again. We have sex on the kitchen floor, again. But this time, he's much more tender. Our love making is softer and wholesome and warm, more like what I'm used to. I'm happy to have one area of my life return to normal.

We have a sweet family dinner together. The kind we used to have every day. The kind we used to make a priority. The kind that reminds us how loved we all are.

Everything feels almost monotonous again. I'm not thinking about imps or kitsune. There are no shadows or Jinn. I'm even back to feeling just as exhausted and out of shape as I did a week ago. And I take some solace in that feeling instead of letting it scare me.

Chapter 14

Miranda

George wasn't kidding when he said he wasn't going to take it easy on me. Even though he chose a different warm up today, my feet still burn with numbness ten minutes into our time together.

On top of that, every muscle screamed at me when I woke up today. My butt and back are bruised from all the roll falls I did yesterday, and the sex on the hard kitchen floor isn't exactly helping either.

Oh, Jake. What was with that man? Before his trip, I couldn't even get him to come home in time for dinner, much less a few minutes earlier so he could fuck me silly on the kitchen floor before the kids came down to eat...

"Okay, time to spar." George throws a padded helmet at me.

When I go to put it on, I discover a cased mouth guard tucked inside.

George's eyes follow mine. "I can't have you getting a concussion here."

After our conversation at my car yesterday, his cold demeanor and short communications with me are jarring. I put on the gear and go to guard stance, waiting for him to start.

To say "he kicks my ass" would be a gross understatement. When we're done, I'm curled in a ball on the floor, gasping for air.

"Get up." His voice is devoid of all the joy and warmth we've shared until now.

I have tears running down my face from the pain I'm in. He lowers his hand to help me up, but I hesitate to accept the offer.

"Miranda, I'm not going to hit you again. I promise." Once I am standing, he looks at me, and his face softens a bit. "I needed to see what you were capable of without training. I told you I can't take it easy on you."

I don't have enough air in my lungs for a retort. Although I'm barely on my feet, I'm holding my stomach and curling in.

"You're not going to get any air in that way. Stand straight. I know it's hard right now, but you'll feel better. Trust me." He moves my shoulders back, "I'm going to teach you how to breathe when you don't think you can." He tightens his abs and moves his arms in a sweeping motion that appears to physically open his lungs.

"Do this three times, when I say, Nogare... Nogare... Nogare..."

I do as he says, and by the third time, I can actually breathe again. So I smack him in the arm. "What the actual fuck, George?"

Now he can't help but laugh as he shies away from my weak assault. "What? I told you I can't take it easy on you."

"There's a difference between 'not taking it easy' and 'almost killing me.'"

"I needed to see what you could do instinctively, without training. Now we know, it isn't much..."

I roll my eyes and cross my arms, reminding myself of Jessie. "I could have told you that. You didn't need to beat the shit out of me to find out."

He's laughing and smiling and truly enjoying this exchange. I'm seeing red, but his boyish giggling turns my red more to pink. Damn him.

He moves back to the middle of the room. "Show me your break fall again."

I roll my eyes but do it, and it's perfect. I climb back up to my feet, not super gracefully, but functionally, and faster than I could yesterday.

He lays an arm across his stomach and cups his chin with his other hand. "This is fascinating. You do that so much better than you did yesterday. Have you practiced?"

I grimace. "Not exactly."

He circles me while he talks, as if inspecting a race horse he's considering to purchase. "I didn't think so. I don't mean any offense! I just know you have four kids and no place dedicated for practice. Anyway, although your instincts are not as fully accessible as I'd hoped, I knew the odds of that were low. But I wonder if once something is taught to you, it wakes that part up of your background and you can just do it. Let me test something."

And without warning, he shoves me from behind. I fall on my face. Hard.

"Oh, Jesus. I'm sorry! That's not what I expected to happen! Are you okay?"

"George! What the fuck!"

"I guess you still need to be taught each technique individually. Good to know."

"Fuck!" I push myself up. I must be a sight because he is shaking in silent laughter.

We spend the rest of our training time going over more break falls. I learn right side, left side, hard front, soft front, roll fall, and back roll fall. So by the time I leave, in theory at least, I won't get injured being knocked to the ground. Or, ya know, tripping over myself. I guess that's an improvement.

"Tomorrow we're going to work on self-defense techniques. Then we'll get into offensive stuff. Okay?"

I nod because it's all I have the energy to do. Then, walking toward the door, he decides to sweep me so that I fall over to the side. I'm not expecting it, and apparently my instincts have not kicked in yet, because

I yip and fall over. He catches me, one arm around my waist and the other grabbing my wrist that I framed in front of me. Some kind of static electricity buzzes between us in that moment, right when I know he won't let me fall.

Then he stands me up and smirks. "You good?"

I roll my eyes and contemplate punching him, but I'm too tired to lift my arm. He pats me on the back and then nudges me toward my car, and as I drive home, I'm left wondering when I'll be able to knock him on his ass. With that thought, I smile the whole way home.

***

When Jake comes home, I am almost asleep on my feet, stirring a pot of chili. His hands are all over me.

"I just can't tonight, okay?" I push his hands off me and continue cooking. My arms are screaming for more ibuprofen.

He pouts his bottom lip out. "No. I want my wife." He starts by massaging my shoulders and kissing my neck, which actually feels pretty good right now. But when he lowers his hands and grabs my ass, I whimper in pain.

"Jake, please stop." I feel my hand tighten on the wooden spoon to keep from lashing out at him more.

But he doesn't stop. He goes back to my shoulders and neck, trying to get me to change my mind with a seductive, "Oh, come on, Baby. I don't need to take long."

But he can't change my mind. I don't think I have ever felt this level of pain and exhaustion in my life. I turn around and rip his hands off me. "Back off!" I shove him back, harder than I intended.

Jake stumbles backward. His eyes open wide for a split second, then narrow and darken as he glares at me. "Fine, whatever." He grabs his keys and storms out. This is a side of him I have never seen before.

My eyes start leaking of their own volition. I need to calm down before the kids return to the kitchen to eat. I take a couple deep breaths, grab my cell phone, and text Eliza.

> Hey. Something is up with Jake. Any chance you can take the kids for an overnight Friday night, so he and I can have a chance to talk about whatever it is we need to discuss?

The three dots pulse and then,

> Of course! You know Tabitha adores them all! Can't wait!

Thank god for best friends. I try to get through the rest of the week, focusing on my training and not my marriage. But Jake isn't the only one who's being cold right now. George has become all business.

Thursday is mostly self-defense. He dedicates all morning to showing me how to evade and defend against a slew of different attacks. He also shows me a bunch of blocks and parries, as he calls them. At the end of the day, I learn a few different kicks and punches. I particularly enjoy the front thrust kick and the jab, cross punch combo. I feel like I know what I'm doing quickly and that I have a lot of power behind them. Well, for most of the techniques...

"I don't understand why this jumping side kick is so hard for me!" I slam my fist on the tatami after landing on my ass for the millionth time today.

George is patient with me, more patient than I probably deserve. Finally, I detect a hint of warmth in his voice when he speaks to me. "Miranda, you've been doing karate for three days. Maybe give yourself a grace period before you expect yourself to do it all perfectly? Even with your gifts, it's amazing how fast you're picking this all up."

I shake my head. "Nope. That's unacceptable. There are creepy ass jinn thingies and little red bat people and I'm the one who is supposed to stand in the way of them. I need to get this shit down now. I can hear softer sounds than I could before, see things clearer than I could before, and kill giant monsters. Why can't I do this kick?" I walk in a big circle, shaking my limbs out, trying to get out of my head, and just do it.

"I'm glad you can't." George stands perfectly still until I stop pacing and glare at him. He lowers the body shield he's holding and picks at the stitching so he doesn't have to look at me while he talks. "You're special, but so are the martial arts. They are to be respected. If you could do everything perfectly right away, you'd be missing out on all the fun."

I'm floored. "The fun, you say? Really? You know, you're right. Getting my ass kicked by a blackbelt, not to mention the fucking minotaur, so much fun, George!"

"Okay, I get it. Try again." He regains full control of the shield by wrapping both forearms through the straps on the back. Then, he raises the shield so the top edge is in front of his cheek, and he braces himself in guard stance. "Hajime."

I jump into guard stance myself, take a deep breath, and start running. I run as fast as I can, which admittedly is not very fast, before pushing off hard with my right foot, left leg extended to my side, foot flexed. I know I'm going to make it this time. I can feel it. He got me all charged up, and I'm going to. I know this truth, right up until the moment I crash to the mats and swear loudly, two feet shy of my target.

***

Thursday night, Jake gets home after I'm asleep and barely speaks to me in the morning before taking the kids to school. Being home so late isn't out of the ordinary for him, but giving me the silent treatment is unheard of. He hates going to bed when we're still fighting. I don't think we have in years. And if we do, he wakes up extra early and forces us to hash it out before the kids wake up. He's not okay when we're not okay.

But not this time. This time, he's more distant than ever, and all because I said no to sex, which makes no sense to me. He's never acted this way before.

Friday, when I drive up to George's castle, he's already outside, waiting for me. He's straight out of a winter catalog in his dark wash jeans and medium gray cable knit turtleneck. With his hands shoved casually in his pockets and the way he leans sideways against his car, he should get a contract with Burberry.

I am sure George's mom must be insanely proud of him. I look forward to the day I get to beam with pride over a confident Sammy, all grown up. If I get to see him that way... But then the passenger door opens, surprising me out of my meditative state. My eyes pop open at the sound.

"Umm, hi."

"Good morning. We're going on a field trip." He buckles himself in and looks at me. A moment of silence fills the space when I'm still too shocked at his sudden appearance in my car to start driving. He widens his eyes in response. "Turn right at the bottom of the driveway."

I salute in response. "Aye, Aye, Captain."

His narrowed eyes and clenched jaw make me face forward and restart my car. When we've merged onto a highway, and he's indicated we'll be on here awhile, I decide to inquire further.

"So, George, where are we headed today?"

"We're going to go meet with Joanna."

"Joanna? Should I know who that is?" Then the memory hits me, and it takes everything in me not to slam on the brakes. "Um, Joanna, my predecessor?"

"Yes. You are in the rare, actually, unprecedented, situation where you have the opportunity to meet the previous Guardian. How can we pass that up?"

"You could have let me known ahead of time. I would have dressed more professionally or something."

"Dress for the job you don't want but were born into anyway?"

"Something like that. Hey, was that a joke?" I glance at him and see the hints of a smile on his lips.

"Maybe. Don't get used to it. I'm not here to be funny."

"Yeah, yeah, yeah. I know. You're not my friend. You're my docent. I get it."

"Yup. Plus, you're in your gi. Doesn't get much more 'for the job' than that."

He has a point. The rest of the drive is quiet. Aside from his navigation, we don't have much to say to each other. He's made it clear that ours is only a working relationship, and even though I'm obviously not the kind of person who can compartmentalize that way, I'm trying really, really hard to respect the choice he's apparently made.

After about an hour, we reach our destination: a sprawling blue Victorian farmhouse separated from the road by a manicured lawn that is bigger than my entire property. The white wraparound porch leads to a small screened-in gazebo at the corner on the far side of the facade, away from the driveway and garage, and off-set from the house enough to look out over the expansive fields in the back of the property.

I let out a low whistle. "Does being Guardian come with some kind of paycheck that you failed to mention? I just assumed since it's my birthright and not really an option that it's a free gig. But damn."

George rolls his eyes. "Um, no. When the League of Docents came to the decision that Joanna was, well, to put it bluntly, surviving past the normal life expectancy of a Guardian, they realized they should take care of her. So, they bought her and Benjamin this farm. They figured that since it's remote, they would be out of harm's way, for the most part. That is, unless they need her to jump back into harm's way."

My eyes instinctively roll. "They sound charming, really. Can't wait to meet these League guys. Who's Benjamin?"

He waits until we're both out of the car to answer casually. "Oh, uh, Benjamin is her docent…and her husband."

I don't have time to ask any of the many questions that little nugget brought to my mind because just then a woman, older than me but not by as many years as I'd expected, comes out of the red front door and down the first of the four front steps. She smiles to us and waves her hand, indicating for us to follow her to the gazebo. And we do.

It's eerily quiet here. I'm not used to being so far from the sounds of traffic, or from neighbors fighting with one another, or from kids fighting with one another. The tranquility is kind of nice but more off-putting. I feel like I've entered one of those soundproofed rooms that no one can stand for more than a few minutes without losing their mind.

When we enter the gazebo, Joanna leans over a wrought iron and glass table and pours lemonade. She lifts a glass in each hand and brings them to us. "Well, hello there. You must be George. And you, you must be Miranda. It's a true honor to meet you, dear." After handing me the glass, she puts her hands on my arms, just below my shoulders, and closely inspects my face with a broad smile.

I smile back. Her eyes are warm glowing pools, even with all she must have seen in her life. Her skin has the sort of earthy look only earned by working in the sun for years. I suspect her dark grey hair once looked similar to mine, both in color and style. She wears it pulled back in a low braid, but the few flyaways tell me her hair's natural state is frizzy curls, just like mine.

After a minute, she releases me and turns back to the table, pointing to the chairs surrounding it with an open hand as if she works at an amusement park and doesn't want to take the chance of insulting someone with a true pointing gesture.

I force myself to speak as I take a seat. "Hi, Joanna. It's really nice to meet you."

She smiles and nods her head once slowly, proudly. Now that I'm here, it's hard not to fangirl. George was right. One Guardian getting to meet another is unprecedented; I cannot waste this moment. I have to think of good questions and not to embarrass myself.

"So, how did you live so long? I mean, not that you're old, because you're not. I just mean, how did you keep from being killed at a young age? You know?"

Yeah, good one Miranda. Way to go.

In the chair to my left, George audibly groans from my ability to make quite that big an ass of myself. Joanna smiles sweetly, staring off into her fields and remembering back to the times my questions evoked.

"It wasn't anything I did, to be honest. Things just kind of settled down around the time I was called up. I had a few years of hard work, and then, it just sort of fell off. And even the years I worked, I never had to deal with anything too big or dangerous. It's like they all knew to stay hidden, or they were hibernating or something."

I nod. "So, your docent never, oh, let's just say, threw you into a maze with a minotaur, for example?"

She laughs deeply, straight from her soul. Her eyes crinkle at the corners. Then she claps her hands together and rests her thumbs against the dip in her upper lip as she regains her composure. "Oh, Benjamin sent me into all kinds of places with all kinds of creatures." She leans toward me and stages a whisper. "And I'm including him amongst them!" Her tone tells me she's joking, but also not. "But the creatures were all domesticated and threw only their species' signature moves, so I had real life practice."

"Oh, sure. Of course. Domesticated. Did Ben just pick them up at the local farm and horse show, or...?"

"Well, no. Back then, the League had all sorts of connections and resources. They basically had a whole catalog of domesticated creatures they could get their hands on fairly easily if a docent wanted to use one to train their Guardian."

My brow furrows. "Were there more of us then?"

She looks a shade more serious in response to my own change in demeanor. "No, not more of *us*, although of course your successor has already been Chosen, even if she's not ready to be called up. But more creatures, and more...let's call it bureaucracy. Everything had to be done just how the League of Docents wanted."

An idea pops into my mind, a spark of hope igniting. "So then...do I even have to do this? I mean, I'm sure the next one in line is at a better stage in her life to take this on than I am. Can't I just...pass?"

She shakes her head. "You can't. And you wouldn't want to! You're about to embark on the most amazing personal journey anyone could ever hope to endure. You're going to become so much stronger and better as you go. Trust me, if I can do this, you can do this."

I nod. "Rightrightrightrightright... I hear you. I do." I smile weakly. "But let's just say, I'm totally okay being weak and subpar...I mean, I just, I have four kids. I think I'm done with the part of my life wants to go on a personal journey. I don't have all that much free time for that kind of thing, you know? Also, I'm really happy for you and your retirement and all, but, um, every other Guardian in the history of Guardianship has also gotten so much...you know...deader...as they went."

George buries his face in his hands. But Joanna keeps the smile on her face, and her eyes lock on me until I start to squirm. My heart is racing, and just when I've decided I'm never going to get out of this moment, she reaches out and takes my hands in hers.

"Miranda, I know you're scared. This has to be the single strangest thing you have ever had to come to terms with in your entire life. But you know this is real." Then she sits back, picking up her own glass of lemonade and reclining as best she can in the iron chair. "It sounds like you're processing this all pretty well though, if you're already up to bargaining."

"Bargaining? Like, the stage of grief?"

"Of course, the stage of grief! Miranda, you just lost your life as you know it. Your future. Your plans. Your control over your destiny. And your core belief of how the world works. How could you not be going through a grieving process?"

When she puts it like that, I almost feel normal again. I force my lips to turn upward, but I'm not feeling it at all.

George takes over the conversation, asking questions about Benjamin and Joanna's training regime, their relationship beyond that, and creatures she's had to confront.

I lean back into my chair, withdrawing into my own mind. I revisit Joanna's words, about how she's certain I wouldn't want to pass on taking this personal journey. But in actuality, I really would. If only I could.

Chapter 15

Miranda

A little over an hour later, George and I drive back to his house. He stares out the window in complete silence for the entire ride, obviously disappointed in my behavior, in spite of the fact that Joanna assured him, multiple times, that (most of) my behaviors and reactions were completely normal and to be not only expected but also commend-ed because I was so open and honest with myself, and with him.

And honestly, as much as experiencing growth beyond my wildest expectations, both physical and emotional, through my training and experiences sounds cool, I can't help but wonder if I'll get to see my children experience the growth they will surely attain just by living their lives. If I'll be around to see the people they grow up to be. If I'll get to dance at their weddings. If I'll ever be a grandma. I know this job's not my choice, but damnit, if it was...it's not the life I would choose in a million lifetimes.

Joanna must have known what I was thinking though, because even when I got quiet and introspective, she didn't seem to mind. I really like her. I hope I can be like her one day, happy with this lot in life. Also, you know, alive, retired, and living out my life in peace, not fighting dangerous creatures as my day job.

***

Because Eliza's picking up the kids and bringing them home to pack before taking them to her house for the night, George and I still have time to train when we get back to his house. But before we get started, I text Jake.

> Eliza took the kids for the night. Please don't come home too late. I'm out running errands but will be home around 5. Love you.

I vacillated about whether or not to send the "Love you." In the end, I send it to encourage his ass to come home at a reasonable time. I don't want to give him any reason to be tipped off that this evening is going to be a battle. It appears to work because less than a minute later, I receive back:

> Can't wait.

Okay. The trap is laid, so to speak. Now to finish my training.

George and I review everything we've worked on all week. Then we spar. I'm a lot better this time. I still don't beat him, and I make contact offensively only one time. But I block almost every technique he throws my way, and I'm not dying at the end, so I consider that a win anyway. On the way out, he gives me a high five and my first homework.

"I want you to use the weekend to put together a playlist so when we're sparring, you can get out of your head. I think it'll help you."

"Umm, okay. What kind of songs?"

"Whatever you could lose yourself in."

"That's not very specific."

"I can't be more specific, Miranda. It needs to be music that'll work for you."

"George, you may not know this about me, but I'm not particularly good at these kinds of open-ended assignments."

His only response is a smile, and as he turns to go back inside, he yells to me over his shoulder "You did good today. Have a good weekend."

Homework to obsess over aside, I'm feeling pretty damn good about myself by the time I head home. In the car, I blast the 90s channel through my phone, making mental notes of which songs I think I can lose myself in so I can make a playlist later.

When I get home, Jake's car is already in the driveway. That was fast. I wonder if I did too good a job selling the fact we would be alone tonight. I didn't think I did, but then again, that man does not seem to need much encouragement nowadays.

I walk in to see the lights dimmed, and a trail of rose petals leads into the house from the mudroom. I bend down and pick one up. I rub the leathery velvet between my fingers and smell the sweet floral musk. They're definitely real petals.

"Oh shit."

Definitely not what I was going for. Still in my gi, I duck into the laundry room. Digging through a basket of clean laundry, I finally find and change into a fresh pair of leggings and a T-shirt. I stash my gi in the drawer under the dryer and then continue on my path.

I follow the petals. How are there so many? I check my phone. I sent him that text about two and a half hours ago. I struggle to calculate how did he get out of work, buy these flowers, get home, and set all this up so fast. I feel a little weak and winded as I climb the stairs, but it has nothing to do with exertion this time. I don't see how we're supposed to have a serious conversation when he has our house set up like a proposal scene from a TV show I would have watched in high school.

The lights upstairs are off, and as I walk down the hall, I see a flickering glow coming from our room.

There's no way those are candles... Jake hates candles. He won't even let me light one in the bathroom.

But they are.

Several ivory-colored candles illuminate every flat surface. They don't look brand new either. They look like they've burned for a while, prior to today. But that makes no sense. Maybe he's having a mid-life crisis. That could explain this side of him I've never seen any hint of before. That could also explain why my husband, who has never even liked when I use scented wax melts, has all these previously used candles.

Then I see something laid out on the bed. A... Does this qualify as clothes? It's some kind lingerie, black and lacy.

"Go put it on." I jump when his voice comes from a dark corner.

"What?"

"Take that. Go in the bathroom. And. Put. It. On."

There is no question in his voice. He's not making a request. A familiar tingling starts between my legs, and I know my body is going to betray me.

Holding the...garment...out on the fingertips of one hand, I look in the direction his voice came from. "This isn't exactly what I had in mind for tonight, Jake. We need to have a conversation."

"After. It can wait. This is exactly what I have in mind for tonight. So go put it on. Now."

I still hesitate.

I think he realizes maybe he's approaching, or has crossed, a line because he softens a bit. "This is going to be different than our usual love-making. Do you trust me? Are you okay to continue with what I have planned?"

I nod and let out a meek, "Yes."

I hear the smile in his next words. "I prefer, 'Yes, sir.'"

Sheepishly, I smile back. "Yes, SIR."

Surely, this won't take long, and then we can talk. And maybe he'll even be more receptive to what I have to say once he's sated... I go into the bathroom, shut the door, and turn the light on. Dear god. Now that I can see the thing in full light, I can't imagine where he would have bought it.

After twisting and bending and contorting my arms, I manage to get the piece on correctly, although I don't know how he could possibly think this is an attractive look for me. The entire time I'm changing I hear his impatient breathing outside the door. I don't want to leave the bathroom, but I also don't know what the hell is going on with him and don't want to make him wait any longer. I put my hand on the doorknob, so I don't have to find it in the dark, and turn off the light. The less light shown on me right now, the better. Taking a deep, bolstering breath, I open the bathroom door and step out into the candlelight bathed bedroom.

He's sitting on the bed, and although he's fully dressed, I can see how hard he is through his pants, even in the semi-darkness.

"Come here."

I'm not usually one to take commands without a smart-ass retort, but for some reason I don't dare to disobey. I try to hide myself strategically with my hands and arms as I walk.

"Stop. Stand proudly. I want to see you."

I have never seen this side of him so strongly before. Maybe glances of it here and there, but the only times I can recall when he's been remotely dominating were when I asked him to be. Because *I* like it. This is something else. I put my hands to my sides and force myself to keep them there the rest of the way to him.

When I am standing right before him, he looks up at me. His big brown eyes are sweet and sexy at the same time. "I'm asking you again, are you okay with this?"

I nod, with more confidence this time, perhaps because I am standing above him. But also because this has always been a sort of fantasy of mine, and I'm excited to be acting it out. "Yes. I am. Sir." I add the last word almost as an afterthought, partially because it was and partially just to test him. I wonder, if I act a little bratty, what more will happen?

He puts his hands on my buttocks and grabs forcefully, pulling them apart slightly. I am acutely aware of my nipples hardening against the lace, and so is he. He stares straight at them while he bites his lower lip, trying to control himself from giving in to some dark impulse. He slips one hand through a hole in the material under my right breast and with the other pulls my left toward him, licking and biting the nipple through the fabric. Then he pulls away and looks up at me, the wetness on his chin echoing that between my legs.

"Lie down. I want to look at you." I do as I'm told. He adjusts my arms and legs to be where he wants them so he can get the best view. Then he grabs the closest candle. He holds it several inches above me and runs it slowly up and down every part of me. Once in a while, he pauses to look closer, and a bead of melted wax drops onto my body. It stings, but it's not intolerable. I'd even call it pleasurable right now. When he's had enough of this strange ritual, he puts the candle down and comes back to me. It is not lost on me that he is still fully dressed while I am laying on full display.

He straddles my waist and reaches up toward the headboard. He grabs my left wrist and buckles it into a tight, fur-lined cuff, then repeats with the right.

My eyes go wide. "What the fuck are you—"

He shoves his tongue in my mouth to quiet me but pulls away too quickly for it to count as a kiss. "No questions. Just answers. Are you still okay?"

I nod again.

But he's not satisfied. "I need an answer."

"Yes, sir." I have to yell it because I can't get the sound out of my throat any other way.

He smiles down at me again.

Why did that just make me hotter? I'm distracted by the new wave of tingling down low when he grabs my right ankle and pulls it toward the corner of the bed and buckles it into a cuff as well. Then he moves to the left and repeats. I'm now splayed out like a starfish in nothing but strips of fabric that don't cover anything important. I'm completely at his mercy, and he knows it. He climbs off of me and just stares down at me from the foot of the bed. He looks hungry.

I may climax just from that sight, from being wanted that badly.

Then he walks around to the side of the bed and whispers to me, "No one is home but us. You better not hold back your screams. At. All."

It's all I can do to make myself nod.

"Miranda, I can't hear a nod. Are we good to move on? If we are, say, 'Yes, sir.'"

"Yes, sir."

"And do you understand that I do not want you to control your screams or moans in any way?"

"Yes, sir."

"Good. Then I can continue with what I have planned to do to you."

That is the last dialogue we have for a long time. I lose count how many times he brings me to orgasm with his tongue and fingers. Then he stands next to the bed, smoothly pulls his shirt over his head, and finally releases his rock-hard erection from the pants that were not doing much to hide it anyway. I bite my lower lip, wanting so badly to have him in my mouth.

He climbs on top of me, facing my legs. He keeps his shoulders and head in the air and does not reciprocate what he expects me to perform. He feels so good as I run my tongue over the smooth head, down the shaft. Because I can't use my hands to assist as I normally would, I have to concentrate on doing all I can with my mouth. I get the impression I'm doing more than a decent job though.

He starts to moan and shake, and then he pulls away, abruptly leaving me tied here, cold without him as my blanket. I can't believe he doesn't want to come. It's not like he would waste the night, not after how fast he recovers lately. As if he heard my thoughts, he chuckles to himself, out past the ring of light that encases the bed.

"What's so funny?" My quiet words shake because I am actually a little afraid of the answer.

"You are the most amazing, beautiful, sexy, powerful woman on this entire planet. And you're all mine."

I had not been expecting that.

"What?" My response is much less elegant than his.

"Shhhhhhhhh. I just want to look at you." He comes out of the shadows and stands over me, taking in every inch of me once more.

If I didn't know any better, I would think this is the first time he's looking at me so naked. There is something so primitive and animalistic in his hungry stare. If I wasn't tied to the bed, I would curl up to hide. But I am tied to the bed, and he is looking at me with such a hunger that I am starting to believe maybe I am sexy. I arch my back a little so my breasts push up. I part my thighs the slightest bit more, and his eyes drift down my body. He bites his bottom lip when he sees the wetness dripping there, the wetness I will him to see.

I moan slightly through my mouth in what I hope is a sexy O shape, "Oh, Jake. I want you so badly."

He smiles. He knows he has me right where he's wanted me all along. He sits next to me on the bed, out of my reach.

"I thought you wanted to talk, Miranda... Is now a good time for that talk?"

My jaw drops. He can't possibly mean that. "Don't you dare."

He laughs. "Don't worry, my love. There will be plenty of time for our discussion, but now is definitely not that time."

He leans down and kisses me, hard. I taste myself in his mouth, which makes me writhe more. In one smooth motion, his legs are between mine, and he enters me. My back arches again, this time without my intention. My body is completely out of my control as he presses his hips in again and again, pounding deep into me with every thrust.

At first, I fight against my bonds, wanting to wrap my arms around him and pull him deeper. Soon nothing matters to me but the endless crashing waves I feel within as I climax over and over. Reality slips away from me as lose track of everything but my pleasure, but he eventually cries out with his own and collapses on top of me, spent, but only momentarily, I'm sure, given his recent history in this area. After a couple minutes, he loosens my shackles and suggests I use the bathroom. I can barely walk once I roll out of bed, but I eventually reach the door and hear, "Oh, and Miranda, don't take that off just yet."

I smile as I close the door behind me.

Chapter 16

George

I'm happy to say that Miranda has officially begun her training! While her body is learning everything it needs to do, it isn't responding as quickly as it really should be. Even at her advanced age, she should be able to do more of these techniques as soon as she's shown. It shouldn't take until the next day. I don't know what else I should be doing to get her moving the way she should

I'm anxious about our relationship, too. Being a docent is proving difficult, or at least more difficult than I expected and hoped. I think my greatest challenge will be staying professional. Maybe it is our bond getting stronger, I don't know. I don't usually open up to people, but she has this warmth to her that makes it easy to relax around her. Her sarcasm cracks me up and it is hard to keep things serious in the dojo. The problem is, if we're not serious when we train, it's going to get her killed. She is nowhere near as disciplined as she would be had she started as an adolescent instead of as an adult with a fully formed, larger-than-life personality. She's not as disciplined as she needs to be to survive.

Knowing this keeps me focused on her training. I also sometimes act more responsible than her, regardless of our age difference. For instance, when we went to meet Joanna. I cannot believe the way she spoke to her predecessor. My father must me rolling over.

Maybe bringing her to meet Joanna was a mistake. Maybe, instead of an opportunity to learn, that meeting was a tease, a glimpse at a remotely possible future that we both silently know she most likely won't attain.

Maybe I'm making a mistake, letting myself get too casual and too attached to a Guardian. But that's part of the spiritual bond, I guess. That's the one part of this my dad never really explained. I know he loved her, but I never knew the depth of that love. But I need to stay more detached, if for no reason other than I know has she such a small chance of surviving much past her first *real* confrontation. Especially if I can't find and figure out how to stop these jinn.

I haven't been able to find out much besides the fact that the imps summoned the jinn. I've returned to the dive bar half a dozen times, but, other than being propositioned by what I believe was a poorly disguised harpy, I haven't had luck making contact with any creatures of import there. I need to make some more progress.

Chapter 17

Miranda

I wake the next morning feeling sorer than I have ever been in my life. I'm sure some of it's from my training this week with George, but most of it...most of it is from the sex last night. So much sex. Sex like we were newlyweds again. Sex like we have never had before. The kind of sex where two people know what to do to make their partner scream as well as knowing what their partner can do to make them scream and it all comes together, just as they do. I don't know how I kept up, but I'm guessing it's one of the pluses to this chosen one thing.

I'm thinking about all the positions we tried and how some worked and many did not. This one particular position we tried, successfully, and, wow, I think it is my new favorite. Jake is whistling in the shower. I'm content. And then it suddenly hits me.

"Mother fucker!" I bolt to sitting from my lazy sleeping-in position. We never had our conversation. What the hell, Jake! That's it. We need to talk as soon as he's out of the bathroom. I get up, put a T-shirt on my naked body (eventually the lacy thing just got in the way), and begin to pace.

He's still whistling when he opens the bathroom door, towel wrapped around his waist. I bite my lip when I look at him and force myself to ignore what I know is under that towel. He looks me up and down and grins. "Ready for more?"

"No, no, no, no. No." I put my hands up in front of me to keep him from getting any closer. I didn't even mean to, but I'm actually standing in guard stance from my training. I hear my phone chime with a text message on my bedside table. "Stay. There." I point to the bathroom doorway, so he can't try to misinterpret where I mean.

I skirt around him to the bedside, keeping as much distance as I can keep to prevent his penis from somehow accidentally falling inside me. I grab my phone and read the text from Eliza.

> Hey, how's it going? Absolutely no rush. Just wondering the plan for today.

I sit on the edge of the bed and sigh, not sure how to explain that I have obtained none of the objectives I set for the night.

> Hey, need a little more time. Sorry!

I put the phone on do not disturb before placing it on the table. I feel his eyes on me and know I have to say something. I can't look at him though because I'll just want to rip his towel off.

"Jake, we need to talk. What is going on with you lately? All you seem interested in is sex. And when I don't want it, you get pissed and storm off."

"Is it such a crime to desire my wife?"

"No, but there is more to life." I chance a look at him because this is serious and I need him to know that. "I'm not always going to be in the mood for it, you know? What the hell happened to you out in Vegas that you're so sexually insatiable all the sudden, anyway?"

He looks a little nervous. "I don't know. I guess I realized there's no reason to put off pleasure. At the clubs out there, people were practically fucking right on the dance floor. So why's it so bad to have my own wife when I want her?"

"Ummm, maybe because that's not real life? It's a club, it's a vacation, or it's twenty-somethings who don't have four children and the multitude of responsibilities that come with them." I'm met with an eye roll as his only response. I try to broach the other subject at hand. I quietly ask, "Where did you go the other night, when I didn't want to have sex?"

He's staring off, far away, and a wicked smile comes to his face. He's remembering something I don't think I want to know. My heart is pounding a warning, like it did when I thought about the candles last night.

He widens his grin. "I just...I needed to get out. To feel sexy to *someone*."

I can only imagine my face. For a split second, he sneers like I'm an insignificant nuisance. "Oh stop, I didn't hire a prostitute or pick up a girl at a bar or anything. I just went to a strip club." Then he shrugs, smiles to himself, and adds as an afterthought, "And got a private lap dance."

"You...what?" My eyes fill with tears.

A private lap dance... I'm twelve again. Listening to my father describe the stripper's body and wanting to disappear. I retreated to my room and gave myself physical pain to distract me from the emotional...

Now this man, my husband, who refused to have a belly dancer at his bachelor's party, went to a strip club and got a private lap dance because I denied him sex one time? We've had many conversations about how we both feel about strip clubs. I run to the bathroom and throw up. I'm still hunched over the toilet when I hear him chuckling to himself in the doorway.

"You know what the funniest part is? I was sure you were losing interest in me. I felt so sorry for myself. But after last night... Well, I guess that worry was unfounded."

I push up from the floor and wash my hands and face, my gut twisting the entire time. While I brush my teeth, he takes one step inside the bathroom so I can see his reflection.

He still wears that grin. "I mean, at least I got an idea of what I'd like to see you in when I went, right? It didn't look exactly like that on Chardonnay, but I still loved it on you."

I put down my toothbrush, wipe my face, and turn to him. In three strides, I'm standing in front of him. I smile sweetly right before my first two knuckles connect with his jaw, a perfect hook punch. I think George would be proud. I didn't even wind up before I let loose, so Jake had no idea what was coming.

"What the fuck, you bitch!" He lunges toward me but I duck under his arm and out the bathroom door. He doesn't follow me but stands in the doorway and glowers while rubbing his jaw.

"Okay, we both need to chill out." George said karate was for defense only; I can't look at my hands without shaking. "I'm going to go get the kids. You do whatever you need to do to calm the fuck down. That is, whatever you need to do that doesn't involve having another woman rub herself all over you, please and thank you."

I pull on leggings and a sweater and storm out of the room and down the stairs where I yank my purse off the hook. I slam the door behind me, leaving all my thoughts about my marriage and our future trapped within that house.

Once I'm locked in my car, I text Eliza, telling her I'll be there soon but not immediately. Then I just start driving. I'm stopped at a red light after driving for about ten minutes when I hear the hissing, the whispering. By the time I cross the intersection, the voices are so loud that I can barely focus on the road. I pull over next to a park.

As I sit in my car and take slow, deep breaths I notice a patch of shadow playing in the grass. A few weeks ago, I would have described the dance as pretty. On a normal day, I wouldn't have thought twice about it. But my days aren't normal anymore, and now I wonder why the patch of shadow is moving in the grass at all. The shadow is too dark and defined to be from a cloud passing the sun. Its movement is nonsensical, and that low whispering is much louder here.

I hope the shadow doesn't disperse when I approach, but since that hasn't happened yet with all the weird things I've encountered, I'm confident it won't. I get out of my car and move toward the shadow but not directly as I try to act like I'm just coming to the park. The whispers are more defined, and I think if I concentrate, I can maybe make them out. I don't chance getting any closer, so I sit on the nearest bench, close my eyes, and tilt my face to the blue sky, basking in the warmth of the sun like any regular person enjoying the weather.

I listen with my newly improved hearing as hard as I can, and the whispers separate into different pitches and tones, so I have no idea how many of whatever I'm listening to there are.

"They are conferencing now, speaking to the human about how Lu needs to behave to fix this."

"This is all very unusual."

"Well, there has never been a husband of a guardian before. Or children."

Woah there! This is about my family. I want to scream and launch into action but I know I need to hear what they say. I pinch my leg with my nails through my leggings to keep myself grounded and focused.

"The ladies believed in him. They believed he must have a special power, too."

"Or how would he have pleased such a woman as she."

"Or even won her."

"But now they are doubting the plan."

"Erato and Cleo believe she needs to take him again. So far, it hasn't been enough. But they still believe it can work."

Take... Jake... *Again*? My mind is racing a million miles a minute and I tighten my fingernails in the soft flesh of my thigh. I have to keep myself at least looking calm. I need to hear everything I can. I need to hear where they are taking my husband.

"Mel disagrees."

"Mel never agrees."

"She thinks we are not doing our part getting the Jinn to do his."

"The Jinn needs to finish what he was summoned to do. The Jinn is too soft of heart and stubborn of will. He is fighting our commands."

"They should have summoned him instead of making us do so."

"That is what Mel insists happens now. They believe they will have more control. They are summoning the Jinn tonight."

"They want the Jinn at the mountain when they take the husband back there. They want insurance."

The whispers and the shadow vanish at the same time, so that all I hear now are actual birds and cars driving by. I stand and stretch casually before walking as slowly as I can manage to my car. I have no doubt that was about me. And Jake. And at this point, I have no idea if the Jinn is causing me to hallucinate or not. The line between real and imaginary has been obliterated.

Once I'm back on the road, I try to call George, but he doesn't answer. So, I text him.

I need to talk.

Three dots pulse for a long time for me to then see,

> Monday. At training.

What? What kind of guide is he if I can only reach him during bankers' hours?

> I don't think this can wait. Something's going on with Jake.

I grind my teeth while I wait for his reply. Finally, I hear from him.

> Is this work related?

Grrrrr. Come on, George! Are you fucking kidding me? I take a deep breath and steady myself. This isn't about me. Well, not entirely. Right now, this is about Jake.

> Yes. What do you know about talking shadows? I heard them talking. Someone or something is targeting Jake, and he's been...weird. Can you look up the names Mel and Lu?

For the life of me, I can't remember the other names. The harder to I try to dig out the memory, the more their conversation deteriorates in my mind. I send George the message anyway, angry at myself for letting the information slip away when it has to do with my own family.

> Okay. I'll see what I can dig up. Sit tight. I'll update you if I find out anything.

Fine. Fine. It'll wait. It's not like I have any other option. I still have to go pick up the kids. Maybe it isn't as urgent as it sounded. I can't quite recall if the voices mentioned Jake by name or if I'm jumping to conclusions and looking for reasons to excuse his shitty choices lately.

I continue to Eliza's house even though I don't feel ready to get the kids. To start, I have no idea what I'll be bringing them home to. I don't know who Jake is right now, and I can only imagine the mood he's in after I sucker punched him and ran off.

Sitting tight and letting George handle the research alone isn't easy when I just heard a bunch of shadows whisper about him. I think. I mean, after punching my husband so squarely in the jaw, I'm pretty confident I'm ready to defend us all, but, still, I don't want this shit coming near my family. Damn it!

I park in Eliza's driveway and pull down my mirror to check my reflection. She'll know I was crying, but I don't think the kids will. At least, I hope they won't...

When I ring the bell, Jessie comes to the door. "Oh man. Already?" She rolls her eyes and returns down the long center hall to the kitchen where they've all congregated.

"Nice to see you too, dear." I roll my eyes back at her, but I do so to the back of her head, so my attitude doesn't make me a bad mom or anything. "Hey guys, how are you all doing?"

The scene I walk into is the opposite of what I came from. The room is joyful and light. Phoebe's feeding Tabitha who's all giggles with her big cousins visiting. "Hey, Mom." Phoebe barely glances in my direction. And here I was concerned they would notice anything about my appearance.

Natalie and Sammy are in a heated but quiet argument about some video game, I'm sure. Because it doesn't involve any screaming, their argument can't be about anything important.

I smile. At least my kids were spared the scene from this morning. I'm not sure how that all would have gone down if any of them had been in the house when I found out everything. I decide to stay awhile, so I put my purse on the hallway table and my shoes by the front door, the way Eliza prefers.

"Where is Aunt Eliza?" I ask when I return. I realized she was absent from the virtually perfect tableau before me. Just then the basement door flies open, pushed by a basket piled high with clean but unfolded laundry being carried by my bestie. "There you are. Let me help you with that."

"Touch the laundry and lose a finger."

"Ummm. Okay... You okay, Lize?"

"Yup. I just like things done a certain way now is all."

"I mean, I get that. I do, but do you know how many times I had to change the way I put my laundry away because you insisted on folding it while you were babysitting, and I couldn't bring myself to refold it?"

She tilts her head and looks off toward the ceiling, remembering. "Yeah, that sounds like you should have been clearer with your expectations of me, which is a *you* problem, not a *me* problem... Sorry!" She looks for an empty seat to set her basket on, temporarily forgetting that five extra asses are currently in her kitchen. At least mine is standing.

"Geez, who pissed in your cheerios this morning?" I turn to my progeny. "Kids, were you all horrible guests last night or something?"

They all do some form of denial, shaking their heads, shrugging, murmuring descent.

"No, no, no. They were all wonderful as always. I just talked to my mother a few minutes ago." She finally gives up and sets the basket on the floor by the door to the garage.

"Oh, yeesh. I get it now. Sorry."

"Yeah, it's fine. I'm fine. It's fine. Whatever..."

"Oookay then. Do you want to talk about it?"

"Nope!"

I nod. "Okay, so I'll gather my children and be off then. Kids, are all your bags packed up?" Groans from everyone in the room, except Tabby, who is entirely too sweet for this world. "Come on. We can't impede on Eliza's life forever."

They file out to get their stuff, Phoebe handing Tabitha off to me on her way by. "I get to hold the baby!" I coo at her chunky little face. Her big brown eyes crinkle as she lets out a deep belly laugh back at me. I sit down, still coochy-cooing her. I notice her hair is finally starting to grow in, a little darker and way curlier than Eliza's. Must be from Rory's side.

"So, how'd it go?" Eliza pours us each a cup of coffee and sits across her round kitchen table, looking at me expectantly.

"Uh, probably should wait to tell you the details... Suffice it to say, I'm literally afraid to go home right now though."

"What? What do you mean?"

"I'm afraid of what state I'll find my husband in, considering I punched him in the face before I left. I also haven't ruled out the state of absentia..."

Eliza nearly spits her coffee back into her cup. "Miranda Gold! You did not!"

My only answer is to sheepishly hide behind Tabby. "He practically cheated on me!"

"What? In Vegas?" She slams her mug on the table, and coffee sloshes over the side. Her mouth still hangs open while she sops up the puddles with a paper towel.

"No, actually, now that you mention it... I don't know if he did in Vegas. Maybe that's why going to strip joint here was so easy for him."

"A strip joint? No way. Not Jake. You know how he feels about strip joints!"

I don't know if I should nod along because I do know, or shake my head because obviously I don't know anything, so I do a little of each and throw a hand up in the air while responding. "He got a private lap dance. Several nights in a row in fact."

"Ok... That's a really stupid move financially, but still not really cheating."

"It was so he could get his rocks off when I denied his advances, because I was sick of his screwing me on the kitchen floor and the sore knees that come from it."

"Sore knees? Oh! I mean I guess that's a better choice than an ice cold back. That floor in your kitchen..."

"Not the point, Eliza!"

Somehow through all of this, Tabitha is still cooing. She distracts us from our topic just in time because less than a minute later, Sammy comes in. And I stand up, handing the sweet bundle of love back to her mom.

"We'll talk later, Lize. Thank you for taking the kids last night. I really, really needed it."

"I love you, Miranda."

"Love you too, Lize."

Sammy and I wait by the front door where I direct each kid in turn to thank their auntie and return to the door. Then we all file into the car to head home. I actually have to psych myself up to be able to turn the car on.

The car is relatively quiet on the way home. The kids are probably tired from having too much junk food and staying up too late, but that's okay. That's the whole point for them. They're kids. It's adults who are supposed to behave responsibly, in theory anyway.

I let out a breath I didn't realize I'd been holding when we pull into the driveway, and I see Jake's car. I'm incredibly relieved he didn't go to a strip club to get over our fight. Again. That would have been the final nail in the coffin of our relationship. The end. But he stayed. Which, I realize, is more than I did in the heat of the moment. So now I suppose I have to get over myself and just go in.

I park, and the kids file out. I get distracted when I notice a bright orange streak run out of sight. I guess the kitsune is still around. Phoebe stays back as the rest go in the house.

"You okay, Mom? You seem a little...out of it."

"I think I'm okay, sweetie pie. Thank you for asking."

I start the walk in. Each step is torture, walking into this unknown future.

Phoebe holds the door open for me. I thank her and cross the threshold, a little shaky. But whatever I expected to find when I walked back into the house, this is not it.

Jake's prepping a snack for everyone, like he's loved doing their entire lives. He's always felt a huge sense of satisfaction and purpose when he creates simple dishes for them, which they love more than a meal from the fanciest restaurant. He places the plates in front of each kid, tussles Sammy's hair, and excuses us from the room. "I just have to talk to your mom real quick in the other room. We'll be right back."

He puts his hand on my lower back to guide me out and across the hall to the living room. When we stop walking, he turns me to look at him and takes my face in his palms.

"I'm sorry. I'm so, so sorry." His brown eyes are soft and kind, which I haven't seen in a long while now.

Wow. Not at all what I was expecting.

"I'm so sorry. I was an idiot. I never should have thought you didn't want me anymore. And even if I did, the way I handled it was beyond stupid and immature. It was hurtful. I know about your family history. I know about your dad. I know the pain he caused. I don't know what I was thinking. I hope, one day, you can forgive me and trust me again."

As far as apologies go, that was pretty spot on, I have to admit.

"Thank you. And, I guess I'm sorry I punched you in the jaw. How is it, by the way?"

He flexes it back and forth a little before smiling shyly. "I think I'll survive. Where'd you learn to hit like that though? I had no idea you had such a great right hook!"

I feel my eyes get big as I realize he still doesn't know about my own new secret, and just how hypocritical that is. "Well, actually about that—"

"Wait, Mom hit you? Are you okay?" Natalie, always jumping to her daddy's aid, runs into the room and up to him to check his jaw. "Mom! What were you thinking?"

"I'm fine! Trust me, I deserved it. Your mom was well within her rights. Don't worry about it."

Okay, I guess the Guardian conversation will have to wait for another, other time. Hopefully he responds better than I would, given the circumstances.

Chapter 18

George

I 've had some luck looking for the Jinn, though not much. They're unquestionably good at blending in with humans, unless the human is really paying attention of course. The signs are subtle, but if you are in on the whole fantastical creatures being real secret, you know. And I'm still having trouble.

Luckily, imps are much easier to find. And track. And intimidate. And they always seem to be hanging about. People who don't know any better tend to see a red bird, assume it is a cardinal, and move on.

I was able to grab a particularly slow one the other day when it hung around after the rest of its swarm flew off. I needed to find out who, or what, they are working for. Imps don't really plan things on their own. They aren't smart enough to think things through that way, so they usually stick to causing minor mischief and being annoying. So when I saw that group of imps intimidating the Jinn at the dive bar last week, I had to find out what was up.

Unfortunately, I was not particularly lucky grabbing the little bugger that stayed behind. Rather, this imp is habitually behind the rest of its group and thus misses out on the most important bits of information. Also, it's not the smartest, not that any can be considered geniuses, and its memory is on par with that of a goldfish.

So, the only new information I was able to glean is that a group of lower goddesses is trying to get rid of Miranda as a threat. He doesn't know what theology they are from. He doesn't know what their bigger plans are. He doesn't think they want her seriously hurt or dead, but he does think they may have multiple avenues that they are pursuing to get this accomplished.

So, I guess the Jinn aren't the only things I have to be looking for now. I plan to cross-reference the names Miranda gave me, Lu and Mel, with goddesses. I also have to try and get a lead on these shadows she heard talking.

I just hope I don't let Miranda down.

Chapter 19

Miranda

The rest of the weekend passes uneventfully, except for positive events, that is. We actually go to the zoo as a family; we haven't done that in years! And, even better, we all had a lot of fun.

George texted me only once, letting me know that he hadn't found anything regarding a creature named Lu, and he's found too many entries for beings whose names start with Mel, but he's looking into it. And even if I can't text him about non-work-related stuff, I'm still grateful to have his help.

Monday morning, everyone wakes up easily, and the morning routine goes off without a hitch. On his way out the door, Jake leans in to kiss me and whispers, "I'll be back after I drop them off so we can talk more."

This sounds wonderful, except I'm supposed to train after they leave. "Um, okay. But I have an appointment this morning, so we can't talk too long."

Confusion crosses his face briefly, but he nods and smiles and heads out the door. And I send a text to George before pouring my second cup of coffee for the day.

Something came up. I'll be a little late.

George still hasn't replied by the time Jake walks back into the kitchen, carrying something. Something white. Something I soon recognize as my prized gi.

"Hey Miranda, what is this? I saw it in the mudroom."

"Oh! That! Remember the talk I've been trying to have about that new opportunity I was offered? Well, this has to do with that..." I trail off, unsure how to connect my next thought to what I've already said.

But then I don't need to figure it out, because he's chuckling to himself.

"You were given the opportunity...to learn karate? I think that's great. Really. But why wouldn't you just tell me about it? Looks like I'm not the only one who has been harboring secrets in this relationship. And this...logo? Is this the logo of your new school? A geisha? That's fascinating. Geishas weren't really known for their martial arts skills, Miranda. So what exactly do you do at this dojo where they've offered you such a wonderful opportunity?"

His words sock me in the stomach knocking the wind out of me, but I clench my fists, refusing to hit him again, because I know that he's at least partially right. I stand in neutral, letting his tirade slam into me, a tidal wave of truth and anger, and then I just let it all flow back away from me.

"You're right." I speak quietly, too quietly for his liking.

He bends toward me like a plant reaching for sunlight, or perhaps more like a flame licking toward the most combustible material in a room. "What did you say?" He waits until I repeat myself, whether for his edification or just to make me squirm, I'm not sure.

"I said, You. Are. Right. I shouldn't have kept this from you. But it's nothing close to what you did. This is nothing sexual. This is who I am. And how dare you insinuate I am exchanging sexual favors for this opportunity."

He straightens his posture, then looks for a moment like he's going to speak, but shakes his head instead. His mouth opens and closes a few times, a fish taking in gulps of air he doesn't realize are actually killing him. Then, finally, he finds his words. "I don't have time for this. I need to get to work. I'm just glad I know whom I'm married to: a hypocrite who keeps secrets while demanding complete honesty and perfection from those around her." He opens his hand and lets the gi drop unceremoniously to the floor.

My entire body trembles and I gasp involuntarily. I want to rush to pick the gi up but my feet don't move when I ask them to. I would say I am frozen to the spot but what I feel is white hot anger, so maybe melted to the spot is better.

He turns and grabs his briefcase from where it's leaning against the doorjamb. Then over his should he announces, "My boss is sending me back to Vegas Thursday. He won't let up until I get that group to sign with us."

"Okay." I can barely get the sounds out between my gritted teeth, much less make them audible. My hands won't unclench.

He exits through the mudroom where I had clearly not concealed my gi well enough Friday night. I wait until I hear the door slam to bring my now empty mug back to the coffee pot for a third cup. I down it like it's a shot of vodka, grab my keys and gi, and leave.

I need to go hit something. Luckily for me, that something is George, the person who brought me into this upside-down world.

***

My head is still throbbing and my mind racing when I get to George's place. So, when I see him standing in the open door, arms crossed, and looking annoyed, I push past him into the house and head straight through the dining room. He follows behind me, trying to engage me.

"You're late."

"Whatever." I say it to myself but loud enough that he can hear me.

He pushes himself in front of my path, trying to start a conversation. His brow furrows when he looks in my eyes, which are red from the good cry I had in the ride over. "Did something else happen with the shadows? With Jake?"

My eyes flash for a second. My voice goes completely flat. "Nope." If I show any emotion, I won't be able to stop. I look away from his eyes.

He pulls his shoulders back and lifts up his chin as he erects his wall of professionalism. "Then it's important for you to be on time. Everything else can wait."

"It's also important for you to not be a cold-hearted asshole." I pause to rip my sneakers off and drop them by the door before I bow and enter the dojo.

"You can't let your emotions control you like this. They'll get you killed." He follows me onto the mats.

I stop abruptly and turn to face him, beyond annoyed with the men in my life. "What the—? Why? How can you—?" They are barely even words. My face flushes and my hands flex and clench because I know it would be very bad to sucker punch my karate instructor. I pause to try and regain my composure. "You literally showed up at my door one day, telling me how we are spiritually connected and pulling me into this shit show of a world. Now things are targeting my husband, and you're telling me I can't feel angry about it? Grow the fuck up, George."

He nods to himself, probably thinking I'm insane, as he paces in a circle around me. "Did you make your playlist? This seems like a day you'll need music to get out of your head, and out of your own way."

"Yeah, I sent it to you before I came in."

He takes his phone out and fiddles with it for a few moments. I shadow box in my spot, trying to shake out some of this energy. Then my playlist comes on over speakers that must be hidden around the room. It is a mix of powerful female singers and musicians, artists that make me feel powerful myself. I close my eyes and let the anger in the music wash over me as the singer sings about her bad reputation. The validation of the lyrics feels so good.

When I open my eyes, George is across from me. "You okay?" His jaw is set, but there is something a little softer in his eyes.

"Do you even care?"

"No, not really. Ready to spar?" Though his words are cold, his brow remains low with concern. "Okay, let's begin."

I jump into guard stance. We touch fists, as is custom, and I launch myself after him. My round kick gets his sciatic on my first try, and I follow up that attack with a left upper cut to his abdomen and a knee kick to his now dropped chin. My eyes dilate and my pulse quickens. I can't believe I'm finally beating the shit out of him! But it doesn't even feel like enough to turn around my mood. Not yet anyway.

"Wow, Miranda. I'm going to piss you off every time we train. You are so much better when you're mad."

"Whatever." I'm bouncing on the balls of my feet as if I'm half my size. The aches in my knees correct me. I ignore them. "Can we keep going, or you want to have a whole conversation?"

Round after round goes that way. My kicks and punches keep connecting with him. It's beautiful. Maybe he's right. Maybe there is something to getting angry before I fight. Twenty minutes later, he calls for a water and rest break. I keep pacing while he takes a few small sips and does some breathing exercises.

"So, are you going to tell me what's going on with you today?"

I laugh. "Oh, now you care? You can't be serious."

"I always care. I'm sorry. I told you, I *want* to be your friend—"

"Yeah, yeah, yeah. But you *need* to be my teacher. I get it." I can't stop pacing even with the exhaustion setting in from our extended sparring round.

George takes a step toward me. "Do you? Do you really? Because this can't just be a hobby to you." I stop walking and gape at him, hands on my hips. "*I* act like it's just a hobby? Really? Because I'm the one actually living with this shit. And now it's threatening my family, whom *you* said would be in no more danger than the world at large." I'm jabbing my finger into his chest when I finish.

"So this does have to do with Jake. How so?" Massaging his pec, he steps back as he talks, so my finger can't do any more harm.

I drop my hand and look into his eyes. "I'm not sure I should answer that question. I don't know what's only *work-related* anymore." I know I sound like a brat when I snarl that last sentence at him. But I don't care.

He rolls his eyes. "Whatever. Let's go again."

"Fine. You're the one that needed a break." I bounce on my toes a bit to make sure my muscles are still awake.

And so we continue. I don't know how long we're sparring again when the music switches to a country song about the revenge the singer is getting on her ex as he cheats on her. Something in me deflates. My power maybe? My strength? Or maybe just my will.

George's expression softens. "What's with this song? It doesn't charge you up like the rest. It seems to be doing just the opposite."

"It normally does. These lyrics just hit a little too close to home today is all." I walk away to get a drink, so I don't have to see the pity I'm sure is on George's face.

"Well, you need to be able to handle emotions like this when you're fighting out there, in the real world."

"The real world? The one where fairies and unicorns actually exist you mean?" I roll my eyes. "I'll take my chances." I'm not facing him. I can't. I pretend to be drinking, but I'm trying not to cry.

"Don't take too much. You'll throw up." His voice is warm and soft. I wonder for a moment if he would let me in, if I could talk to him about Jake. Would George be a friend and let me lean on him while I cried? Or would he continue to be cold and hard like the marble he looks to be cut from?

Finally, I feel ready to go back to sparring. I replace my bottle of water on the floor next to his and straighten back up. I walk slowly and deliberately back to the floor and almost casually position myself in guard stance.

"Hajime." His tone is as relaxed my approach.

I whirl toward him, planning to do a spinning back fist to his jaw, but he sweeps me, and I fall over. I close my eyes, ready to break fall on impact the way I've learned, but he catches me. He doesn't let me fall. Then he swallows hard, stands me up, and turns away to collect his water and phone. He talks to me over his shoulder, as if he can't bear to look at me. The music cuts off.

"We've trained enough today." George grabs our bottles of water and heads toward the door. He calls backward, "We need to have a chat."

I stare after him, until long after he disappears. With a loud huff that echoes in the dojo, I cross my arms and follow after him. In to the kitchen. Where he's making coffee.

George gets out the half and half and sets it on the counter. "I need to know what is going on with you. You need to tell me the whole story, or as much as you know, as calmly as you can, in a way I can actually follow, without having to hot-wire my brain first."

I take a long look at him, my face set like an angry teenager's. It's impossible for me to see where the line is between personal and professional. But I can't solve it alone, and this is kind of what he's here for. I take a deep breath, sit down, hug the fresh cup of coffee to my chest, and let it all spill out. "Okay, so...Jake is acting weird, or was acting really weird, then got kind of normal again, but then we...had an eventful evening, but afterward we had a big fight, and that's when I heard the names that the shadows whispered about and—"

George holds up a hand to stop my ramble. "Hi, again. Do you know how to talk slowly?"

Once more, I roll my eyes and take a deep breath. "Not right now, I don't!"

"Okay, tell me about how Jake has been acting."

I blush. How am I supposed to talk about all the kinky sex we've been having and how mind blowing my orgasms have been? And I'm supposed to be complaining about it? "Well, he's just been more...affectionate...since he came back from Vegas."

George furrows his brow and takes another sip. "I don't understand the problem."

I blurt out, "He's been super horny and sexually insatiable, okay?"

George chokes on his coffee and grabs a napkin to wipe the dribble off his chin. "Okay...got it. Okay... So, he's...more affectionate." He seems to gag on the word as I nod. "Anything else?"

"Um, crueler? About anything not having to do with sex, that is. Actually..." I think back to the dripping the candle wax. "And maybe more adventurous too."

George's face looks strained, as if he wants to ask me details but decides he can't deal with them, so he gets up and starts to pace instead. "Okay, so he's more affectionate, but cruel...and," he twists his head and scrunches his eyes closed before choking out the word, "*adventurous.* Anything else with Jake?"

I shake my head. "I can't think of anything."

"Okay. What happened next?" He sits back down.

"I found out he cheated on me, and I got so—"

"I'm sorry, what? Jake cheated on you?"

"I mean, I guess not technically, but he went to a strip club and got private lap dances a few nights in a row because I wouldn't have sex with him."

His face shows no emotion aside from the slight red tint his cheeks take on.

I toss my head back and screech, "This isn't what he's normally like, George! I'm telling you whatever they did to him in Vegas changed him."

"Okay, fine. What happened when you found out about the stripper?"

"I punched him, then stormed out, and went for a drive." I see George's eyebrows raise "That's when I saw the weird shadows in the park and heard the whispers, so I parked and got closer to hear them."

Pulling a pad of paper and a pen out from a drawer near where he sits, he is poised to take notes. "Okay, you said whispers. So there was more than one shadow? Was it in the shape of a person? Did they stop whispering when you got closer?"

"No, I pretended not to notice them, and the shadow was more like a big blob. But with sharp edges, just not any specific shape." I peer over George's pad to see his notes, that is, until he pauses and arches an eyebrow at me. I sit back down and sip my coffee. "Anyway, I heard them gossiping about how the chief, whoever that is, should try taking Jake again because it didn't work the first time and how some other women thought it just would take more times, but Mel disagrees. And no matter how hard I try, I can't for the life of me remember the other names! Damn it!"

George stares into my face with slightly squinted eyes. His look reminds me of the expression Dr. Grant would assume when examining my symptoms while diagnosing an illness. Like father like son. "Isn't your memory usually better than that?"

I toss my hands up in the air. "Yes. Thanks for the reminder!"

He stares a second more before jotting something down and moving on. "How do you know they were talking about Jake? Did they say his name?"

"No, they were saying things like how the husband of the guardian should be special in order to win her. Something like that."

He stops writing and rests the pen under the cleft in his chin. "I mean, I can't say they're wrong there. The husband of the guardian *should* be special...whether he is or not." He trails off as he takes more notes.

I blink hard and stand so I can return to pacing around the room. Better than getting distracted.

But my motion is too much for George. "Please sit back down." Once I've glared at him and collapsed back in my chair, he continues. "As promised, I looked into what the shadows could have been. There are some freaky options out there, but I think the most likely culprits are hikey sprites. I had no idea they were such gossips though. Can you tell me what happened this morning?" He looks into my eyes, and it shows this isn't just for professional purposes.

I chew on the inside of my cheek for a few seconds. My cheeks redden with the embarrassment of my hypocrisy. I can't look him in the eye when I tell him this. "Jake found my gi and pointed out what a hypocrite I am for keeping secrets myself while being mad at him for the same."

George doesn't say anything. He walks away from me, places his cup in the sink, and then pours me another cup of coffee. My mind tells me he's disappointed in me just like Jake is, even though there is no proof. I feel cold suddenly, though there is nothing to indicate the temperature has changed. Leaving me alone, he disappears into the library and comes back with two dusty books he's been flipping through and places both in front of me. "This is what I found over the weekend. Shadow people are like ghosts, shadow demons have wings, but you described a big blob and lots of voices. That sounds more like a group of the hikey sprites. What do you think?" He points to a sketch of a thin figure, made entirely of shadow but for its bright green eyes the exact color of grass.

"That sounds about right. But we *are* talking about hikey sprites and imps, so what do I even know about anything anymore? And how does this help us?"

George shakes his head. "Okay, let's forget the sprites and concentrate on what they said. Give me the names again."

I close my eyes and try to remember the feeling of the sun on my skin while I sat on that bench listening. "There was something about the chief, something that sounded...erotic? I just remember Lu and Mel."

George looks at his note pad. "And Mel doesn't think that whatever the chief is doing with Jake is helping and wants them to stop?"

"Yeah, something like that. Fuck. I'm so useless!" I push out of my chair and pace again. A primal scream escapes me. Out of the corner of my eye, I see George look down, probably in completely disappointment that his guardian is such a screw-up.

He tries to calmly reassure me. "You're really not. I promise if this didn't have to do with your family, you'd be way more on top of the details. I'm sure your emotional involvement is making you doubt yourself."

"Um, no. My ineptitude is making me doubt myself." I stop pacing and cross my arms, pouting.

"Yeah, about that..." George switches out the book containing the hikey sprites entry for another volume and puts his finger where he wants me to look. I walk back to the table, bend over the text, and recognize the passage about the Jinn from our first day in the library.

...they can also invade a human body through possession if they feel they have been wronged. Jinn are known to be summoned by sorcerers to possess and afflict their enemies. These afflictions often manifest as epilepsy, apoplexy, and hallucination, as well as many other mental illnesses.

I have to read the words three times to understand what George is getting at. Once it clicks, my eyes widen into floodlights, and I gape at him. "You think my husband is possessed by the Jinn? And you expect me to be okay going back to that house now?"

He stares back for a moment with his head tilted before he responds. "You have to go back because of the kids. But the good news is I found a way to know for sure. I think... Any chance you have access to a wolf?"

I furrow my brow while I contemplate if he's the one who's afflicted. But my face relaxes, and I actually smile when a possibility pops into my mind. "Do you think a fox would work?"

Chapter 20

Miranda

When Jake gets home at dinner time, he doesn't try to initiate sex. He kisses me on the cheek only, with his hand resting gently on my waist and no lower. He tells me dinner smells delicious and asks how my day was. It's completely different from how he has been behaving lately. I'm not even sure how to respond. I try to be civil back, but I feel like I'm being cold. I am just still so hurt and embarrassed by what he said this morning.

We have dinner as a family, as usual, but for the first time in a long time it feels like we're all truly present. Everyone remembers their manners and the kids don't even fight, with each other *or* me. Jake remains respectful of my personal space while showing affection by holding my hand and winking at me at opportune moments in the conversation. The whole time my conversation with George is replaying on a loop in my mind. But Jake is back to being Jake. He can't be possessed by a Jinn.

I'm legitimately scared of how the night will go once the kids are in bed. I don't know how I will pull off this test, even with the blessing of Minori (I had no idea kitsune could speak or had names).

Once the kids are in bed, I start cleaning the kitchen. Even though my body's not sore from today's practice, my brain feels like a slushie, which might be because of Maybe-Jinn-Possessed Jake. As I'm cleaning the counters, I hear Jakes' footsteps approaching me. I suck in my breath and go rigid, bracing myself for yet another fight. He walks up to the sink, and I eye the towel I left out next to the sink. (The towel I will definitely be throwing out after this evening.) I know his nightly routine.

Come on Jake... wash your hands... you know you want to...

My lungs are starting to burn from the breath that wants to escape when water hisses out of the faucet. Just a few more seconds and I can breathe again. I hope. I feel a trickle of sweat forming on my chest.

The water shuts off, and I hear the familiar schluffing sound of terry cloth on dry hands. I look at my husband over my shoulder and hope he will still be my husband in a moment.

"Ew gross." He begins by sniffing his hands and then moves to the towel. "Miranda, what the fuck is wrong with this towel?" He isn't angry or scared. He's...amused.

I turn fully around to face him, a look of confusion plastered on my face. "I don't know what you're talking about."

He laughs. "This towel smells absolutely horrible." He tilts his head patronizingly and inquires, "Did you leave the laundry in the washer too long again?"

I want to punch him in the face, even though it appears he is not a Jinn. Instead, I mirror his head tilt and retort, "Oh, you know me. I'm sure it's not *that* bad. Let me see." I take the towel from him and pretend to inhale, already aware of how bad it reeks.

Minori was more than willing to empty her glands on it when I asked her the best way to get her scent inside my house. Apparently kitsune really love a good practical joke. Or, at least, my new kitsune friend does.

She didn't run away when I approached her in my yard earlier. She spoke clearly and calmly. "I have watched your family for longer than you have noticed me, Guardian. I see the changes in your mate. What do you need of me?"

I looked around quickly to make sure no one would see I was conversing with the fox. My voice quaked although I tried to sound as strong as I'm supposed to be. "There is a test I need to do. Jinn are afraid of wolves. I know you're not a wolf, but I am hoping your scent will elicit the same response from a Jinn?"

The graceful canine thought for a moment, her bright fluffy tails swooshing behind her. "Yes, I *think* that my scent should be sufficient."

I smile to myself as I remember the exchange but outwardly make a show of gagging and quickly throw the towel in the garbage. I am washing my hands for longer than is probably necessary when Jake comes up behind me, and his hands surround mine under the water. When we are sure neither of us still smells, he gently rests his hands on my hips and begins rocking side to side, coaxing me to dance with him.

He calls up our wedding song on his phone, and soon Billie Holiday's voice fills our kitchen. He starts to sing along, and we dance in earnest, right there in the kitchen. He leans his forehead against mine. I close my eyes. And every time he sings about the mere idea of me, about his longing for me, about the moments that go oh so slowly until we're together again, I remember how sweet and loving this man I married has always been. Maybe he's just been under a lot of stress at work over that group he's supposed to be courting in Vegas. Maybe this Callie girl is just giving him a hard time or playing hard to get or something. It's not like I asked him.

I open my eyes and see his are still closed. I think I see a tear in the corner of his eye. "Jake?" I speak softly, and his eyes open slowly to focus on mine. "Are you okay? I haven't checked in with you to see how you're doing. Emotionally, I mean. I've been so wrapped up in my own shit—"

He quiets me with a kiss, gentle and warm, not anything at all like the deep, forceful kisses I've started to expect. It's perfect. The moment is perfect.

"It's okay, Miranda. You've been my rock for the last twenty years. You're allowed to have your own shit. At least once in a while. I mean, maybe don't make a habit of it." He winks and smiles. And I melt. "I'm sorry for how I acted. I know that the severity of our secrets wasn't even comparable. This domestic shit is just so hard. I'm so sorry." He kisses me again. I move my hands to his face, one on his cheek and the other around his neck, pulling him closer and trying to become one with him. On my terms. I love this man, and I want to celebrate that.

We will have to have a real talk soon, about what we each want, about what my gi truly symbolizes, and, you know, eventually about the fact that I'm a mythically chosen superhero who needs to defend our world from all sorts of creatures that originated in folklore... But for tonight, we are just Jake and Miranda, the way we were always supposed to be.

We do make love on the kitchen floor again, but this time instead of frenzied it is slow and methodical. I have the time to feel the cold tile under my back and enjoy the contrast of his heat on top of me. The dichotomy only enhances the pleasure I gain from every movement inside of me.

We hold each other right there on the floor, no longer cold because of our shared body heat, for a long time. We even doze off once before we stand up, stretch our aching bodies not used to such hard accommodations, and move to our bed.

As we drift off to sleep for the night, back in each other's arms but this time in the cloud-soft comfort of our bed, I am strong enough for this. I have to be. I will protect my family, whatever it takes.

Chapter 21

Miranda

I daydream while the dish soap begins to dissipate in the sink. I'm cleaning up the breakfast dishes while the kids finish getting ready for school. Jake sidles up next to me and wraps his arm around my waist. But then his phone rings, cutting into my happiness. I bite my lip and look down. He apologizes and moves away, holding my hip a moment longer before letting go to pull the phone from his pocket. I return to my dishwashing duties, only this time I'm frowning.

"Yes. Okay boss. I get it." He comes rushing back into the kitchen. "Yes, just get us on the flight. I already talked to Ryan. He's picking me up in ten minutes, and we'll be at the airport in plenty of time. We won't let them get away. Don't worry."

By the time he hangs up, I've stopped washing dishes, dried my hands, and am standing where we were dancing last night, my back to the sink, arms crossed impatiently. He looks at me sheepishly.

"Well? Are you going to tell me you're leaving?"

"You already know. I have to. I'm sorry."

"Yeah. I know." I wipe a few tears that have betrayed me from my cheeks. I try to force a smile. "To be continued?"

"Always." When he kisses me, it is warm and gently but also abrupt and rushed. "You're good to get the kids to school, right?" He yells the last bit as he rushes out of the room to go upstairs and pack.

"Oh goddamnit." I mumble to myself as I turn around and rinse the last of the soap from my hands. I switch from wife mode to mom mode and call out, "Kids, Mom's taking you to school today! Time to get a move on!"

Five minutes later, he's back, lugging his suitcase and rushing past me with a wave while he's on the phone. "Ryan, I'm on my way out. I'm really not that worried though. I understand that Callie wants to run the group like a democracy, but we just need to show her that as the star, her opinion should have more weight than Mel's does. Erin and Cleo will follow her. I mean, they call her The Chief for Christ's sake! Obviously, they view her as a leader."

Why do those names sound so familiar? My blood runs cold the same time Jake presses a soft kiss into the back of my head and whispers in my ear, "I'll text you when I land and call you when I can. I love you."

I can't even answer before he leaves. I'm too... I don't even know what I am. But my hands move on their own accord, and I grab the closest scrap of paper and write down the girls' names before they start disappearing from my memory again.

"Mom!" All the kids are calling to me at once from the mudroom. I drag my fingers through my hair, holding onto the ends as if they are my only line back to our ship as I drift off to sea. I want to curl into a ball and sob, but I have to be here for my kids. So instead, I take a few deep breaths to keep from having a full-blown panic attack and follow them to the car.

In hyperdrive, I get the kids dropped off as quickly as I can. As soon as Phoebe closes her car door, I race to George's house while I try calling Jake again. I need to tell him to stay here. It isn't safe. Whatever they did to him the last time he was out there, they're going to do it again. And I don't want to see what he's like after because whatever it was before, it will probably be more intense this time. Oh god. What did they do to him? To my sweet Jake. To make him so different. To turn him into that horrible sex addict. (Okay, maybe horrible is too strong a word.)

I practically screech to a stop at George's front door, and, because I'm earlier than usual, he isn't yet waiting for me in the open door. I slam my car door closed, run to the giant oak doors, and bang with my fists until he opens them.

He looks confused and checks his watch. "You're not normally here for at least twenty more minutes. What is going on?"

I don't have patience for his propriety today. "Shut it. We need to find out who Callie, Mel, Cleo, and… Ah!" I pull out my note. "Erin. That's the fourth one."

"What are you—"

I hold up my scrap of paper. "Callie, Mel, Cleo, and Erin. Who the fuck are they?"

He takes it from me and knits his brow as he reads the names. "I have absolutely no idea."

I shove past him and start heading to the library. "Well, we have to go figure it out then."

Forget the Jinn. Forget the shadows. I need to somehow find out more about who these bitches are.

***

George cracks the egg against the hot skillet and waits for the yolk to droop out of its shell. I cannot believe he's insisted on making breakfast before we find out who these women are.

"You realize my husband is already on his way out there with whatever these things are, right? Are you enjoying this?" I'm standing before him, tapping my fingers on the counter and my foot on the floor while staring him down.

He looks up with just his eyes and glares at me across the island. "I need something in my stomach so I can tolerate your particular brand of unhinged this morning."

"You have got to be fucking kidding me! Fine! Do you at least have a pot of coffee made?" He tilts his head, considering something. "It's a simple question, George."

He pauses in his motion, evaluating my posture and demeanor. "I'm trying to decide if I want to caffeinate you or not..."

"Go to hell." I push off my counter stool and walk to his fancy silver coffee maker. I peer inside and see it's full, so I open the cabinet he pulled mugs from before and help myself to one. Thankfully, even though he is much more fit than I am, he also indulges in half and half, so I can prep my cup the way I prefer it. I've poured, lightened, and drank my first cup before his eggs are on the plate. I roll my eyes and make another cup.

I'm pacing his kitchen while he tries to eat. The fork is halfway to his mouth when he pauses to watch me, his eyes look how I imagine they would if he was watching a tennis match. "Can you, just, sit down, please. Our research keeps going in circles. I need you to back up and slow down. Did you do the Jinn test? How did that go?"

I continue pacing. "Yeah he passed. Or failed. I don't know which is which. But he's not a Jinn. He didn't freak out when he smelled the kitsune."

He thinks while he chews and speak only after he's swallowed down his bite of eggs. "That definitely a good sign, although it's far from concrete since it wasn't a wolf and it was a magical being. But I think we can put that aside for now at least. So what else is going on?"

I stop in front of him and put my hands on the back of the chair opposite him so I can ground myself while I speak. "Okay, so last night Jake was sweet again. He was like he used to be. It was like always. And then this morning, his boss called and sent Jake back to Vegas." I point to my note he has next to his plate, having already forgotten the names. "The group is Callie, Mel, Cleo, and Erin. Those are the same names I heard the shadows mention, I think. And Mel doesn't want to use Jake's firm, but Callie does. And they have to be something, right? And, doing something *to* Jake? I mean, to make him act that way?"

He looks at me as he finishes his eggs. "Let's go to the library and see what we can find."

About. Damn. Time.

Surrounded by books once again, I pour over the giant index in the mammoth volume of docent journals while George looks up the names I gave him. The deepening silence tells us we're both coming up empty.

"Argggggggggg! This is hopeless. And my husband is out there with these psychopaths right now." I rub my weary eyes.

George walks to an island in the middle of the room that has cabinets under a marble slab. Opening a drawer, he pulls out a laptop and returns to the table where he was working. "Let's try this a different way. What's the name of this music group?"

Wow. I don't know if I'm more mad at myself for not thinking to look the group up before now or for never even bothering to ask what the name of the group is. "Uh, I have no idea."

He steeples his fingertips around the bridge of his nose and presses the pads of his pointer fingers into the inner corners of his eyes, trying to find patience for me that just isn't coming today. He sits back in his chair and looks at me. I'm sure he is wondering what I can expect of him if I don't have anything to even use as a jumping off point for research.

"Don't look at me like that! Aren't you supposed to be my guide? So, guide me. What am I looking for?"

He stands so forcefully that his heavy chair flips backward as he yells, "I have no idea what you're looking for!"

I finally stop pacing and look at him, surprised and impressed that he had that in him. "Okay, can I use that for a minute?" I point to his laptop.

"Be my guest."

I move toward the table carefully. I pick up the chair and look at his back as he walks to one of the only windows at the far end of the aisle where the tables and counters are all in a line.

Once seated, I look at the search bar in the browser window he has opened. I lightly tap my fingers against the keys not only to activate them but also to get my brain and finger tips connected and awake. I think about potential keywords: Girl group, Las Vegas, Callie. I tap the return key. I read, "Callie and the Celestials."

He walks back, but his legs are long so it doesn't take many strides until he's leaning down behind me, looking over my shoulder. "What did you say?"

"Callie and the Celestials? That's the band. They're beautiful. And young. I think I may be sick..." I stand up and pace again. As soon as I see her shiny apricot hair in its edgy shaggy style, I know. He definitely slept with her.

"You have got to be kidding me..."

"Umm, no, I'm not." I cradle my stomach. "Wait, have you heard of them?"

George jogs down one row of bookcases. He's back, a moment later, a shiny red book in his hand. He walks to where I'm pacing while flipping through the pages. He finds what he's looking for and turns the book around, handing it to me with a giant boyish grin on his face. An elegant, intricate, black and white illumination of nine beautiful women looks up at me. "Have I ever heard of Calliope, *Chief* of the Muses? Yes. Yes I have."

We're back in the kitchen, surrounded by discarded books that have proved useless and a growing pile of dirty dishes and coffee cups.

"Fucking Muses? Jesus. Can I just fight another minotaur instead?"

"Afraid not, hon."

"Thanks, *dear.*" My sarcasm makes him look up from the book he's been intently studying.

"I think this explains a lot. Everything, in fact. According to Hesiod, the Muses brought to people the gift of forgetfulness of pain and cessation of obligations. So, if Jake did...you know...while he was out there, the Muses theoretically could have cause him to just not care about much else, and he was probably chasing that sex high because, let's face it, we're talking about sex with a goddess."

With my left hand covering my mouth, I hold my right up to signal to him to stop talking. "I finally stopped throwing up. Please stop."

A sheepish but self-satisfied look takes over his face. "Sorry."

I close my eyes and put my hands on my stomach, feeling them move in and out with every deep breath I'm forcing into my lungs. But I'm also shaking my head because I just can't believe it. Any of it. How could he? And how could I be so stupid? How did it never occur to me that he could have slept with her, them, who really knows whom!

George seems to read my mind. "If this happened, it may not have been completely in his control."

"Yes, because so many men would turn down the chance to fuck a literal goddess."

"I thought you said he was a good guy?"

I stare blankly at him. "They're goddesses, George. Goddesses!" Just then the alarm on my phone goes off. "Damn it!! I have to leave to get the kids."

"Go, I'll keep researching. I'll keep in touch via text." He doesn't look up from the text he's currently pouring over.

"Really? You'll text me? But only if it's work-related, right?" I stand stock still until he glares at me.

When he does his eyes are the only things to move. "You're going to give me a hard time on this now? Go!"

So I do, but I also look back once more from the doorway, truly wishing I could stay. I need to learn everything I can about these things. Can they even be defeated? Do I just need to talk to them, or will there be fighting? I'm not sure I can take on nine goddesses. I know karate is for defense first, but I really want to kill them if I'm being honest.

I don't know how I'm supposed to just collect my children without somehow giving away that their father has been abducted by beautiful, bonafide goddesses. I guess I'm about to figure it out.

***

I make it through pickup and the ride home okay. I'm a little ornery once we're home, constantly checking my phone for news from George, but no updates come through. The kids notice something is up but decide to give me a wide berth. While dinner is cooking and they're all doing their homework, I do some research myself.

I open the browser on my phone and type "How to defeat a Muse." Apparently, they are the daughters of Zeus, so hopefully I don't piss him off too badly when I beat their asses. They won a singing contest against Thamyris, whoever that is, so I guess they would be good for Jake's firm to have them as clients, you know, if they were not psychopathic abductresses. Speaking of which, I haven't heard from Jake since he left last night. I've been so wrapped up, yet again, in my own thoughts. So, send him a text.

> Hey Sweets, just checking in since I haven't heard from you.
> Hope your flight was good. Hope to see you soon!

My phone tells me he read the message, but I don't see any dots. He's simply not writing me back. So, I go back to pacing. I have a thought to check my watch because I'm curious how many steps I've taken with all my pacing today, but then I get a text message.

Flight was fine. Busy here. Will have to be here longer than last time, fyi.

Yeah, I bet you will...

Chapter 22

Miranda

When the kids are in bed, I call Eliza. Because she answers, I open up about everything, sobbing to her over the phone.

"Honey, do you need me to come over? Rory is here. I can. It's okay."

I shake my head but then remember she can't see me. "No, it's fine. I'm fine. I just don't know what to do. I don't know what these crazy chicks are doing with my husband right now. I don't know how to find them. If I did, I wouldn't know how to fight them. They are goddesses for fuck's sake. I never signed up for this. Jake certainly never did… I seriously don't know what to do."

"Okay, here's what you're going to do. Get yourself a ticket to Vegas for Friday. I will come over and take care of the kids. You are going to spend the next two days figuring out exactly what you need to do to beat these bitches down, if there are any special weapons you need or anything. Then you're going to fly to Las Vegas. Track them down. And get your sweet, kind, would-die-for-you-and-your-children, and would-never-cheat-on-you-if-he-wasn't-under-the-influence-of-some-floozy-goddesses husband and bring him home. Yeah?"

"Yeah… That sounds about right… Okay. I need to buy a plane ticket. Thank you. I'll talk to you later. Love you."

"Love you, too."

As soon as I'm off the phone, I send George a text.

Work-related text: Friday I am flying to Vegas. I am not coming home until I have my husband back... Do with that information what you will.

Three dots... Three dots... and then,

Buy two tickets. I'll pay you back. And tell me what time to pick you up.

I smile to myself. I knew he wasn't all that bad. I buy our tickets and text him the details. Then I take a Xanax so I can get some sleep. Tomorrow, as soon as the kids are dropped off, it will be time for some heavy lifting in the library. I need to find out how to bring these bitches down.

***

"This is so stupid. And pointless. No guardian has ever had to face a Muse before." I slam the docent journals shut and slide the book across the table. The heels of my palms pressed into my eyes are the only things holding me together right now.

George lifts his face away from the book he's reading and looks at me over the stack of books he has already attempted and rejected. "Maybe you're right. Maybe we can't find how to beat them here. Maybe it has to be all you and your instincts."

My hands drop to the table so my eyes can properly glare. "Well then, Jake is definitely screwed if that's the case. My instincts are total shit."

George rolls his eyes. "One of these days, do you think you'll start to believe in yourself?"

"Not likely, no. I've spent forty years doubting myself in everything I do. I don't see that changing anytime soon." I slouch down and lean back with my arms crossed in front of me. I look more like a teenager sulking in detention than a grown ass woman who is supposed to save the world on the regular.

"Fine. Once again, I'll be the one to say it: I believe in you. Don't roll your eyes at me! Whatever, act like a child... Do you know where are they performing? Do they have a casino they are the regulars at right now?"

Ashamed that I hadn't thought to look at that, I pull my phone out and check. "Apparently they perform six nights at a week at the Colosseum." I groan, "Of course they're playing the Colosseum... These chicks are not predictable at all."

"Okay, so I guess we know where we're staying." He grabs his phone and starts typing. "I'll call and get us a room."

"*A* room? Don't you think that's crossing over into the friend zone?"

He's really good at turning his blue eyes to ice when he glares at me. "I'm not letting you out of my sight while we're there. We don't even know what their plan is. For all we know, this is just a trap to get you there."

I think for a second, then nod in agreement. He walks to the kitchen to make the reservation.

***

The kids are all prepared (and super excited) for their weekend with Aunt Eliza by the time I drop them at school Friday. She's coming to our house and setting up the portable crib I hung onto all these years, because who knows if this weekend is going to stretch into more. But as far they know, I'm just flying out to surprise their dad for a romantic weekend.

At 9:00 a.m., George is outside my house ready to go. I throw a couple more pairs of underwear in my suitcase (you can never pack too many pairs, particularly in my line of work) and head out the door, taking a long look around the house as if saying good-bye.

Walking through the airport with this guy is like being with an alien from outer space.

"What is this crazy line for?" He points rudely while he asks.

"It's to get through security." I look in my bag, making sure I can easily grab my liquids when we get to the conveyer belt.

"Is there a way around it?"

I can't believe he's serious. "Not unless you want to be arrested."

"Huh. Interesting." He's on his tip toes, trying to see the line's destination.

I shake my head. When we get to the X-ray machine, George's bag is pulled for further inspection.

"Please, tell me you didn't bring any Guardian weapons."

"I didn't. I swear!"

"So, what did you bring?"

"I don't know. Normal trip stuff?" He looks confused.

"Sir, is this your bag? Do I have permission to look through it?" Once the TSA agent gets the okay from George, he pulls the bag to a table to rifle through it. "Sir, are these yours?" He holds up full-sized bottles of toothpaste, shampoo, and shaving cream."

"Um, yes... Are those considered weapons?"

I smack his arm. "You can't bring liquids that size onto planes! I don't think you've been able to since before you were a baby! Why don't you know that?"

He whispers to me through gritted teeth. "I've never flown on a commercial plane before. Anytime I had to fly, I would just take a private plane."

My jaw drops. "Oh. Of course. And, why aren't we doing that this time?"

A slight blush rises to his cheeks. "Well, my parents were always the ones to arrange those flights. I don't know anything about how to do it."

I nod. Hating him just a little bit. Someday I'll find out how exactly this guy is so wealthy. "Okay, well, next time we have to fly somewhere, I'm happy to figure the logistics out so we can travel in the way that you're more accustomed to."

Two hours later, we are on the plane, getting ready to take off, and I desperately search my bag for the motion sickness wrist bands that I clearly forgot to pack.

"Oh shit shit shit shit shit."

Meanwhile George is having a blast playing with the TV on the seat back in front of him. "This is so cool!'

"Dude, you have got to get out more."

"Did you just call me Dude?"

My only answer is to glare at him. Then I realize I need to give up this search and collapse back, closing my eyes momentarily. "Okay, we need to switch seats."

"What? Why? I want to look out the window."

Since he's acting like a child, I speak to him like he's one. "I know that, Buddy, but I have nothing to do to control my motion sickness, and if I'm not in that window seat, I'm very likely going to puke all over the both of us, multiple times, during this flight."

"Yup, okay. Let's switch." He unhooks his belt and we awkwardly climb over each other to switch positions.

It doesn't really help that much. I still end up feeling like a Xenomorph chestburster is getting ready to emerge from my gut most of the flight. Somewhere over Colorado, I can't take it anymore. I grab the airsick bag and make good use of it.

"You okay there, Miranda? You're looking a little green..."

"I would turn my head to glare at you, but I don't want to take the bag off of my face prematurely and go Linda Blair all over the plane."

His look of confusion reminds me how young he is and that he's probably never seen the classic horror flick.

We finally land, and I am so grateful to get the hell off that plane. On the way to pick up our rental car, we pass a newsstand with a whole display of wristbands. George nudges my shoulder and points. "Want a pair for the trip back?"

I consider it but ultimately shake my head. "Nope. Don't want to jinx there *being* a trip a back."

"Fair enough."

We get to the car rental center and find George Keating on the board with the parking spot number next to it. As we approach the spot, I immediately regret letting George handle this piece of the trip.

"George, what is that?"

He shrugs and unlocks the bright red mustang we're going to be driving.

"Okay. I guess we're not going for inconspicuous?" I can't help but break out in laughter, which ends up snowballing until I'm on my knees, hysterically laughing and crying in the middle of the parking garage.

George looks confused and terrified and doesn't know what to do with me. Until he also starts laughing. He doesn't reach the same level of hysteria, but he is definitely laughing harder than I have ever seen him laugh.

After a ridiculously short drive, we arrive at Ceasar's Palace in style in our zippy little red rental car. George self-parks so we will have access to the car whenever we need it. We are still experiencing the aftershocks of our fits of laugher in the airport parking garage as we walk into the hotel. As we walk through the Forum Casino to get to the lobby, my jaw drops and my eyes open wide as I take in the shimmering lights in the room that looks too dark for this time of day. I remember reading somewhere that they do that on purpose so people don't realize how long they've been gambling. I want to cover my ears to protect them from the bombardment of beeps, clicks, and voices surrounding me. This is nothing like what I expected! Having never been to Vegas before, I had zero idea what to expect here. This was really something!

There's a line three parties deep at the check-in stand, so George and I pass the time by people watching and chit chatting about what we hope to see on the strip while we're here. I don't know if our conversation is for show so the people around us will think we're just on a normal mother-son trip, or because we are trying to pretend to ourselves that we're not here to do what we're really here to do.

Finally, it is our turn to check in. George confirms that the room has a sofabed before he accepts the keys, and I give him a pat on the back.

Then I lean on the counter and ask the clerk, "Oh! I'm so sorry. I almost forgot. We're meeting a friend here, but we're not sure where his room is. Could you look him up for us? His name is Jake Gold."

"I can't tell you his room number, but I can tell you if he is staying here." After a few keystrokes, she says, "No, I'm sorry. Jake is not a registered guest with us."

I'm lost. I don't know what to do now. I have no way to find my husband.

Luckily, George is thinking more clearly than I am. "Is there a block of rooms the music group The Celestials use for guests? He's here as a talent manager trying to sign them, so maybe he's in one of their rooms?"

The clerk's face lights up. "Oh, no! They don't have a block of rooms. They have use of one of our villas since they are headlining at our Colosseum.. They have all their guests stay with them there. So, I'm sure this, Jake, is staying there as well."

I beam. "Oh! That's great! Well then, you just direct us to that, and we'll go after we stop in the room to freshen up!"

"I'm sorry, ma'am. I cannot do that. Even if we were talking about a regular guest, I could not disclose this kind of information. And The Celestials are *certainly* not regular guests. We need to protect our customers. I'm sure you understand."

I smile sweetly. "Really? There's nothing you can do?"

She smiles back. "There's really nothing. I'm sorry." And she signals for the next customer in line to come up and take our place before her counter.

But I'm not moving that easily. "Oh, one last question. Would you be able to get us tickets for The Celestials' concert tonight?"

She grimaces but nods curtly, her lips pressed into a tight, colorless line. A few more strokes on the key board, and she's printing our tickets and handing them to us. "They are the best seats available. I hope you enjoy your stay, and the show."

I nod and take the tickets. Mezzanine seats, but first row mezzanine. At lease we'll be able to see what they're like. Hopefully, their music won't make my ears bleed.

Finally finished checking in and no closer to achieving our end goal for this trip, we head to our room. On our way through the casino, George grabs my elbow softly and tilts his head to a table. "Wanna play some poker?"

I furrow my brow and am quiet for a few seconds. "Umm, I think we're gambling enough this weekend just taking this trip, don't you think?" He laughs, and we continue on our way.

The room is elegantly done in gray and white with a few sparse yellow accents. I push my suitcase against a wall and collapse across the bed. "I need a fucking nap."

George raises an eyebrow. "Seriously? Already?"

I look up at him. "This day has lasted a week. Shut up. Please."

George orders a pot of coffee and some burgers to the room as I close my eyes.

Chapter 23

Miranda

I wake up completely disoriented and look at the clock to see an hour has passed and it's now four o'clock. We have four hours until the concert. I stretch and stand. I see George doing some kind of slow dance by himself in the sitting area. Shaking my head, both in confusion and because I'm trying to shake the sleepiness away, I pour a cup of coffee from the silver carafe on top of the dresser. Still piping hot. Nice. On the desk is a room service tray with two cloche covered dishes. The first one I open has a half-eaten burger, so I pick up the second. Bingo. As I sit in the swiveling desk chair, my stomach growls, loudly, and I begin eating the burger like a lion going at a zebra carcass.

"You okay over there?" George's voice is full of amusement.

I swivel around, not putting my burger down. "Yeah, just hungry. You?"

He has one arm stretched out in front of him, palm forward, and he looks past it at an imaginary adversary; the other hand is also palm forward, but next to his cheek. His legs are in what I've come to learn is sumo stance, knees bent low, feet turned out, back straight. Always need to keep that spinal integrity!

"Hey, George? What the hell are you doing?"

He does this weird circular thing with both arms. "Kata."

"Umm, okay. Why don't I do that?"

"You just don't yet. You will. Believe it or not, we haven't gotten far in your training in the whopping two weeks we've been working together."

"Shut up. It has not only been two weeks. Has it?" My mouth hangs open for a moment mid-chew.

He stops, drops his hands to his hips, and looks at me, head cocked to one side impatiently.

I picture a calendar in my mind's eye and trace back the days. "Holy shit, really? Why does it feel like it's been a lifetime?"

"Well, you've had a lot to absorb in that time. I get it. Anyway, do you plan on going back to sleep when you're done eating, or should we walk around the resort a little and see if we find anything that may matter in some way? You know, like maybe the villa that your husband is probably being held captive in."

"Oh, that's not a bad idea! Let me just finish and then take a shower and get changed."

"In that case, I'll go shower now. You enjoy your burger. We do have time. It's okay."

I nod and spin back around to the desk, helping myself to the fries. They're a little cold but still super yummy. I focus all my attention on my food. My anxiety is kicking up, telling me that I have lost Jake to those goddesses.

Once I'm done eating and George is done in the bathroom, I pick out clothes for the concert and bite my lip as I flip through the clothes Eliza brought me for the trip, clothes she said would be more appropriate than my middle-aged-mom wardrobe, as she put it anyway. Luckily, she wrapped each outfit together and tied the bundles with a ribbon so I didn't mess up her hard work. I grab a pack of clothes and my toiletries bag and run back to the bathroom.

I try to take a hot shower to erase my nerves. Much better. Then I unwrap Eliza's bundle. It turns out I'm going to have to kill her when

I get home. I unroll the outfit I brought in with me and search for the rest of it. There's a post it inside.

Great choice! This will snap Jake out of whatever spell those hussies have him under! Don't forget your bold red lip!

Holy Shit. No. How am I supposed to even leave the bathroom in this, much less go out in public? I put on the corset top. The red and black satin damask has black lace trim along the top edge, two black buttons between the cups. The four strips of boning are wrapped in black satin. I actually kind of look hot. I also kind of look like I'm wearing lingerie, but whatever. It's Vegas, right? If ever I had a chance to try out a new sexy fashion, this is it. At least the pants are simply skinny jeans in a dark wash. Nice and simple.

I style and diffuse my curls, carefully draw on my eyeliner and swipe my mascara so people can tell I have eyelashes. Last, I apply my favorite red lipstick. It's really more like a shellack that doesn't come off until I remove it than a true lipstick, but that's fine. If I can be sure of nothing else right now, at least I'm sure my lipstick will last. I'm suddenly afraid of what shoes Eliza put in there to go with this ensemble. I crack the bathroom door open.

"Hey George, I'm going to come out now. Can you please not look at me? Like, at all? For the rest of the night? My friend packed clothes for me and...just, please please don't look, okay? And if you happen to see me by accident or something, please don't laugh."

"Oh stop. Just come out here."

So, I do. He doesn't laugh. His eyebrows go up, and he smiles proudly. "Damn."

"Do I look horrible? Shit." I rush past him to the suitcase to try to find something, anything, else to wear.

"Miranda, stop." He grabs my shoulders, and his eyes lock on mine. "You, do not, look horrible. Also, I'm sorry for being inappropriate. I really have no excuse. But I need you to know I mean this: you look fucking gorgeous. Own it."

I melt into a giggling little girl. "Um, thanks...okay. I have to find shoes now so we can actually go do this thing."

Thankfully, Eliza packed only my own shoes, so I know I can walk in them, for short distances at least. And, bless her soul, she packed a pair of flats with the post it note:

> These are not fashionable, but since you'll probably have to
> walk a lot and kick some fairytale ass, and I don't want you
> to break an ankle...

I grab the zip up black wedge booties, put them in my oversized leather shoulder bag, and put on the flats. When I look at George again, he looks like a sentimental, nostalgic sensei whose student is all grown up. Once again, I see his father in his expression.

"George, do not get distracted now. We have a concert to attend and a bunch of goddesses to defeat. We need to focus, because regardless of the asshole he's behaved like recently, Jake is a good man and a great father, and my children need him back. I need him back. I need to figure out my marriage with him. And in order to do that, we need to focus and get this done. Right?"

He shakes his whole body out, like he's warming up for a fight. "I'm good. I'm focused. On the concert. On the Muses. On Jake. I'm good. Let's do this."

"Okay. Let's do this."

We take the elevator down to the lobby and grab a bite in the grill before we go to the concert. I have a coke and some bread because I can't possibly eat more than that, but I felt the need to fuel myself somehow, so this was my compromise. I switch to my heeled booties when we head into the concert hall.

We walk up to the first mezzanine and are guided down to our seats behind the waist-high wooden wall with the brass bar running along it. Even though I thought we were going to be super far away, now that we're here, I feel like if I jumped with enough conviction, I could make it to the stage. I mean, yes, I'm technically a superhero, but you know what I mean.

I'm anxious for the show to begin, and my knees are bobbing up and down as fast as a hummingbird's wings. A synthesizer strikes a cord. A dance beat starts. And I realize I am completely out of my element here. I mean, maybe it's just because I know the creators of these sounds have abducted my husband and are trying to use him for some nefarious plot, but I do not like this music. Or maybe I'm just old. Who knows. But when I chance a look at George and see his eyes are practically crossed, I cross the age possibility off my list. I shake in my seat with laughter, looking at his disgust.

He asks me something, but I can't hear him over the noise emanating from the stage. I point to my ears and shrug. He leans right in against my ear and asks, "What do you think is so funny?"

I do my best innocent look and shrug again.

And then a booming voice comes on, somehow louder than the supposed music. "Ladies and gentleman, Callie and The Celestials!"

And with that announcement, the red crushed velvet curtain parts, four young women walk onto the stage, and the entire audience goes absolutely berserk. Well, the entire audience minus two people who are clearly not hip enough for this scene.

The Muses are truly exquisite to see. Their skin shimmers like pearls, and their crystal looking eyes are humongous on their faces. Add in their full pouty lips and perfect hourglass shapes and I have no doubt they are in fact goddesses. They're even more beautiful in real life than they were in the pictures I saw online while researching them. I'm sure it's the lighting or their makeup or something, but they seem to be glowing up on stage.

For the next hour and a half, George and I bond over something we both hate on a visceral level. But everywhere else in the room, I see people who are absolutely enthralled. They're barely blinking, smiles plastered on their faces. It's so weird.

The band leaves the stage and comes back for an encore, which I think is a truly stupid custom, but, hey, I'm not a musician. After they thank the audience, Callie then says something that makes one of my eyebrows quirk up in interest.

"So, you guys and gals are a really special audience for us. You're going to be the first of our fans to hear our news! It's going to be everywhere by the time you get out of here though, but do you want to know now?"

She holds the microphone out to capture the screams of the crowd and then gives the required sassy, "I don't know, girls. I don't think they're that interested," while pacing the stage dramatically, causing their fans to scream so loudly I'm sure none of them will be able to speak by the time we all get to leave this velvet-lined hell hole.

Callie stops mid-stage and faces her fans. "Okay. Okay. I believe you. You earned this little tidbit. Ready for it? Next week is going to be our last week here in Vegas. It has been an absolutely phenomenal ride here at the Colosseum, but The Celestials and I are onto bigger things! We just signed a contract with a big shot New York City talent manager, and we're moving up there to be where the action is. Do you want to meet our new managers?" More screams of course. "Boys come on out!"

I reach for and grab George's hand because I'm so scared of what I'm about to see. Jake and Ryan come out, all smiles and clapping. I mean, sure my husband is wearing a black on black suit I've never seen in my life, but if he got the hottest band signed, it's expected he'd need a fancy new outfit to go with the role… But then The Celestials sing their last song (and I use the word *sing* incredibly loosely), and they include Jake and Ryan in their performance. The guys sing along, sometimes in the mics alongside Callie. And they're dancing! Well!

George's eyes are wide and unblinking for a moment before he leans in to yell into my ear, "Okay, I see what you see in him now."

I glare at him and then back to the stage. "What the actual fuck?" George leans in so his ear is right in front of my words. "I just don't get it. I could barely get him to agree to the couple's first dance at our wedding!"

And then the show's over. The song, the concert, not the pain in my head that will last another couple of hours, but at least the cause.

They all take their bows, my husband and his coworker right along with the actual group. Then, as they back away from the apron of the stage to allow the curtain to close, Callie grabs Jake's hand and intertwines her fingers with his in a much more familiar way than if he was just her manager.

She must take him again…

Yup. My husband is definitely banging a goddess.

Chapter 24

Miranda

George runs behind me to keep up. (Guess I'm not so bad in heels after all.) "Are you sure you're okay?" he hollers.

"Yes. I'm fine. I just don't want to lose what may be our only chance to find them!" I speed walk toward where the custodian told us the backstage entrance is. We get there and meet a big burly bouncer dude.

The giant glares at us. "And just where do you think you're going?"

I try to flaunt some feminine charm by batting my eyes and subtly pushing my breasts together before I demurely say, "Well, we're just huge fans, and I heard the band is back here."

"Sorry. No backstage passes, no entry."

I drop the act, yes that quickly; I have no time for bullshit. "Look, the truth is I'm Jake's wife, and I want to see my husband."

"I don't know any Jake."

"Really? The Celestials' new talent manager who Callie was practically humping out there on stage?"

"Sorry, if you don't have proof, you'll just have to catch up with him later." Then he looks me up and down and laughs, "If he wants you to, of course. If your man decided to upgrade, that's not my fault."

"Sir, I demand to speak with your supervisor. That was completely unprofessional." George is so adorable when he's trying to be chivalrous.

Unfortunately, he also looks like he's about six years old, so the bouncer laughs and laughs.

"It's fine, George. Don't worry about it. We'll find them another way."

We turn to leave when the bouncer says, "Yes, ma'am. I'm sure you will. In the meantime, isn't it past your son's bedtime?"

I smile at George, then turn to the bouncer, and give him a quick snap kick to the junk and a powerful uppercut into his face. In my heels! Booya Motherfucker! I stand over his knocked-out body, admiring my handiwork, when George prompts me that perhaps this could be our opportunity. So, we race through the door to the backstage area, trying to find Jake and the Muses.

Instead, we find a confusing jumble of hallways. "This place is worse than that maze of boxes you put me in with the Minotaur. Damn."

"Uh, thanks? I guess? I don't really know what to make of that statement." He seems to be the slightest bit out of breath from running.

We follow the hall around a few more bends and hear giggling in a room ahead to the right, followed by a gravely, soulful woman's voice, "You're a natural, Baby! You were so good up there tonight!"

My eyes roll compulsively. Really, I want to puke, so I'm grateful that's all my body does.

Then I hear Jake's voice, crisp and strong. "Okay, ladies and gents. The ride is here. Time to head into the mountains!"

"Oh, Jakey! We're going home. I can't wait to get you back up there!"

"It's magical up there, huh?" His voice sounds almost drugged, like he's in a dream or something. Not at all like it sounded just a second ago.

I slide against the wall until I can peek around the doorframe. My eyes bug out and my brain and limbs turn to mush when I see Jake's back to me, in that black suit and those shiny shoes, and another Jake a few feet away, gazing lovingly into Callie's eyes. And no one else notices or cares that there are clearly two Jakes in the room.

"Off to the mountains!" One of the other Muses chants.

I slip back to George before I'm seen. My eyes and mouth are still frozen, and George is genuinely concerned. I motion that we should go get the car. Thankfully, the bouncer dude is still unconscious as we reenter the public hallway.

"We need to get to the car now. Do you know where there are mountains around here?"

"Uhh, no, can't say that I do… Hold on, I'll search for it. Why?"

"Because that's where we're going."

Conveniently, the parking garage is right near the auditorium, so it only takes us about ninety seconds to get there and another two minutes to find the car, but I feel like an hour has gone by, and there's no way we'll be able to track down Jake and the Muses. (Oh god, that sounds like its own music group. I really hope that's not the end game. He may be cute, but the man cannot carry a tune…)

On our way out of the complex, we have to drive around the Colosseum, and as we approach, we see a few figures getting into a white stretch SUV limo. The last person in line is one of the Jakes.

I elbow George and point, "Hey! Check out that luck!"

He doesn't share my enthusiasm but nods an acknowledgement before finding an inconspicuous spot to pull over our very conspicuous vehicle while we wait for the Muses' limo to start moving. I have to give George credit. He's really good at tailing them through the city. We stay behind them, albeit at a distance, for the rest of the drive into the mountains.

After what feels like a day and a half but is really only forty-five minutes, we reach the base of a huge mountain. George pulls over and cuts his lights while we watch the stretch Hummer limousine transporting my husband ascend the monster in front of us.

"So, how do you think we should do this?" The question is as much to me as it is to him. He looks ahead pensively. "Come on, oh mighty docent. My husband is up there with some over-sexed goddesses and a weird ass doppleganger, and we need to get him back." I watch George as he watches the limo getting smaller and smaller. "Hey, George. What is that?" I point to a ball of green glowing energy slowly descending toward us.

George's shoulders slump. "Oh, no."

I look back and forth from the light to George, trying to read his mind or discern what it is, and suddenly my voice is three octaves higher. "George? What is that?"

"That, Miranda, is the Jinn we've been looking for."

"Oh, shit." The things in the park said they were going to summon him here. "Shit. Shit. Shit."

"Miranda, please be quiet for one second. I need to think." George stares at the dashboard like it's a computer screen and mumbles to himself, willing his recall to pull something up from the depths of his memory. Finally, something pops to the forefront. "A magical object!"

"Come again?"

His eyes are sparkling as he speaks at a faster rate than I have ever heard before. "The Jinn has to be tied to a magical object. You know, like a genie lamp? You just have to destroy that. So there it is; there's the plan!"

I'm skeptical of many parts of this so-called plan. "Um, okay. How do I find it? How close does it need to be to him? What kind of object am I looking for? If I do find it, how do I destroy it?"

He looks at me dumbfounded. "I don't know. You wanna go ask him? This is all I have."

We sit in silence a few more moments as the eerie apparition continues down the mountain road, drifting lazily, as if to taunt us. I start bouncing my knee again and am ready to burst out of my skin. "George, we have to do something. I don't know what is going on with my husband. I need to get up there."

"You're right, of course. Let's think. You need to get up there. Not me, right?" He's spit-balling, but I'm nodding along, hopeful that he's onto something. "Okay, so. Ah! You sneak out of the car." He reaches up and switches the interior lights from *door* to *off* before he continues. "Now, you sneak out, and go around to the side of the mountain and climb up. I'll drive over there and distract the Jinn. Sound good?"

"Sound good? No, George. No part of that sounds good!" I stare at him, jaw agape, for a full minute, maybe two or three. I have no idea how to respond. Finally, I say the only thing I possibly can. "Okay. Fine. I'll try to make it back." I open my car door and start out, then pause and sit back in my seat. I look at him one more time. "Hey, good luck. I know you're not my friend or anything, but I still kind of like you. Don't die, okay?"

He nods with a small smile. "Yeah, right back atcha."

Once I'm outside, I stay low to the ground. It's still warm but not nearly as warm as back on the strip earlier. Tilting my head as far upward as possible, I grumble at the snow-capped mountain. I really hope they're not at the very top of this thing. Even though I changed into my flats in the car, I don't think my shoes are capable of getting my ass to that peak, but I start for the side of the mountain, searching for the easiest way up.

The climb takes less time than I would have expected, if I'd ever considered before how long scaling a literal fucking mountain would take me. But my trek still takes longer than I like. Who knows what kinky shit the happy couple have been up to while I've been slipping in mud and slamming my knees into rocks that jut out in places I don't expect.

Not far from the top, I turn a bend and discover a plateau on the side of the mountain that seems to be man, or goddess, made. About fifty feet away, the parked SUV collects a light coating of snow. I didn't even realize it's snowing! I probably shouldn't think about the weather since I'm still in my corset top and no coat. If I dwell on the fact that it's freezing and snowing, I will not survive this night.

I crouch down again, trying to be as inconspicuous as I can in my all-dark clothing against the bright white snow. I somehow manage to sneak along the ground in my squat until I reach the limo, knowing that regardless of how anything else turns out, I will not be able to use my legs tomorrow because I'm going to be so incredibly sore. I glance around the monstrosity of a vehicle on both sides, hoping I can tell where the hell everyone is before they find me, and maybe I'll get lucky and find some kind of glowing object that obviously belongs to the Jinn lying around. I don't see or hear anyone, so I pray to myself that I'm not going to be discovered and ruin this rescue mission. Then I roll away to my left to try to sneak closer.

Fuck that was cold! Why do movies make those rolls look like a good idea? They're very stupid.

On this plateau, near the top of the mountain, stands a round, open-air room that doesn't have walls, only columns that stretch from the floor to the ceiling and are made of white stone or marble. Fifteen or so massive columns stand around the perimeter, connected by a border of white stone. Two of the columns are shorter than the rest and topped with triangular pieces of stone to create a doorway into the room. In the center of this strange room is the biggest bed I have ever seen. And on the bed, covered by a massive but rather sheer sheet, are a whole lot of writhing, moaning bodies.

Then I see it. Or, him, I should say. One of the Jakes is over by the symbolic doorway, standing guard. My heart stops for a second, and when it begins again, I feel every beat as strongly as if someone is using my chest as their bass drum. As inconceivable as it is that this miniature Mt. Olympus exists, my brain won't let me focus on that bed and who might be in it. Every wriggle, every moan, makes me need *this* Jake to be my Jake more. The Jake who's standing guard at the room's entrance. The Jake wearing the black suit and who danced on stage. The Jake who can't take his eyes off that bed, watching with his arms crossed and his head cocked to the side.

My breathing slows and a calmness settles throughout my body, because running away isn't an option. Pretending that this never happened isn't an option. Leaving my husband here isn't an option. So, I approach slowly.

Each step brings me closer to Jake, one of them that is. The one I need so desperately to be mine. My eyes look at nothing but him, so the bed remains a blur in the background. As I get closer, I expect him to turn around. But he never does. Either he is enjoying the sex scene too much, or I'm too insignificant for him to acknowledge. Or maybe he's just under some sort of spell that has him immobilized. I can't imagine the goddesses dragged my husband out here to police the door to their orgy, but I'm cautiously optimistic that maybe this nightmare will be over soon. When only a few steps separate us, I exhale and find my voice.

"Jake? Sweetie? What is going on? Why are you up here?" I'm careful with the volume of my voice. I don't want to interrupt the party on the bed if I don't have to.

Finally, he looks right at me. And as recognition washes over him, a twisted, sadistic smile breaks his face open, and his throat emits a deep laugh. "Oh, Miranda! How perfect!" He's not so careful with the volume of his voice. In fact, he yells my name so loudly that the writhing on the bed stops immediately.

Among the lump of bodies, the sheet flips back, and the other Jake sticks his head out. I can tell he has no shirt on. There are smears of lipstick cover his face, and his eyes are glazed over, but they seem to clear the slightest bit when he looks at me. "Miranda? What the fuck are you doing here?" His voice is angry, his words short. He is mad at me for interrupting.

My stomach twists into a knot, pushing bile to rise in my throat. How do I ever get over this? This Guardian shit better come with some mental health benefits or at least a lifetime supply of Vallium... Okay, Miranda, focus. Bring him home, and then you can kick his ass.

Although, he doesn't really look like he's in complete control of his wits in this moment. Maybe I'm mad at the wrong person. "Um, rescuing you...I think..."

Then Bodyguard Jake laughs again. "Did you hear that everyone? Miranda believes her husband needs rescuing." He circles me, and his eyes contain nothing but cruelty. "Your dear husband is currently being pleasured by four Goddesses. I'm sorry to tell you this, but you aren't half the sexual partner one of them is. And he's having *four*. Why don't you try and save some face. Let's run home together, you and I."

My eyes flash. This is who has been living with me, who has been fucking me, and it's not Jake. My heart is pounding, trying to break free from my chest to run and hide. I would likely do the same if I wasn't frozen to the spot, getting dizzy as I try to follow Ja—whoever this is that's circling me. "Who are you?" I don't sound like a Guardian when I ask. I sound like a little girl, afraid of the big bad wolf in her grandmother's dressing gown.

"Lu, don't be rude to our guest!" Callie says to the fake Jake as she emerges from the bed. She grabs a white satin robe off a nearby chair and ties the belt into a knot around her petite waist while she walks toward us. I'm not sure why she bothered with the sheer robe. Her perfect perky breasts are still taunting me from beneath it. As she approaches, she shakes her shiny, shoulder-length auburn locks so they fall behind her. "Miranda, it's so nice to finally meet you. Jake's told us so much about you. This, of course, is not Jake, but Lu. We'll get to him in a bit. Welcome to our special place! It's not much, but I wanted something that reminded me of home." She puts one pale, slender hand on my shoulder and uses the other to gesture to the direction we now walk together.

Once past Lu, I see a huge wrought iron and glass table with six high-backed iron chairs around it. The table is spread with an assortment of foods in every color, grapes cascading over the edges of silver bowls onto the table top, platters of olives, cheese and fancy sliced meats, finger sandwiches and pastries topped in pastel-colored frosting. And at the head of the table, near where a chair has been pulled out and angled to face the closest chair on the long side which mirrors it, is a big, beautiful, glowing, golden coffee carafe.

She leads me to that last chair on the side, angled to face the head and with a great view of the giant bed, and gently guides me to take a seat in it. The food looks so good, and I know I should be hungry after climbing a fucking mountain, but the idea of eating makes bile rise in my throat again.

Coffee on the other hand... There's always room for coffee. As if she's reading my mind, which she probably is, Callie turns her doe-like eyes to Lu and signals for him to pour us coffee. I'm too numb to argue even though I usually would want to do it for myself.

"I hope Lu has been taking good care of you." Callie sits in the chair opposite me, takes her coffee cup from Lu, and adds just a touch of cream and sugar. "He's an incubus, you know."

If I were not a Guardian, I'm sure her sultry voice would have hypnotized me. Maybe that's what's going on with Jake. I add the half and half to my coffee and take a big sip before I respond. "I'm sorry. He's a what?" I keep expecting Lu or a griffin or a cyclops, something, anything, to jump out of nowhere and attack me. Instead, Lu-Jake pours me another piping hot cup of coffee.

Callie blinks her long, thick lashes repeatedly as if in disbelief. "An incubus. A sex demon. Shouldn't you know that? Were you not born to know what all of us are?" She offers me a small bowl with lumps of sugar. There is something off about her hand. It looks almost sheer, like her gown.

I shake my head at the sugar and keep my tone flat and neutral. I scrunch my nose as I answer. "I'm a late bloomer."

Callie nods and then takes a sip of her coffee. "I see. Still, I hope he's been on his best behavior. Demons can be rather tricky to tame, but I had every faith you'd be able to handle him. After all, no demon's had the honor of loving The Guardian before."

Real Jake sits up a bit and scratches his head. "Um, what's the Guardian?"

Without looking over to the bed I tell him, "I'll explain it later Jake, when we're home."

He shrugs and disappears back under the sheet with the three goddesses still in bed with him, and the writhing resumes.

Callie pouts her luscious lips, and her graceful eyebrows slope downward as she humbles herself to show me pity. "Oh, Sweetie. I'm so sorry you think Jake's going home with you. I was hoping to spare you this whole ordeal. Mortals are so fickle, and Jake's no exception. In *that* regard. That's why I sent you Lu in the first place, but I suppose I'm going to have to help you understand."

My hand tightens on the handle of my mug as I try to keep my face neutral. "I am bringing him back with me. I am sure he misses us, his family, his life." I wonder what her perfect face would look like with coffee splashed in it.

She sighs. "If only that were true. No father cares that much about his children. Do you know how many half-siblings I have? Besides, one of my specialties is helping people forget their obligations. Men want me for that very reason. Sorry about that." She shrugs. Behind her perfectly shaped lips are teeth too large and five shades too white. I see them when she smiles at Lu and signals for him to make me a plate.

I refuse to eat this skank's food, even if all I want to do is go home and bury myself in a pint of chocolate cherry ice cream. I try to keep a calm demeanor, but inside I'm contemplating what the downside would be to throwing myself off the side of this mountain. "Why do you even want Jake? He can't be *that* good. I know. I mean, he's great in every single way. I just don't get why you'd choose him to be your sexual partner over every other man in the world."

Her laugher is like the tinkling of wind chimes. I feel a little woozy. Then again, I did just scale a fucking mountain on my own...in clubbing clothes...to interrupt the orgy my husband was having with four goddesses. Perhaps that's why I feel like I'm going to pass out.

Callie furrows her brow in sincere confusion. "Oh, you don't know? Because *you* did, Guardian."

"Come again?" Now I'm the one confused.

She shakes her head, looking at me with stars in her eyes. "You have no idea of your power, your potential. You can do so many great things. Really, you should give yourself more credit. More attention, too! I've seen so many Guardians come and go, and I've always admired their strength and courage. It makes me so sad that you've spent the years you should have been kicking ass stuck in a house, wiping runny noses and shitty asses. You really should try the pomegranate danishes; they're exquisite." She puts two pastries with red centers on my plate.

A few giggles jostle the bed, and Callie glances at the outlines of her sisters with the corner of her mouth quirked up. She leans back in her chair, crosses her long legs, and rests her delicate hands on her thigh. Her expression wilts. "Our powers are waning, Guardian. We are fading. Much as your powers have been wasted while you play house, ours are wasted because people have stopped needing us. We are already less than half of whom we used to be. Our sisters, Thalia, Polyhymnia, Terpsichore, Euterpe, and Urania, have faded completely. There's nothing left of them. People forgot them, and the same is happening to us."

When she holds up her hands, I can faintly see through them. I gasp, not because I'm surprised but because I can start forming a plan.

Callie, however, nods as if she's gained my sympathy. "You see? I knew you'd understand. Guardians are protectors afterall."

Her words make me choke on my coffee. Protector? Of her? Fuck no! But I keep my face emotionless so she continues her Bond villain speech and I can continue to plan.

Callie sighs. "No one needs the old gods and goddesses any longer. To them, we are fantasies. People find their own muses in the world around them. So I needed to try something, anything, to make me, make *us*, relevant again. Make it so we stop fading away."

"Okay, and how exactly does my husband fit into this?" I use my peripherals to search for Lu-Jake. He's on the far end of the table, awaiting another command from his mistress. He looks completely bored, but he's playing a good lap dog while eying the tarts.

Callie smiles while she places her elbows on the glass table top and leans her cheek against her balled up fists. "A Guardian's never had a husband before. Guardians don't tend to reach the age when they would want to get married, and if they do, they don't want to drag anyone into their world with them. You're..."

I mirror her posture and pretend I'm enthralled with her. I need to keep her talking until I can think of what else to do. "Special? Unique?"

She looks up, trying to find the right word to pull out of the air. "Selfish. You're selfish."

I drop my hands, feeling the sting from her word choice as concretely as if I'd just been slapped across the face.

Callie either doesn't notice or doesn't care, and she continues like nothing happened. "We decided Jake must be pretty fucking amazing if he managed to attract, and keep, a Guardian. But he served his purpose with you. He gave you your kids. So, you see why we need him more than you, right? We hoped that when Jake inevitably fell in love with us, he would prevent us from fading away. Getting him to moan our names has been invocation enough, and we've been able to manifest so much stronger than we have in centuries! But we need to stay close to him for it to work." She lifts one eyebrow and smiles down at her coffee cup. "Even goddesses sometimes have to use sex to get what we want."

I shudder. Okay, eww. "So you replaced my husband with someone who looks exactly like him because...?" I glance at Lu who makes kissy face at me, making my face scrunch up in response.

Callie catches my reaction and snaps her head to Lu. "*You*, behave!" She turns back to me and grins.

Callie grins. "Oh, dear Miranda! I had a Jinn whip up Lu's amazing disguise to *spare* you. You mortals have such a romanticized view of love, and mating." She takes a tiny polite sip of her coffee.

I cross my arms and cock one eyebrow, appraising her. "You're really going to tell me you did this all for me? Why, really?"

She taps her fingers on the glass table, but slowly, deliberately, controlled, with none of the anxiety my movements usually ooze. In fact, I bet she's never been anxious about anything, ever.

"Oh Miranda, you can really be dramatic, you know? If your husband didn't come home, you'd search for him or alert the police, and that would make it quite a challenge for us to take him anywhere public. That's the first why."

I nod. "And the second why?"

Again, that smile. "Did you know that every time an incubus seduces you, they suck a little of your life force out of you? Lu has been making you weaker, keeping you from achieving that true potential you were born with." Movement on the other side of the table reveals Lu is making himself a plate of treats. He freezes and locks eyes with me before smiling awkwardly.

That's a nasty surprise. Here I am, having my first official Guardian gig, jet lagged, in tight jeans and a corset, after climbing a mountain, and all this time I've been having my powers drained, right as I was learning to use them. Damn it. Maybe my abilities have rebounded since Lu left, but last Friday night alone probably drained them more than I could hope to recover quickly.

I go to take another swig of coffee, but my mug is empty. I set it down harder than I mean to, and Lu quickly refills it from the carafe. I thank him, because if I don't have my coffee right now who even am I and how will I possibly get out of this.

"What are you wondering, little Guardian? You look confused. It's been so nice getting to know you this evening, but truth be told, I want to get back to my lover." She stands, smoothing her robe along her thighs as she does. "Any last questions I can answer before Lu takes you home?"

I hold up one finger, trying to think about what I want to know most. I mean, I'm curious if Friday counts as one seduction, or if he drained a little more each time I climaxed, but that information isn't going to help me now. "I have one last question. Jake's moans are keeping you around for now, fine. But he's mortal. He won't be here forever, and then you'll be back where you were. You need a longer con. You know, like a 10...hundred...year plan. So, my question is this: How do I get my husband back?"

She rolls her eyes impatiently. "We know he's mortal. That is why we just signed a contract with his firm. We are going to be stars all around the world, Miranda. People everywhere will know our names and hear our music, forever." She crosses her arms with a self-satisfied look.

I can't imagine their music being more than a fad. "I think you might be overestimating the longevity of public opinion. You didn't answer my question though. How do I get my husband back from you?"

She stares at me for a long minute, then pouts. "That's just mean, Miranda. But fine. You want Jake back that badly? Let's just ask him. Let's see if *he* wants to go back with you. Oh, Jake? Lover? Please come here."

My eyes dart to the bed I had been trying to ignore. Jake climbs out, naked, which shouldn't surprise me nearly as much as it does, and covered in four shades of lipstick all over his body. The three other muses pout that he isn't warming their bed for the moment. I close my eyes against the wave of intense nausea about to take me down and breathe deeply, in my nose, hold it, let it out slowly through my mouth, and hope that my coffee and the single bite of pastry I choked down don't come back up.

Jake stands next to Callie, who links her satin clad arm through his bare one. Her voice is as sweet as ambrosia when she speaks to my husband. "My love, I am going to ask you something. You can answer honestly. I won't be hurt or offended. Do you want to leave with Miranda, or would you rather stay with us?"

When he looks at me, his expression is pained. He knows he's supposed to say he wants to be with me. Then he looks between his harem in the bed and Callie, the four sexy, young (looking), literal goddesses he's been fucking for the last couple of weeks. Callie smiles sweetly at him, and as the pain on his face evaporates. I know Callie was right, that his need to have his wiener wanked by four gorgeous women has won.

Jake doesn't even take his eyes off of her. "Miranda, I'm sorry. I'll always love you. But I can't leave this! Bring Lu home. Have your cake and eat it too. He'll be a fine partner." And with that absolute bullshit answer, he walks back to the bed, now full of grinning and giggling goddesses, and climbs back under the sheet.

Chapter 25

George

As soon as she slams the car door shut, I regret it. We should have stayed together. I know I'm supposed to be her teacher above all else, but how can I expect her to do this alone?

And now, I'm watching this woman, who couldn't walk up a flight of stairs without getting winded a month ago, scale a mountain. When her footing slips, my breath catches in my throat. But then she regains control and keeps going. So high up, I pray she doesn't look down. She seriously is incredible. This is the woman who is going to save the world time and time again. This is the woman I get to know better than almost anyone else. This is the woman who, against my better judgement, I'm allowing to get to know me better than I have ever let anyone else.

She has to make it through this. I know she feels like she can't go back home without Jake, but if it comes down to it, I hope she does just that. She is the one who has to get through this. She is the one who matters. To her family, to the world, and to me. The connection between the Guardian and her docent does not sever with death. Docents have been known to lose their minds, become catatonic, or even die of broken hearts upon the death of their Guardians.

I wish I could sit here and watch her until she reaches the top, but the Jinn is still descending, and I need to make sure he doesn't see her. I slowly drive up the road and toward the Jinn's light as he approaches me. I stop when he does; he's in front of the car's bumper. Even though his entire body is radiant with green light, I leave the car running and the headlights on, partially for light, partially so if I need to, I can try to make a getaway.

The first thing I notice as I slam my own car door is how much colder the temperature has gotten since the sun went down. I'm sure it's even colder at the top of the mountain. I don't know how she can be moving up there in that outfit, much less how she can fight. Maybe she won't need to. I wish I could hear or see something. But I can't. And I need to get my head back in the fight that is about to start here.

Chapter 26

Miranda

'm unable to move. He picked them. He picked the great sex over me, over our children, over our life together. Sex with goddesses. Huh. I did not see that coming. This man who was always so disgusted with anyone who cheated or was non-monogamous in any way... I would never have guessed we'd come to this moment.

As I stand there, my body starts to shiver. Warm, masculine hands slide over my shoulders, then rub down to my back and arms, over and over, trying to warm me. But I fear I'll never be warm again. Maybe I should just lie here, on this mountain, just curl up and freeze. The hands pull me out of my chair, and the arms wrap around me. My eyes are open, but the world has faded to black. Then the blood in my veins begins pumping faster, telling me it isn't time to freeze, not now, and my brain wakes up. My eyes refocus, and I realize the body embracing me is wearing a black suit. I tilt my chin up, and Jake looks down at me, smiling. My mouth forms a smile too.

"Let's go home, Miranda."

I begin to nod. Ready to accept this. Until my heart takes its beating up a notch. I drop my brow and shake my head. "Lu?"

His smile widens as he hugs me close and says into my hair "Let's go home, Baby."

"Lu?"

He pauses and softens the look in his eyes. In Jake's eyes. The eyes that I looked into as I batted my own at that college coffeehouse, the eyes that teared up when he forgot to drop to one knee during his proposal, the eyes that watched as our babies came into this world with complete awe that his wife had just handled that like such a badass. How *dare* he look at me with those eyes.

I step in front of Lu and place my hands on his chest. "Lu. Fuck. Off." I shove him back, hard. He stops about four feet away and scowls at me. "You will never be in my bed, in my house, or around my children, again!"

"Miranda, don't make this harder than it needs to be," Callie says. She's discarded her robe next to the bed and is about to climb back into the orgy.

I jump into guard stance, ready to strike. Lu laughs and mocks me by waving his arms around in a similar stance. The memories of every technique I worked on with George flow into my muscles. I don't even think. Lu charges at me. I parry, change position, and grab his head to pull it down exactly as my left knee swings up, connecting with his face hard. As he straightens, I use an outside crescent kick to get him right in the temple. He staggers.

"Wow, Lu. You're definitely a lover, not a fighter, huh?"

When he glares at me, something about his face is off; he is not quite Jake anymore. I hesitate for a second, trying to figure out what it is, and unfortunately that's all he needs to get himself together and punch me in the face. Luckily, the pain is almost bearable after the sparring sessions when George beat me so soundly. Where the hell is George, anyway? No time to think about that now, unfortunately. Nor the blood pouring from my nose. I need to just act.

Callie stomps her foot, and the whole room shakes. "Lu, how dare you! Stop this immediately, and show Miranda your undying love. Right. This. Minute."

Lu bounces around like a professional boxer, looking proud of himself. I charge with a superman punch and by sheer luck move faster than even I thought possible. To both our surprise, my strike connects with him. Unfortunately, he's much taller than I am. I didn't get enough height in my jump, so I hit him in the throat instead of the face. Still, it's effective. He grabs his neck and spins away from me, coughing and sputtering.

When he turns back to me, he's not Jake anymore. At all. Two giant, bat-like wings have busted through and shredded that beautiful (and expensive) black suit jacket and shirt, and his skin has turned dark gray. His pants slipped off his legs as they shriveled into skinny, goat-like limbs. Nothing about him is human anymore, not even his screams; they're straight from the depths of hell. When he opens his mouth, his jaw seems to completely detach, and his yellow teeth point inside his foul, sticky maw.

I cringe and stumble backward, both at the sight of him and the knowledge that I slept with that thing—multiple times. But at least fighting this creature will be easier than when it looked like my husband, even if my husband is not at the top of my favorites list right now.

Callie screeches from beside the bed, and the sound makes my ears almost bleed. "No! Come on! Play nice, and just go home together!"

Pull yourself together, Miranda. You killed a damn Minotaur with zero training. You've got this. Granted, you had a machete for that fight... Stop it. You can do this.

I do Nogare breathing to center myself, slow my breath, and clear my mind. Then I jump back to guard stance and look around at my surroundings to look for something I can use as a weapon.

Callie shakes her head like a parent disappointed with her progeny. "I tried to make this easy for you, Miranda, but you had to be difficult. Lu, end this quickly. Don't keep teasing your playtoy." Callie finally slips back into the bed. Apparently, she's so confident in the eventuality that Lu will finish me off she'd rather just go back to fucking my husband than stay and watch. She'd rather participate in all the moving and moaning and nasty noises coming from that bed. Yuck.

Just when I start to think all hope is lost, I see beside the bed a statue of Zeus, king of the gods, holding a golden lightening bolt. I run to the statue and try to grab my new weapon, but it's much larger than I estimated. The bolt is not only as tall as I am but also securely set into the stone hand. I pray Zeus isn't watching this all unfold (or if he is, that he's at least on my side and not his daughters'). With Lu laughing in the background, I yank the bolt toward me. Lu stops laughing, and we're both surprised by the little effort I needed to break the whole hand off the statue.

I try to spin the bolt like a bo, but getting my hands in the right place proves difficult with Zeus's still holding on tight. So, while Lu takes a moment to reconsider his expectations of me, I smash the stone hand against the corner of the marble headboard. Zeus's fist shatters, freeing the bolt, which turns out to be not just golden but actual gold, considering it's now bent. Luckily, it's also incredibly pointy.

When the Muses hear the crashing sound over their bed, the sex noises stop, and everyone snaps back the sheet. I am once again left nauseated, this time at the sight of their naked bodies intertwined with Jake's.

Gently but quickly, I bend the bolt back into its former shape and then spin it freely, feeling the weight in my hands and wishing I knew how to accurately throw a javelin, though I'm not sure which target I'd choose first—Callie or Lu. The twisted bat-man glowers. I don't think he's quite sure how to react to this transition.

From the bed, one of the sisters screams. "You bitch! What did you do to our king and father's statue?"

Callie, however, exhales loudly, climbs out of bed again, and examines the broken wrist closely. She cocks an eyebrow as if she's a little impressed with me. "Erato, calm down. It's a clean break. Hephaestus can fix that easily. Let's see where Miranda goes with this."

All of them watch me while in their naked, sweaty, nasty glory.

While I've been trying to keep my coffee down, I've been careless with allowing them to distract me. When I turn my head forward, Lu has halved the distance between us. About twenty feet still separates us, but, you know, he has actual wings, so I can't let myself get comfortable. I hold my bolt like a spear, and I pray for it to stay in one piece for the duration of this fight. That is, unless Lu tries to use it on me. If that happens, I want the fucking thing to fall apart like wet tissue paper.

I charge at him, a primal scream coming from my chest, bolt held out before me, hoping to pierce the demon through the heart. Unfortunately, he also remembers he has wings and simply flies up into the air and over me, landing behind me, while I have to take a few moments to stop, turn, and get my bearings again.

Lu laughs that deep throaty, echoing sound. It makes the whole room shake, if not the whole mountain. Whatever I do, I'm going to have to keep him on the ground somehow. That's my only chance. I review my training in my mind.

Only one option comes to me, but I can't do it. If I miss, it will be goodnight. Except, it's really my only choice. Okay, fine. Let's just get this massacre over with...one way or another.

I estimate the distance between us. Should be right...in theory. I take off, running as fast as I can. He thinks I'm just charging him again, because a second later, he spreads his wings. When I think I'm close enough, I push off the ground with one foot, getting better height than I expected. Midair, I twist my torso so that I fly at Lu sideways. I extend my other leg and flex my foot while I press the bolt securely against the extended leg. The pointy end reaches slightly beyond my heel that I aim at Lu's boney chest. His eyes go wide, but he flaps his wings once and rises off the ground. The bolt misses his heart, by a lot, and he smirks for a split second, until it punctures one of his leathery, veiny wings. As I fall toward the floor and Lu continues his upward ascent, the bolt slashes the length of his wing. I fall to my feet just as Lu's blood curdling scream pierces my ears.

Immediately I turn back to face Lu. Ah Lu. Poor Lu falls on the ground in a heap and writhes in a pool of his own ink black blood, wailing.

"Now, this. *This* is music to my ears." I call to Callie, who squints her eyes and tilts her head, but that is her only response. I guess she's not so attached to her demon errand boy.

I walk to him slowly, savoring the pain I have caused him, maybe a little more than I should. But I know I have yet to unearth, experience, and deal with the pain he has caused. Pain that's going to change my life. And my marriage.

I stare down at Lu, shriveling into himself as he reaches for his torn wing. He's twisting on the ground in a puddle of black, like an evil snowman melting away. Every time he tries to flap his good wing a fresh spurt of blood pulses from the one I tore. He looks up at me. Are those tears in his eyes? Oh well. He lets out one more intensely evil scream from the depths of his soul as I ram the bolt into that disgusting hole in his face.

And then, silence. No screams. No taunts. Not even moaning from the bed. The only sounds I hear are my own heart, beating steady and calm, and the wind beginning to batter the top of the mountain. I turn toward the bed, aware of the fact I am, once again, soaked in the blood of a mythological monster, and face my husband and his cohort. During the battle, he moved to sit at the edge of the bed while the sisters huddle against the headboard, as far away from the pool of blood as possible.

Jake's jaw is on his chest. "What, what, what, what, whatwhatwhat-what—"

Callie spins to face my husband, her features are cold now. I think I see a bead of nervous sweat forming on her brow. "Oh, shut up, Jake." She's not so sweet and friendly now. "Yes, your wife is a badass superhero. But I'm a goddess!" On her last word, the skies flash, and thunder sounds. I jump a little, and she lets out that laugh that now sounds more like wind chimes stuck in a hurricane.

I steady myself and stare at them, huddled together on that bed. "Jake, we're going home. To our life. To our children."

At the mention of our kids, something flashes across his eyes. He furrows his brow and looks downward at the bedsheet, as if trying to pull at a loose string of the shroud covering a long-lost memory he can't quite make out.

"Our children…" I move closer. "Yes, Jake. Our children. Jessie, Phoebe, Natalie, and Sammy. Do you remember them? Or has this bitch somehow managed to wipe them completely from your mind?"

Callie giggles. "There's no need for name calling, Miranda. I would never disrespect *you* like that. And I don't wipe minds. I just cause a cessation of obligations. That means he wants to be *here*. You should walk away now, before you get hurt more. You are the Guardian. You don't need this man to find your true power."

Now I laugh. "I don't need that man, but you, a goddess, do? And for the record, the only way to cessate the obligations of being a parent would be to make someone completely forget they are one."

She rolls her eyes. "You're such a fool. Cessate is not a word!"

Color rises in my cheeks. "Whatever."

Jake softly repeats, "our children," in a tone that hints at emotion, but only confusion at that.

Sitting naked on the edge of that massive bed, he suddenly looks so small. He's innocent in this, a pawn. Granted he's a pawn that got to sleep with four goddesses for a few weeks, but still. He didn't choose this life.

Moving briskly to kneel before him, I take his hands in mine and look into his eyes. I hope he's in there somewhere. I hope when I wake his ass up from this, he can forgive himself. I also hope I have it in me to forgive him, because, on some level, he did choose those women. Between forgetting about our family and the massive amounts of infidelity, this may be a difficult reawakening for us to handle. But that's all later. Right now, I need to get him off this mountain.

I look him in the eyes, and even though his eyes move to lock on mine, I can tell he doesn't actually see me.

He keeps whispering, "Our children. Our children. Our children."

"Yes, Jake. Our children. Jessie…Phoebe…Natalie…Sam. Do you remember them? They're home, and they miss you."

"Our children. Our children. Our children."

To my left, Callie watches, biting her lip shakily. "Oh my dear, naïve, Miranda. You're just dragging out the inevitable. You know how weak-minded men can be."

I glare at her. "It will take your father to help you if you broke a good man."

Her face becomes a mask devoid of emotion, but when she swallows hard, I know she's nervous. I scootch closer to Jake and speak softer, hoping only he will hear me.

"Jake, do you remember the day we brought Jessie home from the hospital?" Hope calms my heart when he stops his quiet chant. "We'd had only an hour of sleep the two nights we were there. Remember? She wouldn't let us put her down without wailing, and we couldn't bear to leave her in the nursery. She nursed all night, and the nurses yelled at me for keeping her on me for so long. And then it was time to go home. They had us exit that hospital with this brand-new baby in her car seat. No owner's manual. No real instructions. We had no idea what we were doing. But they let us take her home. That was it. And we've been scared every day since. Every single day!"

The harem behind Jake whimpers, and Callie's lips press into a white line. But Jake tilts his head to the side as if to hear me better.

I rub the back of his hand. "The fear that we wouldn't know how to keep her alive turned into the fear that we would screw her up. And let's be honest, we did screw her up. We screwed up all our kids, but they're still pretty fucking amazing regardless, and that's got to at least be partially because of you, right? I mean, yes, I am a ridiculously amazing mom. Top notch really. But we're a team in this."

Jake stares at me in silence, a coin spinning on its edge, and no one knows which way it's going to tip. I need to control the fall.

I let out a brief laugh, hoping it sounds convincing. "Oh my god! Do you remember when we were driving home from…I don't remember from what. But both Phoebe and Jessie had reached their limit with the car ride. So, Jessie started one of her long-ass tirades. And after six solid minutes of Jessie whining, yelling, and flailing while spewing her three-year-old stream of consciousness, Phoebe just let out a tiny 'Meh' from her car seat. And Jessie screeched, 'No! You don't get a turn! Ever!'"

I have tears in my eyes when I finish the anecdote. My laughter isn't real, but the tears are, because behind these memoires I keep thinking, what if this is all for nothing? Maybe I need more heartwarming stories, less amusing ones. Think, Miranda. Think!

"Oh! Remember when Jessie and Phoebe would fight over who got to snuggle you first at bedtime?" The corners of his mouth twitch, but not enough. I need to go more personal. And fast. I want to get out of here.

"Remember how excited Phoebe was when we brought Natalie home from the hospital? How she bounced around in her tutu, chanting, 'I'm a little sister *and* a big sister!' We were so afraid of how she'd feel about not being the baby anymore, but she was so in love with *her* baby from the moment they met." I stare into his face. Silently, a tear rolls down his cheek.

One more... come on Miranda, think. "Remember catching Sammy as he would jump off the couch, yelling, 'Look Daddy! I can fly!' in his little superhero pjs with the Velcro cape?"

More tears are seeping out of his overflowing eyelids now.

Callie notices too. She takes a step toward us and uses her silky, sultry voice. "Jake, come back to bed. Miranda can go take care of the kids. Miranda, honey, you know as well as I, while decent as lovers, men make shitty fathers." She's not entirely wrong, and I do know that first hand.

I think back to my eighteenth birthday. Instead of coming to my last ever band concert, my father was off fucking his girlfriend. He was home in time to cut my cake with my friends, but we all knew the cheap perfume clinging to him was not my mom's. My friends dispersed quickly after I blew out the candles, not wanting to be a part of my twisted memory. He laughed in my face. "Some friends." I could actually smell the sex in his breath, mixed with the sweet icing from my cake. I spent the night in the bathroom, throwing up and finding more ways to distract myself from the emotional torment he put me through.

But every birthday with Jake has been different than that. Flowers sent to work, cake under moonlight, always with a "Happy Birthday, Baby. Make a wish." And he has *always* been there for our babies. He's missed flights, business trips, calls, and deals, just to make sure he is always there for our kids' birthdays and events. Every concert, every recital, every conference. He is there.

Callie takes my long silence as my compliance. "You see Miranda, your kids are better off without him. They're old enough that they don't need him anymore."

I stand and face her. "The fuck they don't. *Your* weakness, you demented narcissist, is that you underestimate the importance of a father. You underestimate the love a father has for his children, and theirs for him. I guess that shows what kind of father Zeus has been to you, and for that I feel sorry for you. Jake is the best father in the entire world. His children are his oxygen, and he is theirs. Even a goddess can't sever that bond. So, and I mean this with all the respect I would give to a wad of gum that is not scraping off the bottom of my shoe fast enough, Go. Fuck. Yourself."

A rough hand takes mine. "Let's go home, Miranda." I turn and see my husband smiling down at me. He cradles my cheek in his hand. I close my eyes and let my tears starts to fall.

A gravelly complaint rises from Callie's throat, from those smooth vocal cords which until now had only emitted honey sweet tones. "No! You can't go. We need you to believe in us!" She collapses onto the edge of bed, next to her sisters.

He looks over my shoulder and glares at Callie, his eyes void of the warmth they showered on me. "You know what? I think I'm going to give atheism a shot."

A scream sounds throughout the room. Four voices, formerly as light and haunting as sunrays, fade into the hefty groans of haggard crones. They are all kneeling on the bed, frozen in their screams, translucent, but still in this world. They wrap their now withered gray arms around each other, afraid of what will become of themselves if they let go.

Jake and I smile at each other. He chose me. He chose us. How could I have ever thought Lu was Jake? Lu's eyes never had that twinkle I've known since that first night at the coffeehouse. The same twinkle Jake has now as he looks at me, even though I'm covered in demon blood.

"Oh shit, baby. You need some clothes!" I grab the giant sheet from the bed, out of the wrinkled hands of those crones, formerly so glorious. I fold it a few ways and tie it around him in something resembling a toga, but with some extra coverage to hopefully keep his most sensitive areas protected for our descent from the mountain. "That'll have to do for now."

But he raises his eyebrows and looks across the room toward the floor, jutting his chin out to point me to follow his gaze. "Oh. Right."

Lu…

I pick up Lu's discarded pants, shake them out, and hand them to Jake. Sure, there's a little incubus blood on the waistband, but he has lots of other bodily fluids on him already. What's one more? Jake slips them on over the piece of the sheet tied like a loin cloth, under the more dress like part. Then we walk to the side I climbed up, willfully ignoring the pathetic cries behind us, and look down.

"Um, Miranda, how the fuck did you get up here this way?" All I can do is shake my head slowly, not even knowing anymore. After I assess the situation and look around us, I nudge him with my elbow and point at the stretch SUV. "Yes! Now that's what I'm talking about!" He holds up his hand for a high five, and I laugh at the goofiness of it all, so happy he's still my Jake. But my laughter soon shifts into tears.

Now that we're back together, the dam has broken. He grabs my face in his hands and kisses me. That's the kiss I've been needing. "Miranda, we can fall apart in each other's arms soon. Right now, we have to get down a fucking mountain and away from four psychotic goddesses. Yeah?" I nod and we turn and walk, hand in hand, to the SUV.

Chapter 27

Miranda

George is gouging a groove into the earth with his pacing by the time we reach the bottom of the mountain. And the Jinn is sitting on the roof of the mustang? What the hell? George freezes when he sees the SUV, a deer in headlights, because he doesn't know it's us in the limo. I roll down my window and stick my head out the passenger side.

"George! It's okay!" But we're still too far away for him to hear me. I sit back down, and Jake looks at me questioningly. "It's a long story. I'll explain later. For now, just know he's on our side. At least the human is. Not sure what the Jinn's story is." I pull my phone out of my pocket, but it's dead. Oh well, we'll both just have to squirm for a little while, I guess. Although it feels like hours, a few minutes later we pull up next to the rental car.

Jake rolls down his window. "Howdy partner. You having some car trouble?"

I lean forward and smile at my docent. "We won, George! We won! You can relax now. You should have seen me though. I killed the incubus!"

His concerned look split into a grin. "Of course, you killed the incubus!" He turns to his new green glowing friend. "I told you she'd kill Lu." Then to me, he adds, "It had to be easier than the minotaur, and you killed that thing super-fast."

"Why do you know who Lu is already? And why are you buddies with the Jinn?"

George looks a couple times from me to the Jinn and back. "Well, *this* is Frank. Yeah, don't look at me like that. Just trust me that you can't pronounce his full name. He has been doing everything he could to avoid distracting or flustering you like the Muses had planned."

"Hello." Frank gives a wave. "Callie ordered the imps to summon me to find you. But imps are so stupid; that's all they commanded me to do. And I did find you, that day in the pharmacy. They weren't happy I followed their directions so exactly. Luckily, I came across George here on the mountain. I had heard about him and H.A.A.M. from my nephew."

George's cheeks blush slightly.

I furrow my brow. "What about ham?"

George cuts off my questions. "I'll explain later. The main thing is that Frank doesn't want to be used against you. Can you find his vessel in the limo?"

I disappear into the back and dig around while Frank's description floats through my window. "It's green and made of glass and..."

"Um, is it this?" I hold up to the window what I thought was a bong.

"Yes! That's it! You need to destroy it." Frank says while looking at it like it's a bomb.

"I need to what? How?" I ask as I climb back into the front seat. The whole time Jake watches us this with a look of utter confusion.

"Well," George interjects, "correct me if I'm wrong here, Frank, but I believe it needs to be destroyed with another magical object?"

Frank nods. "That is correct. Luckily, Miranda counts."

I look between them. "What do you mean Miranda counts? Miranda is a magical object?"

George tilts his head, eyebrows raised, and crosses his arms. "Um, yeah you are. What have I been telling you?"

I look back to Jake. "I think I'll be right back? I'm assuming this won't take long."

Jake looks at me with his brow so furrowed that his eyes are barely more than slits. "Miranda, wife of mine whom I know better than anyone, or so I thought… Did that kid say you killed a Minotaur? And you're magical now?"

I blush and bite my lower lip. "Yeah…I'll tell you everything. I promise. Just, I have to go do this thing now…"

I push the door open and jump down from the high passenger seat. "So, do I just smash it or something?"

Frank nods. "That should do it. That will sever the link between myself and the magic. And I can live out my life as a normal person."

"And you're sure that that's what you want? I have a feeling this can't be undone." I don't know much, but I'm pretty sure severing magic is forever.

"Trust me, I'm sure. I don't want to be used against you, or anyone, ever again."

"Okay, here it goes then." I hold it high above my head. Then, because I don't know what the immediate effect will be, I move a few feet away from our getaway vehicle. I look into Frank's and George's faces, shrug, and throw the vessel at the rocky ground.

It breaks open with a small explosion, glittering dust bursting out in a pouf of green. I cough. A lot. I can't see as the cloud moves past me. Then everything is clear. Not even broken glass remains on the ground. And Frank looks like a normal human. Well, for the most part. He's no longer glowing, not even his eyes.

We all stand there looking at each other for a minute before Jake honks the horn and yells, "Can we get moving, please? I'm not really comfortable hanging out here, especially in these clothes."

I look at George. "So, are we good you think?"

He shrugs. "Yeah, I think that should do it." He walks me over to the limo and holds my door open as I climb back in. "Do you guys want to leave that beast here and go back in the car?"

Jake and I look over our shoulders, back from whence we came, then to each other. Jake takes the lead on this one. "Um, George, is it? I think we're going to go ahead and take their only form of transportation...just in case..."

George looks panicked. "Are they...not dead?"

"They're goddesses, George. No, they're not dead. I think that's a little beyond my training as of now, don't you?" I'm hoping the humor I'm trying to inject into my words comes through.

George rolls his eyes. "Okay fine. We'll meet you back at the hotel, I guess. But you will have to tell me everything that I missed!"

Jake doesn't like this. "My dude, I think I deserve to hear everything *I* missed first." They stare at each other for a few moments.

George realizes he's not going to win this one. "Yeah, okay. That's fair. See you in a bit then." And with that, George and Frank get into the rental car.

The drive back to the strip is almost physically painful as we sit next to each other in the cloud of palpable tension.

"So...how've you been?" Jake glances at me when he asks the casual question.

I can't help but laugh. He's always good at breaking through to me when I need a laugh. "So, I guess you're wondering what the fuck is going on?"

"I mean, it would be nice to know why a bunch of goddesses kidnapped me to basically be their sex slave for weeks while my wife apparently learned how to fight demons... If you're up to sharing, that is."

I take a deep breath. "I am. I'm just trying to figure out where to even begin at this point. I feel like it's been years since I actually talked to you."

"Okay, let's start there. How did you not know that an evil sex demon wasn't me?"

"Why would I ever have an inkling that when you got home from a business trip you had been kidnapped by goddesses and replaced with an evil sex demon doppelgänger?"

"Fair point."

"Yeah. Thanks."

"But did he kiss like me? Did he make love like me?" My silence is all the answer he needs. "I see. And you didn't think anything was up?"

"Honestly? I thought you'd cheated on me while you were on your trip."

He slams on the brakes so fast and hard that I'm not surprised to see George almost swerve off the road behind us. "You thought I had cheated? I would never cheat on you, Miranda!"

"Oh, okay. Says the man who spent the last few weeks having an orgy with a bunch of goddess rock stars..."

His face is red with anger and his arms are flailing as he yells, "I was under some kind of spell!"

"That's not how they work! They don't mind-control; they just make people feel less obligated to their responsibilities!" I hadn't thought of it like that until the words came out of my own mouth, but that truth knocked the wind out of me. They hadn't made him have sex with them. They just made him not care that he shouldn't be. If he didn't want to, he wouldn't have.

I start to fumble with the handle on my car door. "I need to get out. Now."

"Miranda, don't go." Jake is pleading with me desperately.

"I need to get air." I finally find the right lever and yank, feeling the door spring free. I practically fall out onto the road and immediately get to my hands and knees and begin to throw up. I throw up Callie's leftovers, again and again. I'm staring into the bright yellow puddle, wondering how long it will take the burning in my esophagus to stop, when I feel a hand on my back. I turn as quick I can, my fist starting to fly. But it's George, kneeling beside me, and he traps my hand before my knuckles can reach his face. I collapse into him, crying.

"What the hell happened, Miranda?"

But I can't answer. All I can do is sob. I knew I would have to deal with the emotional ramifications of this battle later. But now that Jake is safe, Lu is dead, and the Muses are hopefully fading into nothingness, I have no more reason to stand.

With his arms around me, George pulls us both to our feet, together, in one graceful move. He leans back to the open door of the SUV. "I'll take her back to the hotel."

A heavy sigh emanates from the driver's seat. "Look kid, I have absolutely no idea what the hell is going on with my wife, who you are, why you're here, or why I was kidnapped. You think I'll just let her go with you?"

"Jake, you may not know me, but I know you. And trust me when I say I'm exactly who Miranda needs to talk to now. We'll meet you back at the Palace, and she'll be ready to tell you everything. Right now, she needs someone who has been with her through this whole ordeal. Someone she doesn't need to explain anything to right this minute. And, like it or not, that's me."

"Oh, that's you, is it? You know what, fine. Have a good drive. I'll see you back at the Palace."

George closes the door, and the SUV speeds off. I watch it get smaller as my husband drives toward the horizon, toward the strip, toward the sun rising on what I suspect is going to be one of the hardest days I've ever had to live through. But at least I watch it from the inferred safety of George's support.

The rest of the drive back to the hotel is miserable. I stare at a random spot on the dashboard in front of me, and although my eyes make no perceptible movement, my mind is racing. My thoughts keep going around in an endless loop:

You cheated too. You slept with Lu.

But you didn't know it was Lu; you thought it was Jake. That's the difference. He knew the Muses weren't you, and he still slept with them.

You should have known that wasn't Jake. If you were stronger you'd have found out sooner. And they removed his sense of obligation. You can't really be mad at him.

You can't? You just found out that apparently the only reason he's been faithful all this time is his sense of obligation to you. Why shouldn't you be mad at him?

Okay, but the kids!

"Penny for your thoughts?" George startles me out of the cycle, which is good because one half of my subconscious was about to bitch slap the other for daring to bring my kids up as a reason why I shouldn't feel completely betrayed.

"I just...I don't know what to think. It's only because of me that Jake was abducted in the first place. But it's not like they had him under a spell or tied him to the bed or anything. They just made him not feel so responsible, and he stayed there and slept with them for weeks, completely betraying me, and our family."

When I look over at George, his eyes are on the road, but his brow is furrowed and his lips are sort of pursed, like a duck's bill. He's clearly pondering something.

"What? You think I'm wrong?" I ask.

"I think you're hurt, and as a result you're underestimating the power the Muses have. Okay, so they *merely* bring the cessation of obligations... That's not clearly defined though. Not to mention, they are still goddesses, Miranda. And his speaking their names was basically keeping them alive. Maybe they don't use mind control per se, but don't you think that if a group of goddesses want to keep someone from going home, they have the power to do that?" I'm silent for a full minute. "Well?"

"Shut up, George." I pull the lever to tilt my seat backward and close my eyes, finally feeling how exhausted I am. I hear him smile in the silence.

When I open my eyes, we're in the parking garage at the Palace. George dropped Frank off somewhere along the strip while I slept. He was so grateful and didn't want to burden us anymore. I see the massive SUV parked along a wall. It's no surprise Jake beat us back, but I can't help but wonder: Where is he now?

Not that I can investigate because as we enter the Forum, everyone stares at me...and my clothes covered in Lu's blood. When no one's looking, I grab a sword from a nearby statue. George laughs, knowing what I'm going for here, and we walk to our room as if I had been working Vegas as a freaky sideshow character. After I clean up and trash the corset, I leave George to do whatever he wants, and I head back to the Forum, trying not to panic about where my husband has disappeared to.

It tuns out to be a foolish concern because when I walk into the Forum food court, Jake's in line for a hamburger. My stomach growls at the thought, so I join Jake. He puts his arm around me and tucks me into his side. I sink into his well-worn T-shirt from the first concert I took him to. I pull back.

"Hey, where'd you get your clothes? You were in a sheet when last I saw you."

"I went to the villa, took a shower, got dressed, and took my suitcase. See?" He indicates his roller bag on the floor on the other side of his legs.

"Oh, okay."

"I didn't know where your room is, and I wanted to get my stuff out of there." He adds quickly, "No one else was in there."

I nod. I'm glad he showered, honestly. I feel a little bit better knowing that the first thing he did with his freedom was scrub the goddess skank off of himself.

By the time we get to the front of the line and can finally order, I'm hungrier than I've ever been in my entire life. We both get double cheeseburgers and fries. I add some avocado to mine so I can pretend I'm getting nutrients. Jake adds bacon and charges our order to the villa. I think that's a nice touch. Once we're in possession of our food, we find a table and silently scarf down our respective meals.

He, of course, spills ketchup on his T-shirt. When I have smooshed avocado on the corner of my mouth, he reaches over and wipes it away for me with his napkin. It almost feels normal. I mean, aside from the exhaustion I'm feeling deep in my bones, coupled with the fact that my body feels like it's been run over by a combine, then scooped up, threshed, and dumped back out through the ass end of the same piece of machinery.

When we've cleaned our trays and our table, we walk to the elevator for the Palace tower, holding hands. The doors close behind us, leaving us truly alone for the first time since the car ride. He hits the emergency stop and turns to me.

"Okay. So, what is going on?" He's not angry. He's just...Jake.

I take a deep breath before beginning. I fidget a lot while I explain. "There's a lot, but the short version? It's my birthright to be something called a Guardian, which basically means that I'm the quintessential

Chosen One. Don't laugh; I did enough of that for the both of us...trust me. And I'm supposed to protect humanity from all these creatures that people think are just myths and stories, but really people's beliefs brought them all to life. But, I'm obviously not the quintessential Chosen One. I'm me. And I wonder how the fuck I'm not going to get myself killed every time I see anything supernatural."

To his credit, he doesn't laugh. Or freak out. He just looks off and nods for a few moments. "It makes sense that it's you."

"I'm sorry, what?" My mouth hangs open at his response.

"You're the most maternal and protective person I have ever met. It makes sense to me that your fierce mama bear instinct is from something even bigger." His eyes are locked on mine. I never want to not look into his eyes again, but I am also deeply uncomfortable taking compliments, and this was a big one. He actually has confidence in me. I feel my heart unclench from a tension I didn't recognize was even gripping it. Maybe I can do this. After a couple more seconds Jake clears his throat and looks away. "So, who's the kid?" Of course, he still needs to learn about George.

"He's not a kid. He's twenty-four."

Jake lifts one eyebrow.

I roll my eyes. "Whatever. George is my docent, my trainer. Well, technically his father was supposed to be, but he died three years ago. And because all had been quiet for so long on the mythical creatures front, the last Guardian hit the ripe old age of sixty. Then the powers that be decided I should be called to duty since she probably wouldn't be able to fight much off without breaking herself at this point. Not that I'm in any better condition..."

He looks up, his lips mouthing the words "docent" and "creatures". "Okay, I think I got all of that. And the muses kidnapped me because...?"

"They figured you must be pretty damn special and a real tiger in the sack if you managed to snag a Guardian...since there's never been a married Guardian before." I smile at him. It's an obviously fake smile, because how am I supposed to smile? I'm super nauseated again and feel my lip start to curl in disgust.

Jake doesn't smile at all. "But, they were wrong. You're the special one, Miranda. You've always been. You know that, right? I've always known that and even if you've never seen that before, you have to now."

My smile fades the rest of the way as I continue, "They hoped your love making would imbue them with some extra powers or influence or something."

Jake's eyes open in surprise. "Well, that's gross." He takes my hands and makes sure I'm looking into his eyes. "Miranda, none of this was your fault. They were just a bunch of crazy psychos."

While I was explaining, I'd placed myself into a literal corner of the elevator. As he leans toward me and reaches his arm around my waist, my breath catches, my nerves are still a little raw, and I've missed him so much. Jake again presses the emergency stop button behind me to disengage it. Then he looks into my eyes and smiles sweetly as the elevator continues its ascent.

Chapter 28

Miranda

Sunday, we take a morning flight home. We are still exhausted and mostly silent on our way through Harry Reid International. I almost thank god when George doesn't have full-sized toiletries in his suitcase this time, but given everything we just endured, I'd rather not give any more power to any gods. By the time we touch down at Newark Airport, Jake and I are able to interact in a fairly usual way.

Jake and George are also getting along the slightest bit better. Jake isn't quite ready to invite George to a family barbecue, but they're at least able to ride in a car together without making me gag on their mutual disgust for each other.

George drops us off in the afternoon and immediately drives away. To anyone watching, he was our Uber driver.

We stand outside the door for a moment and brace ourselves for seeing the kids, before we've had a chance to work through anything that we've each experienced over the last few weeks. Then we go in.

We still expect the kids to behave like they did when they were tiny, running up with unbridled excitement, unable to contain their happiness now that we're home. But all four are in a heated video game race, and they barely notice when we come in to the room. No one responds with so much as a hello when we gave the requisite, "Kids, we're home!" call upon entry. We find Eliza in the kitchen, doing dishes and listening to a podcast from her favorite author.

"Ah! You're home! How are you guys?" She shuts the water, dries her hands, and then pauses her phone before running over to hug us. I wince when she squeezes me.

She pulls back and looks at me. "What the hell, Miranda?"

I'm still grimacing in pain.

"Sit down," she says. "I'll get you a snack and some ibuprofen. I can't imagine what you must feel like after having to fight goddesses."

"Oh, okay. So Eliza found out before me? That's fair."

I glare at him, then remember, this is not his fault...this is not his fault...We are working through all of this insanity together..."To be fair, I thought I had started the conversation with *you*. I didn't realize that *you* wasn't you."

Eliza looks back and forth between us. "I'm sorry, what? What do you mean he wasn't he? Who was he if he wasn't he?"

"And incubus named Lu," I grumble. I can tell she has more questions. Many, many more questions. "I'm going to have to fill you another time, Lize. Coffee this week? Tuesday?" George is going to suck up me taking a day for myself here and there if this is going to be for the rest of my life.

Eliza nods. "That's fine. I'm not leaving before dinner today though. I don't trust you two to get all these kids fed. You should both go lie down. You look like hell. I'll walk you up the stairs to make sure you don't tumble down. I have to get Tabby from her nap anyway, or she'll never sleep tonight."

She leads the way up the stairs, mainly because Jake and I are both hobbling, and we don't want to slow her down in her mission to wake her sleeping baby.

I take a short, hot shower and then fall into bed as Jake gets into the shower himself. (The sheets are fresh and clean. I love Eliza so much.) A few minutes later, he falls into bed next to me. I turn on my side to face him, and he's already looking at me. We scoot toward each other bumpily, with no grace whatsoever. Then we fall asleep, wrapped in each other's warmth and love, and, at least for me, with tears in my eyes because of the road we have ahead of us.

We needed that nap more than anyone knows. We sleep right through each kid trying to wake us up for dinner, so Eliza decides to stay the night. We wake up briefly when Sammy wedges his way between us, but it is still dark outside. I snuggle up to him, smell his hair, and push the curls from his face so I can kiss his nose before I fall asleep again, his body heat warming my soul.

***

I don't wake again until a few minutes before my alarm will sound to start the school day. The moment I move and stretch my sore limbs, I feel gross again, so I go take another hot shower. Between the blood, the sweat, and the emotions, I wonder if I will ever feel clean again. Then I go make a pot of coffee so I can get started early, figuring out my future.

My phone dings with a text.

> We should still train. Come by today when the kids are dropped off.

I stare at the message, not sure how to respond, when I feel Jake's arm circle my waist and his breath on my neck before he kisses me under my ear. I smile, put the phone down, and then push myself around to face him. I cross my arms around his neck and look into his beautiful brown eyes. They're so much warmer than Lu's. Will I ever forgive myself for not realizing that wasn't Jake? Will Jake ever forgive me? Will I ever forgive him for sleeping with the Muses?

I don't know. I don't know what the future has in store for us. What I do know is that our relationship deserves that we fight for it, so I need to have my head on straight. I can't be worrying about being The Guardian right now. At least, not alone.

At 9:00 a.m., I pull into George's driveway and park the car. He opens the front door and smiles at me as I climb out and shut the door. His smile drops when Jake does the same. I look back at my husband and signal for him to wait one minute. Then I jog over to the house.

"You brought Jake?"

"George, I need to focus on figuring out my marriage and working through everything that just happened. If you want me to keep training, for right now, he needs to be included in this. He won't be here every day, but he needs to feel this isn't some secretive thing you and I share. He needs to be part of it. We have a lot of broken trust we need to repair, on both our ends. I can't have our training oppose that work. Plus, after his abduction, it's pretty obvious Jake needs to learn this stuff as much as I do. This Guardian has a husband, so we need to rewrite the rules a bit."

George harsh glare fades into understanding. He nods.

I hear gravel crunch behind me and know Jake has approached.

George blinks and looks to him. "Hey Jake. Welcome to headquarters. Let me show you around." He steps aside and gestures for my husband to come on in.

Jake looks inquisitively at me as he steps past and over the threshold.

George pats Jake's shoulder and guides him toward the dining room. "I'll show you the dojo. You want to learn how to fight, too? May come in handy the next time someone tries to abduct you, you know?"

Jake looks back at me. I smile at him and nod my encouragement, like I did to my kids on each of their first days of preschool. I close my eyes, take a deep breath, look to the heavens above for some strength, and walk in after them.

I know now just how much power our beliefs have. So if I strongly believe everything will be okay, maybe it just will be.

Epilogue

"Geeorge, it is highly unusual for a docent to request a conference with the League. It has only happened a handful of times in our entire history." Perry Philips is seated in the middle seat behind the dark wooden desk that takes up the entire width of the dais.

I want to ask him why they have this ridiculous setup. It can't be the most effective way for them to conduct their everyday business. The seven men who make up the League of Docents are spaced out, one next to the other, all the way across the room. Doesn't seem like the best way for them to communicate to each other either. But, out of respect and all, I keep my mouth shut on the subject.

"Well, Sir, I think we can all agree that there is nothing particularly usual about the current Guardian situation." I pause, expecting some kind of response, but I am met with nothing but icy stares and silence. I clear my throat to buy myself a moment. Even though the League does not like being told anything, I remind myself that this is all for Miranda, so I take a deep breath and continue. "On that note, I'm here to tell you that, in light of recent events, Mir—The Guardian has demanded that her husband be brought into the training as well."

Muffled chaos ensues. Conversations—no, arguments—break out across the row of usually composed-to-a-fault men. Miranda would love to see the uproar she has caused. I allow myself a brief smile because I know none of them are looking at me anyway. But I haven't said everything yet, so I replace my smile with the impassive expressive I usually keep around them and clear my throat, loudly. They quiet down a bit, enough for me to speak strongly over them.

"I demand you find a counselor you trust for them. Miranda and Jake have a lot of healing to do, and they can't expect any marriage counselor to help them work through one of them being kidnapped and ostensibly raped by a bunch of goddesses or the other unknowingly having sex with a demon."

Once again, I'm met with silence. The only expression I can read is Perry's, and that's because his eyes are silently screaming, "How dare you!" from his position of prestige. But, thanks to my time thus far with Miranda, I know who has the power in this situation. Miranda is all they have. They can replace me, but they won't ever be able to control her the way they're used to, so why bother.

Finally, Perry speaks. "This is unheard of. Then again, as you said, nothing about any of this is particularly usual. The League will honor the request to train Jake Gold, provided that you, George Keating, are willing to take the additional responsibility on yourself."

I nod to show I am.

Perry clicks his tongue. "Very well. As for the other matter, we need time to collect some trusted options for The Guardian to choose from."

"Thank you, Sir." I bow my head slightly. If we were in the dojo, I would have to bow completely to show my respect, so I'm used to the idea of the bow. However, I don't feel any great respect for the League, and that makes bowing at all harder for me, but I fake it well enough.

"If that is all, George, you are dismissed. We wish you luck with your...Chosen...Two." He gives me a smug smile.

I wish I could hurricane kick that look right off his face, but I have a feeling that would not be well received. Instead, I thank them for their time, turn around, and walk out my head held high and a smile on my lips.

I have a feeling this is the beginning of something truly beautiful.

Coming Soon

Miranda's story is far from over! Join as she, Jake, and George all join forces in the second book of the Guardian series, due out in Fall 2023!

Be sure to check out Michelle's latest books, get free excerpts and updates through her newsletter, and connect with her on social media by scanning the code below or going to https://msummerswriter.com/

Acknowledgements

Thank you to my family for inspiring and supporting me through this and all things. And for being okay to live out of laundry baskets the many weeks I neglected our laundry. Sorry about that.

Thank you to Erin and Life Beyond Parenting. Your first workshop back in 2021 reminded me how much I love to write. Who knew back when we were spinning flags together 25 years ago that fate would bring us back together this way? Thank you for being one of my biggest fans, my cheerleader, and for believing in me before I could believe in myself.

Thank you to Maria for popping my editing cherry and being super gentle with my fragile ego during the process.

Thank you to my friends, my Elizas, for all my late-night frantic gut and grammar checks.

A big OSU to my dojo family at AMMA. Miranda wouldn't exist if you didn't show me how strong I've been all along.

Thank you to my All Write Well writer's groups. I've learned so much from you, and I'm excited to see what we all accomplish next.

And, of course, thank *you*! Thank you, my readers. An author is nothing without their readers. Thank you for taking a chance on a new author and reading *The Chosen One, My Ass!* It would be amazing if you could go click some stars on Amazon to help others find my book. A quick rating helps a ton, and if you have the time and desire, a review is the highest compliment I could hope to receive!

About the Author

M ichelle Summers has been writing since age eight, when she wrote a script that she hoped would be made into a movie starring herself, with Tom Cruise and Meg Ryan as her parents. Michelle has a B.A. in Studio Art and years of experience as a manager in retail. These helped her land the prestigious job of an abused executive assistant, which she inevitably quit to be a freelance graphic designer, and, when that failed, a trophy wife.

Michelle is most proud of the three little spitfires she is raising, although she sometimes regrets to have imbued them with all of her sass and smart-assery.

In her free time, which she doesn't really have but pretends to for the sake of her sanity, she loves training in martial arts, even if she can barely get her feet off of the ground for her jumping kicks. She also enjoys volunteering in her community, a suburb in the metropolitan New York area.

You can find Michelle on Facebook (Michelle Summers – Writer) and Instagram (msummers_80). You can catch up with her old newsletters and subscribe to receive them weekly at her website.